I0577364

INTER

EMBERHOLD ACADEMY SERIES
BOOK TWO

FRANKIE JAMES

SELF PUBLISHED

CONTENT WARNING

This book contains sexual situations and other adult themes. Recommended for age 18+. Trigger warnings include (but not limited to): Dubious consent, Non-Consent (rape), Profanity, Sexual situations, Violance, Death, Blood Play. If you have any specific questions please email me at frankie james153027@gmail.com.

CONTENTS

CHAPTER I

NATHAN

AURATHIA

I woke from a restless sleep and slowly sat up, rubbing my eyes. The room I was in was more of a cell than anything else. It was an 8x12 box containing a single twin bed that my feet hung off. (There was no way Hayes slept on a bed this size.) My cell had a tiny bathroom with a sink, toilet and shower, but no door.

I was grateful it was at least partially enclosed by walls, even if the walls didn't quite meet the ceiling. Not because I had anything to be ashamed of, my body was complete perfection, but because I preferred to take a shit in private.

I sighed and stood up. It was hard to get excited for a new day when my Nexi wasn't part of it.

Walking to the sink, I splashed water on my face. I'm sure if there was a mirror, I'd see bags under my eyes and a face that had aged ten years. This place was Hell, exactly like Damien had said. Missing Reverie was Hell all by itself, and I was coming to the end of my patience.

These weeks without her would've been unbearable if

training hadn't taken up every spare minute of my time. I barely had the strength to shower before falling into bed.

Unfortunately, I was plagued by nightmares of Reverie calling out for me, leading to a night of tossing and turning. I had tried repeatedly to contact her, but she was too far away, and our Faction wasn't complete.

I guess I should have been nicer to the gingers.

Each morning I rise before dawn, take a quick shower and put on clothing that feels distinctly medieval. The clothing may very well be my favorite aspect of this world. Pulling up leather pants that made my ass look amazing, I mourn the fact that Reverie isn't here to admire it. I slip a lightweight shirt over my head, perfect for long hours of training. Sitting back on the bed, I pull on boots that lace up the front and stop just below my knees.

There was a knock on the door, "Come in. It's open."

I laughed at myself. Of course, it was open. The knock was purely for politeness' sake. The door had no lock and the slightest touch would have cracked it open. That little fact contributed to some of my sleeplessness.

"Hey, are you ready to head to breakfast?" Taylor asked, running her eyes up and down my body then glancing away quickly as her cheeks heated.

"Yes, just give me a minute," I said sharply. She nodded, then stepped back into the hallway.

Taylor had been assigned as my training partner on my first full day here. I'd protested the pairing to Damien but he said, and I quote, "I have much more important things to deal with than your stupid bullshit."

Taylor hadn't been here long, maybe a week before I arrived and was only eighteen. I had nothing against her but didn't have any interest in having another woman's hands on me, even in training.

Some of the guys grumbled about how lucky I was because she was beautiful and had a body that wouldn't quit. I guess, objectively, she was, with dark brown hair and blue eyes. She was around 5'10 with a cleft chin, full lips, and long lashes. Taylor was fierce on the training field, and I learned the first day not to hold back or I'd get my ass kicked.

But she was no Reverie.

Everything with Taylor was fine at first, but I'd caught her staring at me with "heart eyes" more than once. She also managed to sit beside me at meals no matter how early or late I showed up. The person beside me mysteriously finished their food right as she appeared, giving her their seat.

I treated her respectfully but didn't speak to her outside of training. I didn't want to encourage any kind of relationship, even friendship.

Taylor attracted a lot of attention from the other guys, but she ignored them completely. If I were just an ordinary guy without a Reverie, I'd eagerly grab the opportunity to be with someone like her.

However, I was as unavailable as one could possibly be. My Nexi was the very breath in my lungs and the blood in my veins. I didn't exist without her. I refused to exist without her. There would never be anyone for me but my Nexi and that was that.

I finished getting dressed and left my room to find Taylor waiting outside my door. She'd shown up to walk with me for breakfast the last two days. It annoyed the fuck out of me. I had no problem hurting her feelings, but she was my practice partner and would most likely fight with me in the arena if I was here that long. It didn't seem super smart to alienate her completely.

"You didn't need to wait for me," I said as I shut my door and started walking toward the dining hall.

"I didn't mind," she ducked her head and gazed at me through her lashes. "I can't start training without you anyway."

The blush returned to her cheeks. Taylor reached hesitantly into her pocket and pulled out a hair tie.

"I noticed your hair getting in your eyes yesterday, so I thought I would bring you something to hold it back." I couldn't argue with that. My hair had grown out in the weeks since I'd been here and was starting to interfere with my training. I took the tie from her and pulled it away from my face.

"Thanks, I appreciate that." She blushed again and looked away from me. I couldn't blame her for her good taste but this snack was all for my Nexi.

We entered the hall and I went straight to the food laid out in huge serving platters on a large buffet-style counter. They fed us well because training and fighting took a lot of energy. I grabbed a plate from the end of the table and scooped a huge portion of eggs, potatoes and about ten slices of bacon onto it. I finished my masterpiece with a colossal ladle of gravy over everything.

I walked to a long table that seated about twenty, plopped my plate down and began eating. I'd made sure to sit between two large guys so maybe Taylor would find another seat.

Sure enough, as soon as Taylor walked up the guy on my right quickly picked up his plate and left. What the fuck was going on around here? Taylor sat beside me, placing a large cup of water beside my plate. I looked up at her in question.

"You need to hydrate before training," she blushed again, ducked her head and began eating.

This was getting ridiculous. I'd given her no encouragement whatsoever and what was with these people moving with only a glance from the girl? She was a good fighter but not that good.

I heard Damien speaking to someone as he walked into the room. Glancing up, I saw Hayes by his side, headed for the food.

Damien helped with training, giving advice and tips as needed but always deferred to Hayes when he was present.

Hayes hadn't shown up for three days after we arrived and when he finally did, even with our advanced healing, he was carrying himself carefully. His punishment must have been severe for him to still be in that kind of pain. I tried to talk to him, but he wasn't having any of it, telling me that he wasn't a pussy like I was and to get back to my training. He wasn't a sharing is caring kind of guy.

Since his return, he'd been involved in mine and Taylor's training. His teaching style reminded me of Grumpy's. Both were assholes and had no problem pushing our limits; excuses weren't accepted. I'd trained extensively with Reverie's parents but never with weapons. Swords were entirely new for me, not to mention the other weapons some people here used. I was continuously shocked by the mix of futuristic and ancient that was Aurathia.

Many of the warriors didn't need weapons due to their abilities. Mine was impressive, but I required much more training to use it lethally against other Aurathions. Hand-to-hand combat could become a bit tricky and, in some respects, I'd be at a disadvantage. When fighting a more experienced opponent, they could anticipate my moves and they would be on me before I had reoriented from my blink. Hayes dipped his head in greeting as he passed by but didn't stop. I felt I'd earned some of his respect because of my willingness to train for long hours and listen to instructions. My ignorance of this world occasionally gave him pause, but he never mentioned it or asked any questions. I still didn't completely trust him, so I kept my head down and mouth shut.

I'd collected a lot of disturbing information about this world that led me to believe drawing attention to myself would be dangerous. That wasn't as easy for me as it might be for others because I naturally stood out in a crowd.

Most of the warriors who had been here for more than a year were assigned to a Faction. (I understood the wording now that Hayes had used.) Apparently, new warriors were studied for the first year and then the Factions made their choice of whom to induct. It didn't sound like much choice was involved, at least for the warriors. A few, I'd learned, were sent here by their Faction to train and earn money in the coliseum. They seemed to consider it an honor.

I disagreed.

"When do you think we'll finalize the schedule for the coliseum?" Taylor inquired, continuing to shovel food into her mouth. With only a short time allotted for eating, we had to make the most of it.

"I don't know. You can talk to Hayes about it when we get to the training yard," I kept my eyes on my plate, trying to interact with her as little as possible.

This was probably how Reverie felt when I was chasing her. However, I was much smoother at it.

"That's a good idea." She looked at me like I just gave her the secret to world peace. "We need to spend as much time training and discussing strategy as possible since we'll be battling together in the coliseum."

I could see her looking at me out of the corner of my eye,

waiting for a response. I shrugged and continued eating without comment.

Hayes sat down across from me and started eating without saying a word. I was surprised to see him there until he looked up and said, "You'll be fighting in the coliseum at the early performance on Saturday. We have a lot of work to do, so eat up."

He returned to eating as if he hadn't just dropped a giant bomb on me. Taylor nudged me with her shoulder, misinterpreting my surprise as fear.

"You've got this. I've never seen someone become proficient with so many weapons as quickly as you have." She smiled and fluttered her lashes.

"Do you have something in your eye?" I asked innocently. She pissed me off by thinking I was afraid to fight... I was the tiniest bit, but that wasn't the point.

The smile dropped from her face, and she looked at me in annoyance. Maybe she'd finally get the hint. "Girl, you'd do well to worry more about yourself. Eat your food and quit coddling the boy," Hayes scolded Taylor, then returned to shoveling food into his mouth.

She narrowed her eyes at him, but continued eating. Taylor was a strange girl. Sometimes, she seemed innocent and shy. Other times, I could swear there was a hint of malice in her gaze when she looked at people.

I wasn't worried about my upcoming performance. I was so angry about being kept away from my Nexi that I had a lot of aggression to work out. My ability had finally become more stable, and I was ready to fuck some shit up. Maybe if I won a few battles, fucking Emberhold would consider my initiation complete and bring me back to the academy. I'd kill whomever I needed to make that happen.

I finished my meal before Taylor and headed to the

training yard to stretch. I'd barely started when she showed up and began her warmup.

"What do you want to start with today? I don't think I've seen you try using a bow. I can help with that, if you want. I've had lots of training with it, and I'm more than adequate."

"I appreciate it, but Damien offered to help me yesterday." I stood and walked away quickly before she could ask to join me.

Okay, note to self... subtlety is wasted on Taylor. The gloves were going to have to come off. I knew I was irresistible but damn, get a clue. Now, to find Damien and let him know he'd offered to assist me with my bow skills.

The massive training yard with equipment and obstacle courses made Emberhold's look ridiculous. Nothing we'd done at the academy could have prepared me for what I was dealing with here. I'd established that nothing about this initiation was normal, and I needed to gather as much information as possible. The situation here was fucked. I wish I knew why Emberhold had sent me here and what I was supposed to be looking for.

I saw Damien standing next to a rack of weapons, talking to a guy I'd seen around but never spoke to. That wasn't saying much because I avoided talking to everyone as much as possible.

I wasn't interested if their name didn't begin with an N and end in exi.

"Damien, could I speak to you for a minute?"

He nodded, "Give me a moment to get Chris started and I'll be right with you."

The guy, Chris, smirked at me and gave Damien his full attention. Damien finished up and motioned for me to follow him. He headed to the armory, stopping at the entrance to talk to the guard on duty, "We're going to get him kitted out for his first battle."

The guard nodded his head and resumed scanning the yard. I didn't know what his ability was, but it must have been impressive to be put in charge of keeping these powerful Aurathions in line. I wondered if I could aggravate him enough to use it

"Snap out of it, boy, and quit wasting my time," Damien grumbled, having called my name several times.

"Yes, Your Excellency," I smirked and made a rude gesture behind Damien's back.

The guard didn't smile at all. He merely rolled his eyes at my behavior—tough crowd.

"What did you want to talk to me about?" Damien asked as he walked over to a row of long swords.

"I was wondering if you could help me with my bow skills. I assume you know I'll be in the arena in a couple of days, and a long-range weapon may be useful." I hit him with my puppy-dog eyes.

He scratched his head and faked confusion, "Why not ask your partner? Taylor is excellent with that weapon, and I know she would be more than happy to help." The asshole smirked. It was, apparently, obvious to everyone that she'd be overjoyed to help me.

Now it was my turn for an eye roll, "I don't want to encourage her. We spend enough time together and she's got her training to worry about."

"Fine. But I'm only doing it because, for some reason, Hayes has taken a personal interest in you." He turned and walked over to the wall, which displayed a selection of bows. Damien grabbed a black one with silver designs covering its surface and handed it to me.

"This one should be a good fit. Let's head to the target

area so I can critique your skills and see what we need to work on."

We exited the building. I turned and flipped off the guard for absolutely no reason other than to provoke him into revealing his ability. He frowned and narrowed his eyes, but offered no other response. I knew I shouldn't antagonize him, but I'd never been accused of making wise choices and my curiosity got the better of me.

I could hear Reverie: "Nathan, you good-looking god of a man, please don't aggravate the puny guard. When he keels over in fear, you'll feel terrible."

"Leave Justice alone, he could kick your ass with one hand behind his back, and you damn sure don't want him to use his ability." Damien scolded, never even turning his head to look in my direction. Maybe one of his abilities was having eyes in the back of his head.

Taylor was already there, drawing her bow back, but she stopped when we approached. "Hey Nathan, I can help you if Damien has other things to do."

You had to admire her in a way. Having the balls to keep trying when it was obvious, I wasn't interested. On second thought, maybe she didn't understand social cues. Not everyone was blessed with the ability to read a room like I was.

Before Damien could screw me over, I said, "No that's okay. He's already here and has been doing it a lot longer than you." Taylor frowned at me and nodded her head. I knew I sounded like an asshole, but enough was enough. If I were shitty enough, maybe she would focus on somebody else.

"Come on, Mr. Irresistible. Let's get started." Damien motioned me to follow him.

We walked down several rows until we found an unused

lane. Damien showed me the stance and explained draw length and draw strength. There were no sights on this bow, but given my situation, that would be useless and too time-consuming. Damien had me hold the bow, correct my footing, and go through the stance several times. He then had me draw it back to feel the draw weight.

Next, we spent thirty minutes reviewing how to nock my arrow and deciding whether I was more comfortable using the side-face anchor or the under-chin anchor method. I drew the string back several times, and Damien corrected my stance for what felt like the millionth time. Then, we started going over everything again from the beginning.

"Damn, dude, I'll have to lift my balls to wipe my ass by the time we finish this lesson." I bitched. My arms were getting tired, and I was ready to shoot this damn thing already.

I was slapped so hard on the back of my head that my whole body rocked forward, and I almost fell. Completely taken by surprise, my instincts kicked in. I pivoted quickly and held out my hand in a defensive gesture. The bigger surprise was flames shooting out of my palms.

Hayes threw himself to the side, "What the FUCK?!"

What the fuck, was right!

CHAPTER 2

NATHAN

The fire stopped almost immediately after it began.

Everyone nearby stared at me in awe. Taylor attempted to speak to me, but Hayes handed her my bow and directed her to return it to the armory. Then, he and Damien guided me back into the building, down several winding hallways and into an unfamiliar room.

There was a crude desk that appeared to have been cobbled together from wood scraps. Books were strewn all over it, along with what seemed to be fighting schedules. A dry-erase board, which looked out of place, was mounted on the stone wall and displayed a list of names. I saw my name second from the bottom.

I turned and narrowed my eyes at Hayes, "Why is my name next to last?"

Hayes looked at me in confusion, "After what just happened out there, you're worried about where your name falls on a list?"

"Yes." I was confused by his confusion. "I'm not a bottom-of-the-list kind of guy."

"Forget about that boy and explain why you didn't inform us of your ability to wield fire." He frowned at me as Damien sat in a chair behind the desk.

I opened my mouth to respond, but before I could speak, Hayes said, "And while you're at it, you can tell me why you lied about having a Faction and who they are. Taking the serum wouldn't keep you sane long without a Faction when using that kind of power. Fireballs are one thing but the heat and force of what you just did is something else."

Well, shit. I paced around the room, trying to decide what to do. At this point, I felt I needed to take a chance and trust someone. I'd watched Hayes and Damien over the last few weeks, and if I were going to confide in anyone, I would say these two were my best bet. My decision to keep a low profile wouldn't fly now.

I glanced at the board and stopped, frowning at my placement. I could hardly concentrate on anything else with my name next to last on that stupid list.

"Oh, for fuck's sake," Hayes sighed and headed to the board. He erased my name and put it at the top of the list. "Are you satisfied now, you idiot?"

I smiled in satisfaction, ignoring the "idiot" comment. "Yes, that makes me feel a lot better."

"Get on with it, boy or I'm going to have to 'lift my balls to wipe my ass.'" Damien mocked me from earlier.

"I think we both know that ship has sailed, sir." I looked pointedly at his white hair.

He threw a paperweight at my head, but I ducked, and it hit harmlessly against the wall behind me.

"Start talking before I beat your ass and make you." Hayes narrowed his eyes, clearly done dealing with me.

"OK, keep your pants on." I walked to the door, opened it, looked around, then shut and locked it.

Hayes and Damien glanced at each other and then back at me. "Anything you say stays between us. We both try to keep our fighters safe from the Brummond faction and, more importantly, Selene." Hayes looked at me with concern.

I took a deep breath, "I'm not from here."

Damien stared at me blankly, "None of us are from here. We were brought to the coliseum to fight and bring gold and prestige to our factions."

I rolled my eyes, "No, I'm not from this world." Hayes and Damien froze, looking at me with more interest. "I'm a student at Emberhold Academy and was sent here on initiation."

I expected a reaction, but not the laughter that burst out of them.

"Shit, boy, you almost had me. Emberhold was destroyed decades ago." Hayes laughed briefly. The amusement slowly left his face, "I'll have the truth now, or you'll take an ass beating."

"Listen, old man, I'm a student at Emberhold but not here in Aurathia. It's located in a pocket dimension, and I was sent there through a portal from Earth." He reminded me of Reverie's Grumpy. There was no grey area, everything was black or white. Hayes jumped to his feet and grabbed my shoulders.

"Don't lie to me, boy! Nobody has been able to create a portal to Earth, or anywhere else, for almost nineteen years."

I jerked out of his hold, "I'm telling you the truth. I was raised on Earth and didn't learn I was of Aurathion ancestry until just a few months ago."

Damien stood from behind the desk, "Everyone needs to calm down. Nathan and Hayes, you both need to take a seat."

We stared at each other scowling, but did as Damien said.

It would take some convincing, but if they could help me get back to Reverie, it would all be worth it.

"Now, let's start from the beginning," Damien said calmly. "Tell us the whole story, and we'll listen," He looked pointedly at Hayes. "-without interruptions."

Hayes rolled his eyes but nodded his head in agreement. I would bet Zane's left nut that he couldn't keep quiet. (No way would I bet my nuts. How would Reverie have mini-Nathan's?)

I drew in a deep breath and began my story, omitting Reverie's name. I was aware that her parents had escaped from this world and that two of her dads had died during the ordeal. It's possible they either fought against or had some knowledge of them. For now, it seemed wiser to withhold that information.

After I finished, they stared at me in complete disbelief. I knew it was a lot to process, so I remained quiet, waiting for their reaction. Hayes never interrupted once. It's a good thing I didn't bet my nuts.

"I don't know what to say," Damien sighed. "Why don't you head to lunch and give us time to process this? We'll talk to you later this evening, after training is complete."

I nodded and walked out. The ball was in their court.

Hopefully, they believed me and would help reunite me with my Nexi. But for now, I was starving. Confession was exhausting and I needed to refuel before tackling the training fields again. Upon entering the eating hall, I made a beeline for the buffet. There were large pieces of meat resembling enormous turkey legs. I didn't examine the food too closely. If it looked recognizable, I placed it on my plate and started eating.

Lucky for me, I'd never been finicky. I could eat almost anything. The only exception was pizza, I refused to eat it without pineapple. I wasn't a complete psycho, unlike Reverie, who couldn't stand it. I sighed. It was her only imperfection.

"Hey Nathan, is everything alright?" I jumped. I hadn't been aware Taylor had come up beside me, too lost in my thoughts.

"Yes, everything is fine." I continued filling my plate then turned and walked to the long table in the middle of the room. I deliberately sat between two people, hoping this time would be different and she'd get the hint.

Once again, Taylor stood staring at the person next to me, clearing her throat to get their attention. The guy stood, but instead of walking away, he smiled and tried to start a conversation with her. She ignored him like I wished she would ignore me and took his seat. Her determination was admirable, but she had no idea who she was messing with. I was the most hard-headed person on the planet.

"Did you get into trouble?" Taylor took a bite, looking at me in expectation.

"No, why would I be in trouble?" I kept my eyes trained on my plate.

She placed her hand on my thigh. "For using your ability on Hayes."

I looked down at her hand and frowned. "You know this means I'm part of a Faction, right?" I might as well use what Hayes had accused me of earlier to get rid of her.

She removed her hand and shrugged her shoulders. "We're all part of a Faction, so what?"

That was news to me. I had no idea she was already part of a Faction. Supposedly, that came after you proved yourself in the coliseum. She'd never mentioned it, and I didn't ask because, truthfully, I didn't care.

"I'm loyal to my Nexus and not interested in anyone else."

It felt so good to say those words. I'd felt sickened not being able to tell people who I belonged to. I didn't want anyone to know her name, but it felt amazing to at least be able to say this much.

Taylor rolled her eyes. "Everyone will be assigned to a Faction in another few months. You don't have to be worried about looking bad to any of us. We all know the score and have relationships elsewhere."

I was stunned. I knew most of these people did or would belong to a Faction to keep their sanity because of the serum. I just expected a little more loyalty. I shouldn't, since I met Hayes trying to escape from his.

"I don't give a shit what anyone else does. I'm loyal to my Nexus and I'd appreciate it if you started respecting that. If you can't, I'll get another training partner." I scowled at her.

She reared her head back, her eyes welling up with tears. "I'll respect that, Nathan. I promise. There's no need to find another partner."

The hurt on her face didn't bother me. I'd tried several times to be subtle, but at this point, I knew that wouldn't cut it. "Fine. But there's no need to walk with me to breakfast or try to be friends. Training partners is the extent of it."

I continued eating, and Taylor didn't say another word. Hopefully, she would move on at this point and give her attention to the other men. Plenty were interested, but I wasn't one of them and never would be.

When I was finished, I stood and disposed of my plate. I noticed she was deep in conversation with the guy beside her and I wished them all the best.

I left the hall and went to my room to piss and regroup.

Those two old dicks better believe me. If not, I would be back to square one, trying to figure out what Emberhold wanted, so I could leave.

Being without Reverie was unbearable and became more so every day I spent here. Had she been taken away for initiation? Was Pantar able to go with her? Did Emberhold bring her here? How the hell did I gain the ability of fire? Which one of those motherfuckers bonded my Nexi without my express permission?

I hadn't even been able to put them through the series of tests I had planned. They better be ready for an ass-kicking when I get back. That was the very least those two soulless gingers deserved. I splashed some water on my face and took a deep breath. As long as Reverie stayed safe and was there when I returned, I'd be overjoyed and might go a little easier on the assheads. It was unlikely, but stranger things had happened.

This whole experience had been fucked. There had to be a reason I'd been sent here, but I couldn't figure out what it was. Was I supposed to find out what happened to Reverie's two lost parents? That would be impossible while I was stuck here at the coliseum. I had to put every minute of my spare time into staying alive. Investigating anything had been put on the back burner, but that would have to change. Getting home to Reverie was the most important thing to me. It looked like I was going to learn to multitask. It shouldn't be too hard. Lucky for my Nexi, I wasn't just a pretty face. I'd be back in her arms in no time. Heading back to the training yard, I prayed with my whole soul (thank God one of her Faction had one) that I would return to my Nexi soon. I didn't know how long I could stand being away from her and keep what was left of my sanity.

CHAPTER 3
HAYES

I was stunned. Leaning back in my chair, Damien and I stared at each other in shock. What did this mean for me?

I'd been told by several credible sources that Adelaide had gone through the portal with John and Jesse. I'd tried several times to follow them, along with most Aurathions left behind.

"Do you believe him?" Damien asked, looking at me intently. His Nexus had also gone through the portal. Unfortunately, she was alone.

"I want to. I haven't been able to feel my connection with Adelaide in nineteen years. I'd assumed at this point that she was dead along with John and Jesse."

I rubbed my chest in the spot over my heart that still ached from her loss. Even though other bonds had been forced upon me, I still felt the phantom pain of losing Adelaide. It's much like I imagine losing a limb feels.

Damien looked at me with understanding, "I know the feeling, old friend. Jasmine barely got out, I told her to go with the promise that I would be right behind her after retrieving our baby boy." His eyes welled with tears.

He didn't like talking about this stuff and neither did I. Rehashing it just brought pain and a feeling of complete devastation to the forefront. We had too many lives dependent on us not to keep our heads in the game.

"You know Jasmine would understand. You both left Blaze with her sister to keep him safe. We didn't know that our ability to access a portal would be destroyed that day." I reminded him that he wasn't at fault, as I'd done too many times to count over the years.

"I know in my heart that's true, but finding Rose dead and Blaze missing was devastating. How am I ever going to tell her? How in the hell is she ever going to forgive me for the loss of her sister and our son? All these years, I've searched and never been able to find him." The look of sorrow and loss on his face was heartbreaking.

We'd known each other since before the war. Adelaide and Jasmine were best friends at the academy. Even after all our Factions were formed and we graduated from Emberhold, their friendship remained strong. Lucky for us guys, our friendship with Damien came easy. We just clicked like we'd known each other forever.

Lucky for me, our friendship had grown over the years. Now, we were as close as brothers. Without each other, I doubt we would've made it this far. The things we'd gone through together to survive were unbelievable.

"I don't have all the answers to the questions she'll ask. But I know even with everything I must explain, and the chance Jasmine might not forgive me, I still want to see her face again." He sighed and leaned back in his chair, closing his eyes.

I nodded my head in agreement, "You're right. I dream of it every night."

I understood how he felt. I winced at the thought of the things I'd done and had been forced to do that would bring shame to my Faction. If by some miracle Adelaide were alive, the things I'd have to confess would likely cause her to break our bond. I wouldn't blame her if she did.

Still, the chance to look into her beautiful amber eyes once again would be worth everything. I dreamed of them at night and how they must have looked going through the portal without me and Rue. The tears that must have made them shine in grief... the way they would look when she found out about my transgressions.

As much as looking at her beautiful face and listing the ways I'd betrayed her would kill me, the chance to see her once again would be worth it. Even if she only let me hold her briefly before discovering what a disgusting failure I'd turned out to be, it would still be worth it.

"Even if everything he's said is true, it doesn't sound like he knows how to get back. From our experience, you know that the academy doesn't return you until your task is done, and if Emberhold returns him, it will still leave us here in the same position we've been in," I ran my hands down my face. Damien nodded along with what I was saying, but it was apparent he was deep in thought.

I quieted and waited for him to speak. When he got like this, he was processing all his information and trying to formulate a viable plan of action.

Damien's ability lay in collecting knowledge. He never forgot a conversation he heard or participated in. Anything he read or saw was stored in his brain, and the pieces would come together over time; his reasoning and problem-solving skills were exceptional. He could identify patterns that most

Aurathions could not. His ability had kept us both alive and thriving in this new environment.

Thriving may be too strong a word, surviving was more accurate.

I thought back to the days and weeks after the war's conclusion. I'd stayed back to keep Rue safe; we were in his lab trying to collect all his data and destroy what we couldn't when I felt a stabbing pain in my neck. I blacked out and when I woke up, I was in a cell, in what I now know was deep under the coliseum. There was no sign of Rue and a deep stabbing pain in my chest from a lost connection to my Faction.

Later, I was told by witnesses that Adalaide was seen going through the portal with the twins. The pain in my chest told me she was dead, but I clung to this information with both hands. If there was the slightest chance she was alive, I still had a reason to keep living.

Soon after, I was forced to join the Tempest Faction and its Nexus, Selene.

She managed the entire coliseum for the Brummond Faction, which was the second most powerful of the Dark Factions, only surpassed by Trent Storm. That motherfucker was one of the instigators of this whole thing. I'd love to get him alone for about fifteen minutes.

After my bond was broken with Adelaide, I lost all my power. Our Faction had been made stronger by the fact that we were able to share our abilities. We'd used everything in the war, but it hadn't been enough to defeat the Dark Factions. I blamed most of that on being betrayed by the Council and their families. It was hard to win a war when you had to watch for enemies fighting beside you and not just against you.

I was forced to receive an injection of the serum that

caused the war, regaining my ability to levitate along with new skills. I wasn't as strong as before, but I had learned to cope with it. To keep my sanity, I had been assigned to Selene, not that I had any other choice.

The bitch was going to make me lose my sanity faster than the serum ever could.

Being forced to bond with her left me devastated, as it felt like a betrayal to Adelaide and my love for her. The only comfort I found was knowing that Adelaide wouldn't want me to lose my sanity or die. I never doubted our love and I know I would want her to do whatever was necessary to survive, no matter what that entailed. I felt in my heart that she would want the same for me.

Selene was a cunt. When I wasn't dreaming of my Adelaide, I was dreaming of squeezing her fucking neck until her head popped off. She was a complete sadist, and I wasn't the only one in her fucked-up Faction that wanted to kill the evil bitch.

"What if I could come up with a way to attach us to the boy so that when he went through the portal, we were pulled through, too?" Damien narrowed his eyes at me in question, breaking me out of my dark thoughts.

"I'd say let's do it, even if it's a long shot," I answered with no hesitation. "Since my last attempt, Selene is watching me much closer and the sensor in mine and the boy's neck also needs to be dealt with. I have no idea how it'll react to a portal. I know in the past we've found that certain technology is vulnerable to that kind of travel, but I don't want to be the one to test it."

Damien laughed, "I don't blame you. Adelaide always was partial to your face; I'd hate to bring you back to her without one."

I smirked, "What's not to like about this face? It's a nice face."

"The face is fine. It's the odor you emit from other parts of your body that isn't so attractive. I always assumed Adelaide had lost her sense of smell back at the academy." He scrunched his nose like a prissy bitch...that I absolutely knew he wasn't.

"The same could be said about you, my friend. I've smelt a day-old corpse that didn't stink as bad as you after you've eaten boiled eggs." I gagged at the memory.

Damien guffawed, "True that, my friend. True that."

We both laughed. I appreciated these moments. They also contributed to my survival.

As the laughter died out, Damien grew thoughtful again. "I need to do a little research. Give me a day or so, and I may have the solution to our problems." He stretched and stood up from his chair. "You know there's one thing you told the boy that isn't quite true."

"What would that be?" I had no idea what he was talking about.

"That there is nobody left in this world that can create a portal," Damien smirked. "There is something in this world that still has that power."

Damn, he was right, "Yes, but we haven't seen a Fellat in years. I'm not even sure they still exist."

"I know they do. Some interesting information was brought to me just recently." A big smile overtook his face. "Be ready to leave at a moment's notice and let the boy know to do the same. I'll get back to you as soon as I know something."

After Damien left, I reflected on the years I'd been here. I'd suffered through some horrible things, but every single one would be worth it if I were reunited with my love. I hoped she was alive and still with my brothers.

Now, if only I could find out what happened to Rue. I'd looked for him for years, but without our connection through Adelaide, it was nearly impossible to locate him. Maybe if I were rejoined with my Nexus, we could find him together. I knew he was too valuable to these evil bastards to have been killed.

I slowly rose to my feet. I'd better go find the boy and let him in on everything Damien and I had discussed. The next few days were going to be interesting.

I needed to make sure he'd be able to survive his upcoming battle or all of this was for naught. I knew he would fight with everything in him because he seemed just as anxious to return to his Nexus as I was to be reunited with mine.

She must be one special girl to be able to put up with him. The boy never stops running his mouth. Her father must be a saint because I'd never approve of that pairing. We'd put off having children because of the war and after meeting Nathan, that might be the only good thing that came out of it.

CHAPTER 4
HAYES

I left Damien's office and headed back to the training yard but paused when I saw Seamus coming down the hallway, his sniveling assistant following close behind him. He had his beady eyes narrowed at me.

Shit.

This couldn't be good.

"Hayes, get your ass to Selene's apartment right now. I have shit to do and having to run down your worthless ass just put me behind schedule." He poked a bony finger in my chest.

His assistant, Marvin, giggled behind him.

I fought the urge to shove his head up Marvins's ass. It would be a pleasant change of pace for them since Marvin kept his head up Seamus's ass on the daily.

"Yes, Seamus, I'll head there now." I kept my face and voice expressionless.

No way would I give this fucker the satisfaction of knowing just how annoyed I was. It was almost a tradition with us. He tried to get a reaction from me and I denied him the pleasure.

Seamus narrowed his eyes at me once again. He knew I hated him but couldn't reprimand me on the hunch that I was being a smart ass. Selene was a raging bitch, but I was in her faction. She wouldn't put up with a lowly employee punishing me for no apparent reason. I suspected Seamus was in love with Selene and wanted desperately to become her Faction. He could have the crazy bitch.

When it became clear that I wasn't going to say anything more, he and Marvin turned and headed back in the direction from which they had come.

I turned the opposite way into a long hallway lined with torchlight. The light cast sinister shadows on the stone walls, but I didn't pay any attention to it. All I could concentrate on was getting to my room as quickly as possible. Coming to a large wooden door, I put my thumb on the sensor located to the right and fell inside. I was one of the few to have the privilege of privacy.

The cost was high.

Hearing the door click shut behind me, I staggered to my bed and fell on it, breathing hard. I desperately searched under my pillow for the tattered length of pink material that I kept there. I brought it to my nose and inhaled deeply, calming almost instantly.

The scent of lavender was long gone, but it remained in my memory so vividly that I would swear the smell was as fresh as the day Adelaide last wore it. Closing my eyes tightly, I brought the memory of gifting it to her to the front of my mind.

"Come, my love, the day isn't getting any younger, and we have a test to study for tonight." Adelaide smiled that sweet smile that I fell in love with.

"I'm coming," I grinned as I shut my dorm door. It was rare for us to spend a day alone. If I was completely honest, most of the time, I didn't mind. The men that would soon become part of Adelaide's Faction had become brothers to me in everything but blood.

"What do you want to do first?" She stood on tip toes, trying to loop her arms around my neck.

Adelaide was a tiny thing. At times, I felt like a massive brute trying to catch a fairy. Lifting her off the ground so she could reach my neck, I gave her a quick kiss and then lowered her back to the ground.

"I have a gift to help keep you warm on our walk."

"I was hoping you would keep me warm," she fluttered her lashes at me.

I loved it when she attempted to flirt. She was not very good at it, but I appreciated it nonetheless because she clearly lacked much experience. It made me feel special that I was the first for her to try her feminine wiles on.

"That can definitely be arranged, but when I can't be there, this will help." I pulled the bright pink scarf from my backpack and wrapped it around her neck.

"I love it!" She lifted a length of the scarf, admiring the color.

My angel couldn't get enough pink in her life and we teased her mercilessly about it.

"Just another bit of pink to add to your collection," I smoothed her pale blonde hair away from her face.

I grinned at seeing the joy my small gift brought her. I didn't have the riches some of my brothers had, but that had never mattered to Adelaide.

She giggled and took a flying leap into my arms. I caught her easily and the little tease started biting gently on my lips as I chased her mouth, trying to deepen the kiss. Getting tired of this game, I moved one arm under her ass then took my other hand

and pressed her mouth firmly to mine. She moaned sweetly as our kiss became more passionate and we lost ourselves in the moment.

A door slammed in the hallway and we both broke apart, breathing hard. I slowly lowered her to the ground, enjoying the feeling of her body against mine. Adelaide looked a little dazed, but I had a massive grin. My chest puffed out with pride at how affected she'd been by our kiss. How did I get so damn lucky?

We left the building and strolled toward the nearby forest. The day was beautiful and I breathed in the sweet smell of lavender that always followed Adelaide around. Truthfully, I could be walking knee-deep in a sewer and still find enjoyment if my angel was with me.

Tears came to my eyes as I drew up my knees to cradle the scarf to my body. I knew I had to go to Selene, but I needed this moment to find the strength to keep going.

Hopefully, if Damien came through, I wouldn't have to deal with the bitch much longer.

I spent another ten minutes allowing myself to get lost in the precious memories of my angel before dragging myself off my bed. I pushed the scarf back under my pillow and went into the bathroom to splash my face with water. I'd delayed as much as I dared, so I dried my face and left my room.

The journey to Selene's apartment was a long one…not nearly long enough. She was at the very top of the building with a balcony outside her apartment that looked out over the coliseum.

The only reason I wasn't forced to live there with her and the rest of this fucked up Faction was because I'd convinced her that I needed to stay close to the warriors. Putting on a good show and pleasing the Brummond was more important to her than torturing me, barely.

I stopped in front of the apartment and stared at the massive black doors, feeling a sickness settle in my stomach.

Taking a deep breath, I knocked and arranged my features into a mask of indifference.

The door opened, and Beatrice grinned evilly at me. "It's about time you got here. Selene isn't happy with you."

I couldn't give a fuck if the bitch was happy, but none of the hatred I felt showed on my face. It would give her too much pleasure to inform Selene of any infractions she thought I'd made against her or her cunt of a mistress.

Beatrice had been the first member of the Tempest Faction. She was almost as sadistic as Selene herself. They'd been lovers since before the war. I thought that would make her jealous of the other Faction members, but she loved lording over the rest of us unlucky bastards.

The creepiest part of the whole deal was how similar Selene and Beatrice looked like each other. They had golden blond hair, blue eyes, similar facial features and were nearly the same height. The two could be sisters and seeing them intimate with each other added another layer of depravity to the Faction.

Beatrice opened the door wide and gestured for me to enter. I stepped into the apartment, and my feet sank into the plush red carpet. The walls were adorned with hand-painted wallpaper in deep red featuring black gothic designs, and all the furniture was a matching deep scarlet, accented with fluffy black pillows scattered throughout the room. An immense gold chandelier hung from the white ceiling in the middle of the room. A massive black stone fireplace was on one wall, with a huge portrait of Selene taking center stage, surrounded by a frame of pure gold. It looked like a high-class brothel, and for all intents and purposes, it was.

The rest of my assigned faction was present. It was rare

for all of us to be together because I wasn't the only member who wasn't exactly happy to be here.

"Take a seat. Selene will be out in a moment." Beatrice turned and slipped through the two elaborate gold doors that led into Selene's bedroom.

I couldn't contain the slight shiver when I thought of all the horrible things I'd been through in that room.

Touch was a problem for me now. It made my skin crawl when anyone got too close, but I refused to let that define me. I refused to let my monster win.

I took a seat on a black, plush stool near the bar. The bar was set up along one wall with a white marble counter featuring gold veins running through it. On the wall behind the bar hung a giant mirror with gold shelves; only the most expensive liquor available in Aurathia was allowed to grace them.

Selene demanded the best of everything, and most people were too scared of her ability to deny her.

"Hey man, how's everything going with the warrior sect?" Fabien yawned as he took a sip of the whiskey in his glass.

He was a nice enough guy. I knew he was one of the members who didn't want to be here. The perverse situations we had been forced to endure had made us tentative allies. Neither of us fully trusted the other, but we occasionally exchanged information.

"It's going. Do you know what this is all about?" I hated being caught unawares.

The other people in this faction were engaged in various activities. Some lounging decadently in the nude, some fully dressed with looks of dread on their face, and a few of them fucking on the carpet in front of the fireplace.

He rubbed his hand down his face, then took a much larger drink from his glass. "I heard that Selene had a big announcement to make. No one knows what it entails, and I did extensive digging. Being surprised by her is never a good thing." His eyes looked haunted, and he looked away from me, staring into space.

I didn't need to ask him what he meant. I knew all too well that a surprise from the bitch from Hell usually meant pain and humiliation for the members of this Faction that were reluctant to be here.

"Knowing her, it could damn near be anything," I grimaced at the squelching noise coming from the throuple writhing on the carpet.

Cat was on all fours, sucking Calvin's dick as Steven fucked her from behind. I hated all three of them with every particle of my being. It took all the self-preservation I had to resist killing them every time I saw them. If at any time I found out for sure that my angel was dead, those three would die right after I dismembered Selene and Beatrice. I would find my angel in the afterlife.

"I guess it's time to find out," Fabien said.

We both turned to see Selene and Beatrice exiting the bedroom.

Selene wore a black negligée that emphasized the paleness of her hair and skin. There wasn't any doubt that she was an attractive woman, but to me, her ugly soul shined through, making her hideous.

"Hello, Tempest Faction. I'm so glad to see everyone under the same roof." She paused and cleared her throat, giving the disgusting trio a look of warning. They halted their debauchery and gave her their full attention.

"Momentous changes are coming our way and I wanted to make sure my Faction was going to be a big part of it. Keep this strictly confidential. If you don't, the consequences will be severe." She smiled with an evil twinkle in her eyes.

"You know I love to dole out punishment, so feel free to try me on this."

No one said a word. Even her allies were quiet. We'd all been subjected to her punishments, and no one was eager for a repeat performance.

Selene paused for dramatic effect, then continued, "The Brummond has informed me that our leadership has found a way to finally stomp out what's left of the Aurathion traitors and take control of the world they fled to."

Gasps were heard all around the room. I barely contained my gasp of horror. The carefully crafted mask of indifference I usually wore had fallen, and astonishment had taken its place.

Selene delighted in everyone's reactions and continued, "I look forward to settling old scores." She turned to look directly at me, "Just thinking about the blood of old rivals covering my body excites me."

I felt like I was going to pass out for the first time in my life.

She had hated Adelaide from our first day at Emberhold Academy until the day Adelaide had escaped through the portal. They'd been rivals in everything they did, with Adelaide always coming out on top.

The reason I was part of this Faction and not another was Selene's hatred for my Nexus. Everything she did brought her a twisted sense of satisfaction because she knew how much Adelaide loved me.

I'd been able to endure the torture, knowing that in a small way, I was still protecting my true Nexus. If Selene could get to Adelaide, everything I'd done would be for nothing.

She had to be stopped.

My thoughts were interrupted by a caress on my arm.

Startled, I jerked back abruptly, as I had been lost in my thoughts and was not expecting to be touched. Then I saw Beatrice's smiling face.

"Come, big man. Selene craves a little time with you." She licked her lips as she continued to glide her hand over my muscled chest.

I stood quickly, and her hand fell from my body. She pouted, but followed closely behind as I walked to Selene. I felt like my heart was going to beat out of my chest. However, I had learned the hard way that Selene wouldn't be denied no matter what I did.

The last time I refused her, two new warriors had died. They were both barely eighteen and were slaughtered in a battle neither was prepared for. I couldn't be the cause of that again, even at the cost of my soul.

When I was next to Selene, she ran her hand down my chest on the same path Beatrice had taken. The difference was that she didn't stop there and continued lower until she squeezed my dick through the leather of my pants.

Closing her eyes and sighing, she said to the room at large, "I could almost orgasm just from the feel of his cock and the remembered pleasure it's given me." Opening her eyes, she looked at me, continuing to tighten her grip to the point of pain.

I avoided giving her the satisfaction of a response and simply looked straight ahead. Beatrice giggled next to us as she began to rub and squeeze my ass. Selene turned loose of my dick and grabbed my shirt, pulling me into her room with Beatrice close behind.

As the door shut, I glimpsed Fabien's face; he looked relieved, followed closely by guilt. I'd worn the same expression many times when he'd been in my position. No one wanted to be singled out by these two.

Beatrice began undressing me, and Selene removed her clothes. She then walked over to a large cabinet that held all kinds of small torture devices. Grabbing the cat-o'-nine-tails, she sent me a sinister smile.

"Lay on your stomach on the bed," Beatrice instructed.

I'd done this so often that I didn't know why she thought it necessary to direct me.

I laid down and waited for the first sharp sting to hit. Selene didn't disappoint. I heard the whistle of the leather sailing through the air right before impact.

The pain was excruciating, but I didn't make a sound.

I knew I wouldn't be able to stay quiet throughout the entire ordeal, but it gave me satisfaction to hold out as long as possible. I paid a price for keeping silent, but the small act of rebellion allowed me to keep a tiny bit of pride.

Hours later, when my back was a mass of bleeding tissue and I'd screamed myself hoarse, the true torture began Selene had injections at her disposal that would make me hard and after administering them, both women proceeded to enjoy me for the rest of the night, covered in my blood.

Please, God, let Damien find a solution to our problem. I didn't know how much longer I could maintain my sanity.

CHAPTER 5
NATHAN

Much to my surprise, I didn't see Hayes until breakfast the next morning. He lowered himself slowly in the chair across from me and dug into his food, not speaking until he was finished.

"Meet me in Damien's office before you go to the training yard. We need to discuss your upcoming battle."

Taylor appeared out of nowhere, "Do I need to come also?"

"No!" We both spoke in unison.

She flushed and held out her hands in a defensive gesture. "Okay! I just thought since I'm his partner, whatever you have to discuss probably concerns me."

As she stomped off, I heard her muttering under her breath, and I could have sworn I heard the name Selene. Soon after she left the room, I forgot her and anything she might have said because she was simply that trivial to me.

Hayes used the table to stand and limped out of the room. What the hell happened to the big bastard? This was the second time I'd seen him like this.

The first time, I'd assumed he was punished by this Selene chick that had been mentioned. She must be one badass bitch to put that kind of ass-whipping on him.

I followed him back to Damien's office. Damien was already seated behind his desk, talking to the guard who had been in front of the armory the previous day.

"Take a seat. We have lots of things to discuss this morning." Damien motioned to the three chairs in front of his desk. Yesterday, there were only two. He was so considerate. Maybe snacks would be served too.

I didn't know why the guard was here, but I was going to be pissed if they brought him in on what we discussed yesterday without asking my permission.

"Nathan, this is Razor. You met him when we entered the armory the other day." Damien gestured toward the guy.

"Yes, I did. You told me about his ability, but I don't remember the details." I tried for an innocent expression, hoping to trick him into satisfying my curiosity.

Damien started laughing, "Good try, but I know better. You shouldn't try to gaslight a man with an eidetic memory ability."

Razor joined Damien in his laughter, and I narrowed my eyes at them both. "Why's he here anyway?"

"He's part of the Allbright Faction and has been here at the coliseum since the beginning." Damien leaned back in his chair.

He barely looked older than I was, so I was taken aback by the information. I knew this was due to my human upbringing. Reverie had explained to me how their aging slows down when an Aurathion bonds with their Nexus. Her parents had aged remarkably well and appeared to be in their late twenties, even though they were nearing their mid-forties.

Hayes and Damien were the Hawthorne's age yet seemed much older. Despite having no wrinkles on their faces, their eyes spoke of all they'd been through.

I sat next to Razor, but Hayes walked up to the third chair and remained standing, putting both hands on the back. He and Damien shared a look I didn't understand, and then Damien began speaking again.

"Razor's ability is strengthened by his Faction. They were one of the few allowed to remain whole." Damien's face filled with sorrow.

I'm sure there was a story there, but for once, I kept my questions to myself.

"My Faction didn't participate in the war. We were in the jungles of Nyberie, studying the ancient species of Draxon for several years. The area is extremely remote, and we didn't learn about everything that happened until our return." He smiled at me, "You might find them interesting after your display in the training yard. They're where the Dragon myths originated in your world."

"My world?" I narrowed my eyes at Hayes and Damien. "Did you tell him what we spoke about yesterday without my permission?" I felt my face get hot. I was pissed right the fuck off. If anything these bastards did endangers my Nexi, I'd kill every one of them.

"I did. When you discover the many ways he can help us, you'll understand why we confided in him." Damien explained, not even slightly repentant.

Razor continued, "I can help you with several of your problems, and with the strength of my Faction, the possibilities are almost limitless."

"Why are you willing to help us? You're a guard here, after all." I asked him suspiciously.

"If it weren't for Damien and Hayes, I wouldn't be alive

right now. Not to mention it's because of them that my Faction was allowed to stay together." He looked at both the men in gratitude.

"I'm glad you and your Faction missed the bulk of the war. Being considered neutral was the only thing that saved you. Well, that and keeping most of your ability secret," Hayes said, his voice sounding hoarse.

He seemed off today, but I knew he wouldn't take kindly to me questioning him about it. Maybe he was coming down with something. Though for an Aurathion, that would be highly unusual.

Damien turned to me, "You can also trust him because what we're asking of him could harm his Faction and he's agreed anyway."

I knew that it would be on me no matter what happened from here on out. I just had to have faith that I put my trust in the right people. Putting Reverie's life into anyone's hands but mine was never going to sit well with me, no matter the circumstances.

"Your battle in the coliseum takes place tomorrow and I hope our chance to leave presents itself then. The plan is to leave before you're forced to perform, but if not, directly after." Damien explained.

"You still haven't told me how he can help," I said to Hayes, gesturing toward Razor.

Razor answered me himself, "We'll explain everything, but I don't think here is the safest place to do that."

At that exact moment, we heard footsteps approaching from the hallway.

Damien said quickly, "We'll meet in the armory after midnight."

Before any of us could respond, a woman I had never seen before entered the room. She was beautiful, with blonde hair and blue eyes, but something about her gave me chills. My instincts were reinforced by the stiff posture displayed by the three men in the room at her entrance.

"Beatrice, what can we do for you?" Damien asked in a very formal tone.

She walked around the room slowly, casually running her finger over some of the furniture, stopping in front of the board and examining it without saying a single word or responding to Damien's question.

I could feel the tension rising. I took my cues from the other men and stayed quiet.

She turned from the board, walked over and sat in the chair behind which Hayes was standing. I didn't know how it was possible, but Hayes stiffened even more. No one spoke as she took her time straightening her dress and smoothing her hair.

Just when the tension in the room had reached code red, she crossed her legs and smiled at Damien.

"Selene wanted to meet the man who displayed such an incredible ability yesterday. Imagine my confusion when he wasn't in the training yard and neither were you two." She raised one eyebrow in Razor's direction, "I really can't think of any explanation as to why you're here."

"We were meeting about the performance tomorrow. This will be Nathan's first and we thought Razor could help. Other than Hayes and myself, he's been in the most battles." Damien lied smoothly. "He's also familiar with Nathan's new talent."

We held our breath, waiting to see how this woman would respond.

She stood and placed her hand on Haye's chest, sliding it slowly around his body as she walked to the door, never losing contact until just her fingertips touched him, dropping her arm only when he was completely out of her reach. I'd witnessed many deviant behaviors since coming here, but something about her made the innocent touch raise the hair on my neck. I felt as though I was in the presence of true evil.

"We just wanted to make sure you're not telling tales, big man," Beatrice winked at Hayes. He winced slightly, and then his face turned into the expressionless mask I was accustomed to. If I hadn't been watching him closely, I would never have noticed it.

She paused in the doorway. "Come, Hayes, and bring the boy with you." She winked at me, "Selene's going to like you."

~⚜~

We walked down several hallways until we came to a large staircase. I'd never been in this part of the building, but it had progressively become fancier the further we walked. The staircase seemed to go on forever, but we finally reached the top and took a left. The end of the long corridor abruptly ended in front of a massive set of black doors.

Hayes paused and turned to me. "I'm going to see you through this." He looked down at the floor for a moment, then took a deep breath, "Only speak when you're spoken to and keep the smart-ass remarks to yourself." He stared at me until I nodded my head in agreement. "Anything you see or hear, do not fucking repeat it."

At this point, I'm not ashamed to say that I was somewhat concerned. We both knew the chances of my speaking only when spoken to were unlikely.

Hayes took another deep breath and knocked on the door. A woman in a maid's uniform answered. She bowed slightly and then opened the door wide for us to enter. It looked like a whorehouse from the old west and a French chateau had a baby. Several people were lounging around on the furniture in various stages of undress. They completely ignored us while we followed the maid. She led us through another set of double doors where a massive table awaited us, seemingly capable of seating twenty. The maid gestured for us to take a seat.

A man came through a swinging door carrying a large tray of food, and he was soon followed by several staff members who also had trays of food. We sat on the right side of the table, with Hayes next to the end and me beside him. The food kept coming until I thought the table would collapse under the weight of it all. I didn't think Hayes had taken a breath since we entered the apartment. I'd never seen him so tense and it was starting to freak me out.

Suddenly, I heard footsteps behind us and turned to see several people entering the room. There were three women and five men, not counting Hayes and me.

After they were seated, not a word was spoken. It was strange as hell, especially since several of the individuals who had sat down hadn't bothered getting dressed.

A few minutes later, I heard laughter and two women talking as they entered the room. I felt fingers weaving through my hair, releasing it from the tie that was holding it back from my face. I started to jerk away, but I felt Hayes grab my thigh and squeeze it hard. The woman from earlier, Beatrice, I think she was called, walked around the end of the table and sat across from Hayes. She gave the person behind me an adoring smile. How could someone that looked like a Barbie doll feel so evil?

The hand in my hair tightened and pulled my head back. I felt warm breath on my neck, followed by a sharp bite on my earlobe that made me wince. Blood trickled down my neck as a warm tongue licked the trail clean.

What the fuck? Hayes's hand never let up the pressure on my thigh in warning, so I fought against my every instinct and remained still. There was a tinkling laugh, and then my hair was released, and a blonde woman who could have been Beatrice's sister took the seat at the head of the table.

I assumed this was the infamous Selene. Every instinct urged me to get as far away from her as possible. If Beatrice felt evil, this woman possessed a malevolent aura that surpassed hers by leaps and bounds.

She wore a red dress that was pure steampunk fashion down to a tiny top hat pinned on the top of her golden curls.

Smiling, she looked directly at me. "Go on, handsome, fill your plate. A growing boy needs his protein." Licking her lips, she looked me up and down. "You need to keep up your strength."

Deciding for once in my life to follow someone else's advice, I kept quiet and restrained my urge to lash out. I picked up my plate and filled it with whatever was nearby, not having much of an appetite. This broke the spell around the table and everyone seated began talking and piling food onto their plates.

Hayes put very little on his plate. We had just finished breakfast an hour earlier, but I'd seen him eat many times in the dining hall and he could put it away. It seemed I wasn't the only one with no appetite.

"So, my young Nathan, where do you hail from?" Selene asked as she delicately took a sip of wine from her crystal goblet.

"I've lived all over Aurathia, so I consider myself a nomad." This was going to get dicey quick if she questioned me too deeply.

Selene hummed but didn't speak and took the small sliver of meat Beatrice held up, sucking the finger that held it. Beatrice moaned and closed her eyes in pleasure.

"He's from near the Pulchra village. A small town called Daisetta and a member of the Mills Faction. He was assigned to them at the age of sixteen." Hayes said all of this without any inflection in his voice.

Selene raised a single eyebrow, "Why was he assigned so soon?"

"I believe it was because he was orphaned at a young age. As is the usual practice now." He took a sip of his wine and continued to eat.

What the hell? This was all news to me. If this were a story he'd concocted with Damien, it would've been nice to have shared that with me. I felt like we were teetering on the edge of disaster and I was just along for the ride.

"That would explain why you consider yourself a nomad. I've heard of that Faction and they travel considerably, selling the lovely glass products made with their fire abilities." Selene finally took her attention off me and started eating.

"You better perfect that fire ability before tomorrow. You're fighting some vicious predators. I would hate to see you eliminated before we get a taste." Beatrice winked at me, continuing to feed Selene choice pieces from her plate.

"She's right. If you perform well, we might steal you from the Mills Faction and keep you for our own. You'll be more than satisfied with the change." Selene took a drink of wine and then licked the moisture from her lips, staring at Hayes with heat in her eyes. "Just ask our very own Hayes how much pleasure he's found here with us."

Several people around the table, including her and Beatrice, started laughing. Hayes didn't comment and continued to eat. The conversation around the table picked up, and it looked like my questioning was over.

After we were done, Hayes stood and approached Selene. She rose to her feet and extended her hand; he kissed it and then gave her a deep bow.

Selene turned to me and lifted her brow in expectation. I followed Hayes' example, kissed the hand offered to me and bowed. I felt like an idiot, but I valued my life enough to do what was needed to get through this. Touching my lips to another woman's skin made me nauseous, but coming home to my Nexi was more important than dying if I offended this demon.

We left the apartment, but both remained silent. I was digesting what had just happened, and Hayes was a morose bastard who didn't talk much.

When we approached the practice field, Hayes stopped and turned to me. "Be on time for our meeting tonight." He narrowed his eyes, "And make sure you're not followed."

I nodded, and he left without saying another word.

This world was fucked. I'm so thankful my Nexi's parents escaped this place. The thought of her growing up here was more than I could bear.

CHAPTER 6
NATHAN

T he minute I stepped onto the training field, Taylor ran over to me.

"How did your meeting with Hayes go? Do you have any strategies you need to share with your partner?"

I stared for a moment. This was getting ridiculous. Was she mental? I suppose I'd remained quiet longer than was acceptable to her.

"What?"

It was apparent my lack of response was annoying her. I was well past annoyed, so I'm glad I could share the wealth. "If there's anything I think you need to know, I'll fill you in. Everything we discussed had to do with my new ability and how I can fast-track my training to use it in the coliseum tomorrow," I turned my back to her, ending the conversation and walked to an area where the people with fire abilities practiced.

The most common ability related to fire was the conjuring of fireballs. Usually, they were uniform and could pack quite a punch, but nothing like the one I displayed yesterday. In our classes at Emberhold, we learned about common abilities, those that were rare and those thought to be extinct.

My new ability was rare.

The power behind the flames shooting from my hands felt infinite. There was no lag in energy or fatigue of any kind. If anything, I felt as if I had consumed a six-pack of energy drinks after using it. I'd kept that to myself because even though I hadn't been a part of this world for long, I knew how unusual that was.

I don't know if Reverie bonded with Zeke and Zane or only one of them, but this ability was strong. If she did bond with them both, then I could probably expect another ability to pop up. Hopefully, not while I was in the middle of my battle in the coliseum.

Right now, I needed to see if I could call up my new ability and then try to figure out how to use it. The blast I shot yesterday could have incinerated someone. I needed to find out if I could vary the strength of the stream from completely charring that ass to a precision burn.

I'd fucked people up before, but I'll admit to never being in a situation where killing was called for. Make no mistake, if I needed to kill to defend my Nexi, then I absolutely would. I'd kill to return to her, too. It might be considered selfish, but ask me if I gave a damn. I was selfish. She was my world, and I'd fuck up anyone or anything that threatened that. It was a bitch when your heart lived outside your chest.

I settled on a spot at the very end of the field. There, targets made of fireproof material native to this world were set up.

The targets varied in size and distance, with some even moving to increase the difficulty level. There was no grass on the field, only gravel and rock. It truly was the perfect setup for fire welders.

I spread my legs and bent my knees slightly. Squinting at the target, I held my palms out, straining so deeply I grunted to will the fire to shoot out.

"Are you trying to take a shit or recreate your ability from yesterday?" Razor had shown up at some point, but I'd been concentrating so hard I didn't hear him.

I narrowed my eyes, "If you're not here to help, you can fuck right off."

He laughed, "I'm here to help. I was going to stand back and assess what you needed before I jumped in. But I realized in the first sixty seconds, you didn't know dick. Unfortunately, we don't have time to slowly ease you into this ability. So, you're going to get a crash course."

~�™~

"F uck!" I'd burnt through another target completely. That shouldn't be possible, but apparently for me, it was.

"Watch me." Razor put two fingers on my neck briefly, then turned to the targets in his lane. He held his palm up and a small stream of fire shot out, hitting all three targets in quick succession.

"Damn it! How are you so good at that when it isn't even your ability?" I was frustrated by the ease with which he was welding my ability.

I had discovered a little about Razor's power, and it was amazing. He could literally take another's ability for a brief time and wield it like an expert. The only problem I could see with this was that he had to touch bare skin somewhere on a person's body to make it work. If you had this information, it would be fairly easy to take away his advantage in a fight. But for training purposes, it was invaluable.

"You're forcing it," Razor smirked.

"I'm not forcing it," I scowled at the smug asshole.

I had gotten the hang of calling my fire immediately, so I thought controlling it would come easily. We had been at it for hours and I was still balls to the wall with the strength of my flames.

"You need to breathe. Take a deep breath and let it out." He said calmly.

I took a deep breath and attempted to calm my frustration.

"Okay, that's good. Now close your eyes and picture what you want it to do." Razor kept his voice calm and easy.

I closed my eyes and pictured the targets in my lane, taking my time until I had every detail down pat. Next, I envisioned my flames flowing in a thin, controlled stream from my palms, melting a hole in each target the size of a pencil eraser.

Cracking my eyes open hesitantly, I saw that I had indeed melted small holes in each target—so small that if you didn't know what you were looking for, you wouldn't even notice them. I let out a loud whoop and picked Razor up, twirling him in a circle.

"What the FUCK?! Put me down, asshole!" Razor pushed at me, causing both of us to fall.

Before I hit the ground, I teleported out on the field and shot flames at one of the few targets left, incinerating it into ashes, using both of my abilities simultaneously.

"I'm back, baby!" I yelled, teleporting back to Razor. I moonwalked in a circle, then threw in a few hip thrusts for good measure while he sat on the ground looking at me in shock.

He'd probably never seen dance moves like mine before.

"You've got some serious issues." Razor shook his head and stood dusting the dirt off his ass. "Now, let's go get something to eat and you can practice more before bed."

"Hell no, I just found my groove. I'm going to practice for a little while longer." I waved him on.

"Whatever. Don't burn yourself out." He rolled his eyes and headed to eat.

I spent a few more hours honing my skills before eating and heading to bed. I realized long ago that I wasn't satisfied until I perfected whatever I was doing, especially if it involved doing my Nexi.

～☖～

I woke up a few minutes before midnight and quickly jerked my clothes on. I wasn't worried about getting caught sneaking out because of my ability.

Teleporting to the armory, I startled the shit out of Razor, who was laying his hand on the scanner to open the door.

"What the hell?" Razor yelled in a high-pitched voice, then scowled when he saw it was me.

"You fuckwit. Don't do that again. I could have hurt you!" He scowled at me, more in embarrassment than anger.

That squeal would have made a prepubescent girl at a Lewis Capaldi concert proud. "Sorry, you're right. I could have died from laughter. You should add that noise you made to your list of abilities."

I felt a slap to the back of my head. "This is serious shit.

Try to treat it as such." Hayes said as he and Damien scowled at me.

I rubbed the back of my head, "Why am I the only one you're making that face at? Razor is the one squealing like a weirdo."

Razor flipped me off before he motioned us all to enter the armory. We paused as he stopped to ensure the door closed, then led us into a room at the very back of the building. There was a scanner next to the large metal door. Razor opened this one, too, and led us inside.

The room was huge. I'd only been to the armory once with Damien, so of course, I'd never been this far back. Some weapons I recognized, but most of them were completely foreign. This world felt like Star Wars and Gladiator had a baby and the child was fostered by Charles Xavier and Claire from Outlander. I'd never get used to it. It blew my mind that Reverie's parents grew up here.

"How do they keep people with my teleporting ability out?" I frowned. Why had this never crossed my mind? I suppose it was because being away from Reverie affected me on every level and having abilities was still new to me.

"There are ways to prevent that, so don't try to teleport into a locked room. If you're lucky, it will only repel you; if you're not, you could be cut in half." Razor smirked, taking a lot of pleasure out of informing me of the drawbacks to my ability.

He was like the big brother I never wanted.

"Okay, let's get this done so we can go back to bed. We're going to need the rest." Hayes nodded his head at Damien to begin speaking.

"I'm sure you've discovered some of Razor's abilities. Now he's going to let you in on what no one outside of

Hayes, his Faction, and myself are aware of," Damien looked at Razor to explain.

"Because my Faction has been allowed to remain whole, all our abilities have remained stable and as strong as they were when our Faction was completed. You know I can touch anyone and wield their ability briefly," I nodded. "What you don't know is I can also transfer abilities from one Aurathion to another." I was stunned. That was amazing.

"Our plan is dependent on Razor's secret ability. He's going to mimic his Nexuses' power and bind us together." Damien moved his hand in a circular motion between Hayes, me, and himself. "If you get pulled back by Emberhold, we'll be taken with you." He smiled at Hayes, "If you're not taken back before your battle, we have a backup plan. Razor happens to know where he can touch a Fellat and mimic its ability to create a portal."

Hayes looked as stunned by this revelation as I did. I wasn't even aware that a Fellat had this ability. It looked like Pantar would be even more help to my…. I mean our Faction than I knew.

"What ability does your Nexus have that will allow us to be tied together?" I asked Razor. "I've bonded to a Nexus and she didn't get pulled here with me."

He beamed with pride, "She has the ability to bind anyone, whether person, animal, or object, to a location, person, or thing." His expression turned grave. "Tanya has been coerced into binding unwilling Aurathions into these fucked up Factions, where the Nexus can't support more than two or three members.

Additionally, she has been forced to keep prisoners of war bound to deadly regions of Aurathia, essentially forcing her to perform their executions."

"I promise to find a way to get your Faction free of this

horrible situation," Damien assured Razor, seeing the worry on his face.

Razor nodded, "I know you will." He looked at both Damien and Hayes in desperation. "I don't know how much longer she can live like this. The guilt has changed her, and I'm scared she'll end herself if I don't find a way out for us."

I approached him and gripped his shoulder. "I won't forget what you're doing for me. You can count on my Faction to help also."

Razor's surprised look was a little insulting, but a look of gratitude took its place, and he smiled. "Thanks, Nathan. I appreciate that."

Hayes hadn't spoken for a while and when I glanced at him, I saw that he looked deep in thought.

Damien must have noticed, too, "Hayes, what's up? Is something wrong with our plan?"

Hayes didn't speak for a moment, still internally debating something. He paced the room, then paused and narrowed his eyes, "What if we didn't wait? Why couldn't we get the hell out of here tonight?"

Damien looked stunned momentarily at the idea, then turned to Razor, "Why couldn't we?"

Razor started laughing, "Why couldn't we? It might actually be safer."

"Is there a reason you want to speed things up?" Damien asked Hayes with suspicion.

"There is, but I'd rather not say until we're out of here." Hayes refused to meet Damien's eyes.

I felt my heart speed up at the thought of being reunited with my Nexi sooner rather than later. However, now I was concerned with what Hayes knew that he wasn't sharing with us.

"Could what you know be a danger to the Factions back in my world?" I narrowed my eyes.

Hayes nodded his head but didn't speak.

"Okay, then. It looks like we're getting out of here tonight," Damien said with determination.

◦⚭◦

I couldn't believe that these lunatics were trying to start a Fellat breeding program. Were there no lengths that they wouldn't go to?

Razor had led us to a building at the furthest point away from the coliseum. It was nondescript and didn't look like it was maintained. Of course, I had never been near this place, but that wasn't surprising. What was surprising was that it was obvious Hayes had never been here either.

"I thought you were going to have to retrieve a Fellat. I didn't know the program was right here beneath my nose." The anger in Hayes's voice was apparent.

"I've known about it for some time, my friend. But I was scared to tell you in case you did something rash," Damien said cautiously. I could tell that Hayes was fighting the urge to fly into a rage, but after a few moments, he nodded to Damien.

"You were right to do so. I could have never let this stand and Selene would've had the excuse she's been looking for to lock me to her side."

Damien patted Hayes on the back, "None of that shit will matter if this works."

"Okay, first things first. Nathan, we need to use your ability to get rid of the tracking devices in both of your necks." Damien rubbed his hands together.

"Ummm, excuse me? What are you talking about? I don't know how to do that." I was confused.

"Don't worry, kid. Razor can use your ability to do it. I don't think you're ready for such a precise maneuver," Damien smiled.

Razor walked over and touched my arm. He then gripped my neck with the palm of his hand covering the entry point of the tracking device. His hand sent a wave of heat through me that almost brought me to my knees. It felt as if I were being branded from the inside out.

Razor removed his hand, and the pain stopped abruptly. I brought my fingers up to my neck, the skin felt extremely tender to the touch. Thankfully, it wasn't melted off, even if that's what it had felt like.

Hayes was next and of course, he stood there stoically like it didn't hurt at all. The dude was next level.

"Is it gone?" I asked Damien.

"I've been researching the removal of those devices for years and I'm ninety-nine percent sure this worked," Damien smiled in satisfaction.

"What about the other one percent?" I thought this was an important question to ask.

"Your face will look a lot less pretty the next time you see your Nexus." Damien laughed.

I personally didn't think it was funny.

"Don't worry, kid. It isn't functional anymore. The device is still in your body, but you can remove it after you get home." Damien patted me on the back.

"Enough with the bullshitting! Let's get on with it before someone discovers us out here." Hayes walked over to the door.

Razor followed closely behind and held his hand to the scanner. "This should work. I have authorization to open any building, and just in case this one is the exception, I managed to touch Seamus's hand during the evening meal."

"You can retain his powers for this length of time?" My eyes darted all around as I asked the question.

I was anxious to get into the building. Something didn't feel right, but maybe I was just nervous. The night was quiet, and I didn't see anything unusual.

"I retain the ability until I use it," he said, and then there was a click, and the large metal door slid open. We all entered cautiously, but the massive room appeared to be empty. As we walked deeper into the space, we saw row after row of cages—there had to be at least a hundred or more.

"How are we going to convince one of them to help us? They've been betrayed by our people and are not likely to believe anything we tell them." Razor was looking around in horror.

"I haven't figured that part out," Damien said, just as horrified as Razor.

We all slowly turned our heads to stare at him.

"What? I got us this far." He smirked.

"Fuck. Okay, let's spread out and see if any of the Fellats respond to us." Hayes started walking down the row to the right of us.

I shrugged my shoulders and headed for the row directly in front. The first cage I peered into had a mother and two cubs curled up together. She bared her teeth at me and growled. I held my hands up in a placating manner and backed away. Even I knew not to mess with an animal that had babies.

The next few cages I came across contained cubs, but no adult Fellat in sight. The babies huddled together, a few whimpering in their sleep.

This was fucked up. After meeting Pantar, I learned how

intelligent these creatures were. Their loyalty was incredible and they didn't deserve to be treated so terribly. I didn't think they could be forced to bond with a false Nexus, so death probably awaited most of them.

At the very end of the row, there was a cage that looked different from the others. It was completely solid, with only a small window in the door. I peered inside, but all I could see was darkness. Trying to give my eyes time to adjust, I brought my face closer to the window. Two glowing amber eyes appeared just inches from my face, causing me to flinch and almost bust my ass.

"Why do you smell like kin?"

"What?" I looked all around but didn't see anyone else.

"Why do you smell like kin, boy?"

I turned and looked at the two glowing eyes in astonishment. "Are you communicating with me?"

"Not very bright, are you?" the Fellat growled.

"How am I hearing you right now?" This was crazy. Had I gotten this ability from Grumpy through my Nexi?

"I'm assuming the ability was given to you through your Nexus. What name does your Nexus go by?" The Fellat demanded.

I'd kept this information to myself, but I felt this creature might be convinced to help us if she knew I belonged to a true Faction.

"My Nexus is Reverie Hawthorne." Suddenly, the Fellat started ramming her big body into the door.

I jumped back startled, but my mouth dropped open in shock when she said, *"My Nexus is Adelaide Hawthorne, and you must bring me to her."*

I felt a sudden desperation to get her out of there. "Back away from the door."

I put both hands on the door and called up my ability. Whatever the door was made from, it held up to the heat longer than anything on Earth would, but I was determined to get her out of there. I concentrated on turning up the temperature and finally, the door started melting until it was nothing but ashes.

A Fellat as big as Pantar cautiously made her way out of the prison cell. She walked up to me, sniffed the top of my head, then licked me from chin to forehead.

"What the hell?" I wiped the drool off on my sleeve.

"Come, boy, let's find the men you came here with and empty these cages. Then you can take me to my Nexus." She turned and headed back down the aisle.

I didn't know why I kept referring to her as "she," but for some reason, her movements and voice made me perceive her as feminine.

∼⚠∽

No one was there when we returned to where the guys and I had parted ways. The Fellat paused and then narrowed her eyes. She sniffed the air delicately, then growled low. *"One of the evil ones is here."*

At that exact moment, Hayes, Razor, and Damien materialized out of the shadows. Before I could question them about the distressed look on their faces. Beatrice walked out from behind them, dragging Taylor by the arm.

"Well, what do we have here?" Beatrice gave a tinkling laugh.

"Mira?" Hayes questioned in astonishment.

"Could this moment get any better? I finally get to dispose of this horrid beast and give Selene a reason to imprison you, only bringing you out for our pleasure," the crazy bitch threw her head back and laughed.

I saw Razor edging closer to Beatrice, so I tried to distract her. "Taylor, what in the hell are you doing here?"

Beatrice smiled, "I saw her wondering this way and decided to follow. Imagine my surprise when I saw you three sneaking in here."

Just when Razor was within inches of her, she turned suddenly, dragging Taylor between them. "Watch it, or I'll kill the little twit."

I didn't know what her ability was, but based on how she stopped Razor in his tracks, I was certain it was strong. Razor held out his hands in surrender and moved back.

It was shocking to see these incredibly powerful men so helpless. "You'll be happy to know you would have been too late anyway." She smirked at the three Aurathions. "We have people already in place to remove the most powerful Factions that made it through the portal." Beatrice winked at Hayes, "You can guess who's first on the list." She turned to me, "Now move your sexy ass from in front of the Fellat." Beatrice motioned to me with her free hand.

I shook my head, refusing to let this bitch hurt the Fellat and my chance to get back to Reverie.

"What a waste." She narrowed her eyes and then pointed her hand in my direction.

Taylor's eyes widened. Then she broke free from Beatrice's hold and threw herself in front of me. I was shocked to hear the sound of bones breaking as Taylor collapsed onto the floor.

Hayes didn't hesitate at Beatrice's distraction and took her head in both of his giant hands, cracking her neck with no effort at all.

I dropped beside Taylor, not knowing how to help her.

Both arms and legs were at odd angles, with the bones sticking out. Blood was flowing swiftly; an artery must have been severed.

"Why did you do that?" I didn't understand why she would sacrifice herself for me.

It was apparent she was in a lot of pain, and I had to lean closer to make out what she was saying.

"It's my fault she was here. She promised to make me Nexus and you to be part of my Faction." She closed her eyes and took a ragged breath. "I only ever wanted to love you." Her head fell to the side, and she stopped breathing.

The tragedy was that I would never have been in her Faction. I'd have killed her myself first.

CHAPTER 7
REVERIE
PRESENT

I pulled away from Nathan's arms and dropped to my knees in front of Dad. We stared at each other in disbelief, tears streaming down our faces.

How was this possible? Mom had been convinced he was dead along with my Poppa Rue. Did this mean Poppa was alive too?

I was jolted out of my thoughts when Dad pulled me into his arms. He held me so tightly that I could hardly breathe, but I didn't protest. I never thought in my wildest dreams this would be a possibility.

"My sweet, sweet girl. I'm so sorry." He kissed the top of my head, rubbing his cheek against my hair.

What could this man possibly have to apologize for? I pulled back, and he reluctantly dropped his arms. "We thought you were dead. Mom thought you were dead. She felt the bond break. How is this possible?"

He ran a trembling hand down my face, cupping my chin.

"It's a long story." He looked around, searching for her. "Where is your mother?"

In my disbelief at seeing my dad, I'd forgotten the fire and why we were at home in the first place. "I don't know." I sobbed, grabbing his hand. "We have to find them. There's no way the animals didn't warn Grumpy and Pop."

Before Dad could respond, I heard Pantar growl in warning. I saw another Fellat and a man with dark skin and long, white hair emerging from the portal. The Fellat was a beautiful pale gold, and I could see her amber eyes glowing from here. My view was cut off abruptly by the guys and Pantar surrounding me and my dad.

"They're safe," Nathan reassured everyone. "Damien, come meet my Nexi."

Nathan helped me to my feet as my dad and I stood. Everyone stepped to the side except for Pantar. He cautiously approached the Fellat as she bared her teeth at him.

I was shocked to see him bend his front legs and drop his head in a bow.

"It's an honor to meet the great Mira of the Hawthorne clan. I formally present myself as the bonded companion to your human cub, Reverie."

WHAT?!! This was Mira?

My mother was going to lose her mind. I refused to entertain the thought that they weren't okay. It would be too big of a tragedy for her not to experience the joy of a reunion with her lost loved ones.

The large golden Fellat approached Pantar. She circled him, showing her teeth, and her tentacles pointed at him in threat. Pantar never flinched, holding still for her inspection. After she made a complete circle around him, she nodded her head.

"I accept this bond and wish you great strength and cunning in protecting our family." She then rubbed her head against his body and he did the same.

I didn't know what to think about any of this. I was still stunned at finding out my dad was alive. Seeing Mira appear almost broke me.

"They are scent-marking each other. I would expect that Pantar has done this to every member of your Faction at every opportunity." Dad explained.

His tears had dried, but he hadn't yet taken his eyes off me. How could a man I just met look at me with so much adoration?

As Mira approached, everyone moved back except Nathan, Oren, and my dad. She was beautiful and almost as big as my Pantar.

"I am glad to meet the youngling of my bonded. Many apologies for not being here at your birth." She nuzzled the top of my head, and I wrapped my arms around her massive neck. Even though I wasn't bonded to her, I felt an instant connection.

"My mother has never recovered from the loss of you and my two fathers'. When we find her, she's going to be over-joyed." Tears rolled down my face in joy at the moment, but also in sadness that my mother wasn't present to witness this.

"Do not be upset, cub. I sense your mother is close. Give me a few minutes, and I will retrieve her." She disappeared suddenly.

I glanced around in hopeful confusion. "Mira said she could sense my mother was close, and she was going to retrieve her," I told everyone surrounding me.

My men and Chloe looked overjoyed at the news. Dad, on the other hand, suddenly seemed nervous.

The man that had appeared through the portal with him and Nathan approached and patted him on the back with a huge grin. "I'm so happy for you. Adelaide is going to be overjoyed to see you."

He turned to me and held out his hand, "My name is Damien. I've been friends with your parents since we were at Emberhold."

I eagerly grabbed it with both hands. "I'm Reverie, and it's wonderful to meet you."

Deciding that a distraction would help my dad with his nerves, I thought more introductions were in order. I motioned for Chloe to join me, "Dad, I'd like you to meet my bestie, Chloe."

I heard Nathan growl at my words. Dad narrowed his eyes at him and the growl abruptly broke off. Damn, I needed to learn that trick.

"Hi, I've heard so much about you from my parents. I feel like we've already met." Chloe reached out to hug him, but he quickly stepped back and held out his hand.

Chloe halted her movement and shook his hand. The transition was so smooth it felt like that was her intent all along. "Nice to meet you," he grunted.

It seemed he was a man of few words like Grumpy and Jet.

Oren stepped up beside me and held out his hand. "I'm Oren Storm. Faction to your daughter. It's an honor to meet you."

Damien's eyes widened in alarm just before my dad hit Oren in the nose, knocking him on his ass. Apparently, the hashtags were trending in all dimensions. Nathan and Zane laughed so hard they nearly fell. Being away and dealing with who knows what ,didn't mature Nathan at all. My sweet Zeke, on the other hand, helped Oren to his feet.

Nathan turned to my dad, "That was awesome! Way to go, big g-"

Before he could finish that sentence, Dad hit him in the

nose, knocking him on his ass. Damn, he wasn't giving my guys any slack.

Dad turned to me in exasperation, "You've bonded with a Storm? His family has betrayed our people and caused many deaths. He can't be trusted." His expression was thunderous.

"I can feel his intentions through our bond," I reassured him. "I don't know everything that happened, but I know he can be trusted."

I wasn't lying. There was no doubt that Storm was an asshole, and we had lots to discuss. But his love and dedication to me was warm in my chest.

"It's a true bond?" Dad tilted his head in question.

"True bond?" I wasn't sure what he was talking about.

"In our world, the bond has been perverted to form Factions that shouldn't exist. It's worked to keep our sanity intact, but much of the gifts given to us have been taken in the process." He looked at Oren. "The ability to feel each other's intentions and emotions are just a few."

Nathan was still sitting on the ground with his hand over his nose, looking at my dad in astonishment. "What the fuck? I thought we were friends!"

Dad frowned down at Nathan briefly before returning his stare of death to Oren. "That was for touching my daughter without my permission."

"Everyone believed you were dead. How in the hell could I get your permission?" Nathan asked in confusion.

"That's not my problem." Dad finally shifted his murderous gaze from Oren and looked at the other guys in expectation.

Jet had been quiet up to this point, but when he met my dad's eyes, he stepped up to introduce himself. "Jet Lockley, nice to meet you. I'm just a friend of Reverie's."

Dad said nothing for a few minutes, never taking his eyes

off Jet. "I don't appreciate being lied to," he shifted his gaze to the twins.

Zeke and Zane stepped up, "I'm Zeke, and this is my brother Zane."

I heard Nathan mutter, "No shit."

Dad frowned at Nathan, and once again, he quieted. When Dad turned his back, Nathan stuck his tongue out at him. I covered my mouth to stifle a giggle that was trying to escape. I may have been slightly hysterical at this point.

Nathan winked at me. I stared at him in adoration. I'd missed him so much, and the leather pants he was wearing made his ass look amazing.

Zane narrowed his eyes at Nathan briefly, then turned to my dad. "Hello, sir, it's nice to meet you." Both twins held out their hands.

Dad gave each a firm shake. "Are you both just her friends, too?" He mocked Jet's earlier statement.

"Hell no! I plan on being her Faction before the week is out!" Zane grinned in my direction.

Now, it was my turn to wink, which made Zane's grin grow even bigger.

Zeke slapped him on the back of the head. "Excuse my brother, sir. We're both honored to have been accepted by your daughter as Faction, and we hope to bond soon."

I couldn't leave him out, so I blew him a kiss. He pretended to catch it and put it in his pocket, and I almost swooned.

One of the things I loved most about Zeke was that he didn't care what anyone thought of him. If he felt like being corny with his Nexus, that's what he did. Zane rubbed his head, mean-mugging his brother. "That's what I just said, asshole."

Dad cracked a small smile. I felt my heart warm because it didn't seem like something he did often.

"I'm sorry you didn't get the pick of the litter, but I don't swing that way." Chloe pursed her lips in sympathy. "If it's any consolation, I plan on being around as much as possible."

Dad let out a small chuckle. I loved Chloe Moon. It really was a tragedy that neither of us was at least bi-curious.

We heard screams coming from the direction of the barn. I slapped a hand to my forehead because I couldn't believe I'd forgotten the fortified bunker Grumpy and Pop had designated as our safe house when I was little. Taking off at a run, I didn't wait for anyone else or pause to explain. My parents must have taken shelter there.

Grumpy had drilled us on the escape procedure he'd implemented in case of an attack. He knew they couldn't fight the more powerful Dark Factions with their diminishing abilities. Mom was key in its creation, using what was left of her earth ability to form an impenetrable space underground. She disguised the entrance so well that nobody but us could find it. They had stocked it with food and other supplies, allowing us to stay there for as long as we needed.

How in the hell could I have forgotten it?

When I was cresting the hill about two hundred yards behind our house, I was met by Rubbish, who jumped from the ground onto my shoulder, chattering in annoyance at me for not slowing my pace. He was upset about the fire and angry that I hadn't come to see them sooner. It was amazing that I could interpret his growls and squeaks, but the urgent need to see my parents didn't allow me to enjoy the moment.

I stopped abruptly when I saw three figures emerge, running toward me. Rubbish leaped from my shoulder and darted away, jumping onto the back of a large wolf that was keeping pace with Grumpy.

My eyes welled with tears, and I started running again.

I felt someone rush past me and saw that my dad had overtaken me. He was running so fast that all I could see was a blur heading towards my mother.

When I caught up to them, I saw Dad kneeling and holding my crying mother tightly. Grumpy and Pop looked on, frozen in shock at the sight of their missing faction brother.

Suddenly, I saw a bright white light surrounding them, and they began to glow. All their heads snapped back, and their eyes closed. The look on their faces was nearly euphoric. The light slowly faded, and they opened their eyes, staring at one another in amazement.

I watched tears streaming down their faces and couldn't contain my panic. "What happened? Is everyone okay?

Mom smiled at me in joy, "Our bond with Sly was renewed. With Sly and Mira's return, I have gained two pieces of my heart that were missing."

"I can feel you." Dad was smiling through tears. He sniffed her hair. Closing his eyes, he murmured, "Lavender."

They both held each other for a few minutes more. Then Mom tilted her head back and looked at him in question. "Is my Rue alive too?"

It was painful to see the hope on her face die when tears began running down Dad's face.

"I'm so sorry, my Nexus, I just don't know. I've looked for him for years but wasn't successful in my search." He hung his head in shame.

Mom grabbed his face, forcing him to meet her eyes. "It's not your fault, and I won't have you believe otherwise. You were returned to me, so we must have faith that Rue will, too."

Mom wiped the tears from her face and helped Dad to his

feet. Grumpy and Pop both pulled him into a hug. It was something I never thought I would get to see.

I felt Nathan and Oren step up on either side of me. "Let's give them some privacy, and I'll see if I can collect food and drinks. We can set up an area in the barn to eat and decide where we go from here." Oren kissed the top of my head.

It was nice to have someone, or in my case, several some-ones, to lean on at times like this.

"Sounds like a plan," I smiled, my heart overflowing with joy.

CHAPTER 8
REVERIE

We entered the barn and Chloe and Zeke helped me arrange hay bales in a circle. Zane and Jet cleared the old wooden table in the corner and placed it in the center of the bales.

I felt a heated gaze as I stood looking critically at our setup. Glancing in that direction, I saw Nathan stalking toward me. The look on his face made my panties immediately damp and my heart skipped a beat. I'd missed my psycho with every particle of my being, and I wanted to have him inside me sooner rather than later.

It looked like he had the same idea.

Before Nathan could reach me, Oren grabbed his arm. Nathan looked at him in confusion, his expression changing abruptly to outrage right before they teleported out.

Well, damn! Apparently, he now had Nathan's ability and for Oren, there didn't seem to be a learning curve. As much as I wanted to be in Nathan's arms, part of me was glad for Oren's interruption. My parents were right outside and we had lots of things to talk about. I knew once we started, neither of us would be satisfied with a quickie.

I wanted hours to worship my psycho.

Jet approached but halted when Rubbish ran up his leg and perched on his massive shoulder. He looked at me in panic as the large raccoon began to run his little paws all over Jet's face. I couldn't stop my laughter when Rubbish stuck one of his tiny fingers in Jet's nose. He jerked his head back, and Rubbish chittered in laughter. He climbed down Jet and sat on a hay bale, waiting for the food to arrive.

"What the fuck?" Jet growled, glaring at Rubbish.

"He was just inspecting you. He's usually not fond of strangers. You should be happy he likes you." I was trying to keep the smile off my face.

Jet was still wiping at his nose as he glared at me, "I don't mind him inspecting my face, but he can keep his fingers out of my nose. Now all I can smell is shit!" I lost it.

Tears were running down my face, and I couldn't catch my breath. Rubbish had been known to prank new people. Lucky for Jet, it was probably just chicken shit...probably.

Chloe walked over and glanced at us both in confusion. "What's so funny?"

Her question only made me laugh harder. Seeing I was in no shape to answer, she looked at Jet for an explanation.

"That raccoon stuck his finger up my nose, and now all I can smell is shit." He gestured to me in aggravation, "Apparently, she finds that hilarious." Jet grabbed a paper towel off the table and vigorously blew his nose.

I decided to cut the big guy a break. "It's probably just a little chicken shit." He narrowed his eyes at me and I couldn't resist messing with him a little further. Trying my best to keep a straight face, "But on the other hand he has been known to scavenge dirty diapers from our neighbors down the road." I lost it again.

Jet looked at me in horror and started gagging. Seems our giant had a bit of a weak stomach.

Chloe looked at him in wide-eyed disbelief, then back at me, still trying to catch my breath.

She started laughing harder than I'd ever seen, and the sound out of her mouth stunned me so much that my laughter abruptly stopped.

She sounded like a braying jackass.

Jet and I stared at her in stunned disbelief. We'd laughed together often, but she'd never sounded like this.

Zane and Zeke walked over, and Zane threw his arm around my shoulders. "What did you do to make Chloe break into her jackass laugh?"

I squinted at him, "Her what?"

Zeke grabbed my hand and threaded our fingers together.

"Her jackass laugh." He grinned, repeating what his brother said, "When Chloe finds something really, really funny, that's how she sounds. When we were younger, we would do all kinds of crazy things to get her to laugh like that."

Chloe was still laughing when, out of nowhere, we heard a real donkey start braying. Looking over, I saw that Jack had stuck his head out of his stall and was giving Chloe heart eyes.

"I think she just found her first Faction member," Zane smirked in mischief.

That set us all off, and this time even Jet laughed.

~⚜~

By the time Nathan and Oren returned with the food, my parents and Damien had made their way inside, everyone taking a seat. My dad had pulled mom down onto his lap and didn't look like he had any intention of letting her go anytime soon.

The guys had brought a variety of things back and we all dug in. It was so sweet seeing Dad feed Mom before feeding himself. Grumpy and Pop looked at them in wonder, not showing the least jealousy.

Nathan had likewise pulled me into his lap, nipping at my neck and nuzzling my head while feeding his face.

Dad didn't seem too excited about his actions. He was dividing his attention between Mom and me. Looking slightly dazed, I was sure, at the shock of finding out he had a daughter and reuniting with his family.

When Zane walked over and attempted to take me from Nathan, he growled at him menacingly and squeezed me tighter. Zane raised both hands in surrender and sat on the ground in front of us.

When everyone was finished eating, Pop walked behind Dad and squeezed his shoulders. I noticed Dad flinch slightly. "I think it's time we all caught up on everything that's been happening." He glanced around the room until his gaze rested on Nathan, "Do you want to start?"

"I have a question first. Why have you been using the name Hayes all this time?" Nathan was looking at Dad in confusion.

"I know this one." Mom spoke up. "His full name is Sly... Hayes... Hawthorne." She kissed his lips between each name.

"As usual, my Nexus is correct. I started going by Hayes because I felt like Sly had died after my bond was forcefully broken." He stared into my mom's eyes, "I couldn't stand to have anyone call me Sly, except Adelaide and my true Faction."

"Makes perfect sense. Nathan, do you still want to start?" Pop had a soft smile on his face as he looked at Mom and Dad with affection.

Nathan nodded. "Soon after Emberhold sent me to initiation, I realized I was in Aurathia." He glanced at Dad, "I ran into the big guy almost immediately, and after I rescued him...."

"Boy, I'll kick your ass. You didn't rescue shit." Dad growled, narrowing his eyes at Nathan.

Mom reached up and kissed his cheek. He immediately redirected his attention back to her, raising her hand to his lips and kissing her knuckles.

"We know Nathan can exaggerate things just a bit," Mom said without taking her eyes off my dad.

Nathan grinned back. "Okay, maybe I didn't rescue you right away, but I did get captured on purpose by those girls so that you weren't in that cage alone."

"But was it on purpose?" Dad raised one eyebrow towards Nathan, shifting forward ever so slightly until Pop dropped his hands from his shoulders.

"Girls?" Pop grinned as he walked around to sit at Mom's feet. "Did you get captured by a bunch of girls, Sly?"

"Fuck no! I got captured by the Pulchra." He frowned at Nathan.

Nathan just grinned completely unapologetically.

Grumpy grimaced, "Those women are formidable. Didn't you go up against them during your initiation?" he asked Pop.

"Hell, yes, I did. Unlike Sly, I defeated them with no problem. It's understandable why he couldn't. I was able to distract them with my handsome face." Pop ran a hand down his cheek and struck a pose. "He obviously doesn't have that weapon at his disposal."

"I think his face is beautiful." Mom sighed, still unable to take her gaze off him. Dad smiled and gently kissed her lips.

"He told me you liked it." Damien smiled at Mom.

"He's right. But he may have downplayed how I feel about it. Like isn't a strong enough word." She framed his face in her hands and brought her lips to meet his in a gentle kiss that brought tears to my eyes.

Jet spoke up, obviously at the end of his patience, "Can we get on with the story? After what was done here, I'd like to decide our next plan of action."

"I'm not sure why you think you'll decide anything." Grumpy frowned at him.

"You're just a friend, so why does any of this matter to you anyway?" Dad growled at Jet.

"I don't think they believe you're just a friend, Jolly," Nathan spoke out of the side of his mouth like he was trying to keep his comment confidential but not lowering his voice at all.

Jet scowled at him, but then directed his attention back to Grumpy.

"I misspoke. I meant to say *we* need to decide." He gestured around the circle. "It matters to me because my friend's parents were attacked, and the academy sent my roommate to Aurathia. Nathan bringing back a member of the most powerful Faction ever known seems significant."

"Second most powerful...eventually." Nathan couldn't help himself. I pinched his nipple.

Nathan squealed and jerked back, almost causing me to fall out of his lap. Then he raised his hand like he would pinch mine in retaliation.

Zane had turned when Nathan squealed, seeing him

going in to grab my boob, he thumped him in the nuts. Nathan bent at the waist, dislodging me from his lap this time. I landed on my feet, backing up in one quick motion. Nathan rose from his seat and had a knife at Zane's neck.

Zane, in turn, had jumped to his feet and had his knife pointed at Nathan's nuts. The two stared at each other with identical expressions of menace.

I was holding my breath, trying to decide the best way to intervene, when they suddenly started laughing hysterically. They put their knives away and patted each other on the back. Then they started fighting and roughhousing like two little boys.

Oren rolled his eyes and walked over, pulling me away from the two psychos and into his protective embrace. It was astonishing how natural it felt after everything he'd done. We'd only been bonded for a few hours, but through our connection, it felt as if I'd known him my entire life.

At some point, he would have to be punished for what he'd done. I hadn't decided what that punishment would be, but it needed to be memorable.

"That's enough, brothers. It's time to get serious. The lives of our Nexus and her family are in danger. We need to find out who did this to the Hawthorne home and if any other Aurathions in this world have been attacked." Oren frowned at Zane and Nathan, speaking in his instructor's voice.

"I hate to agree with a Storm, but he's right." Grumpy looked at the two troublemakers with disapproval. "Sly, would you like to continue? Then we'll update you on what happened here."

Nala, a large grey wolf who had been a constant presence in my life, approached from her resting spot and nestled at my feet. When Nathan reached down to pet her, she growled and displayed her sharp teeth as a warning, then lowered her head to her paws and closed her eyes. It wasn't personal; she allowed only my immediate family to touch her.

Even though many animals chose to make their home here, they remained wild. Some only allowed Grumpy to pet them, while others adopted all of us. In the end, it was always their choice, and I had been raised to respect that.

Pantar and Mira both chuffed in laughter and continued eating their meal. Copper, our mongoose, chose that moment to run up Mira's leg and climb to the top of her head, chattering at Nathan and Zane in disapproval. After he finished his tirade, he brushed his tiny paws together like that was that and ran back out of the barn.

We all busted out laughing at his antics. When our laughter died, Dad awkwardly cleared his throat and glanced at Damien.

"I'd like to take it from here if that's okay with everyone." Damien continued after he received nods from Mom and my fathers.

"There are some things that Hayes...Sly would like to discuss in private with his Nexus." Mom smiled gently at Dad in sadness and what looked like guilt, then leaned up to kiss him. "No, Adelaide, wipe that look off your face. Nothing that happened is your fault. I'm the one that left to find Rue, so all of it's on me." He bowed his head.

Mom put her hand under his chin and lifted his head to look into his eyes. "You left to save your Faction brother. We have never resented your decision. I've just always regretted that we didn't stay behind with you."

"Never regret that! I wouldn't have survived knowing the enemy had you. Neither Rue nor I would have wanted that. You did what you should have done, safeguarding our precious daughter." He spoke gruffly to her before sending me a look of love and adoration that brought tears to my eyes.

Damien cleared his throat and began speaking again, "We were assigned to the coliseum in Bellona." He looked at my parents, "You know it as Paradisio."

Mom gasped, "They renamed the capital city."

"Yes. After the Brummond took over the coliseum, he renamed the city after his first Faction member." Damien explained.

"I'm sorry we keep interrupting, but are you talking about Charles Brummond?" Grumpy asked.

"Yes." Dad surprised us by answering.

"He was always such a brutal bastard. I can't imagine him in charge of anything." Pop shook his head in disbelief.

"It was nothing you could imagine unless you were there to experience it," Dad mumbled, then buried his face in Mom's hair.

Nathan pulled me away from Oren and sat back down, holding me tighter than was comfortable. Neither Oren nor I said anything about his actions.

Damien stared at my dad with sympathy, then continued, "We were made to fight, and Nathan was supposed to have his debut performance the day we escaped."

Now, it was me holding Nathan tighter than what was comfortable. As soon as we got a moment alone, I'd talk to him about what he'd seen and gone through. He was the kind of guy that could be in a shit situation and come out smelling like a rose. That didn't mean he wasn't affected; I knew this even without our connection.

"A guard and close friend told us where they were keeping Fellats captive and helped us break in. We had no idea that Mira was there or even still alive." Damien blew out a breath.

Mira raised her head at his words.

"I had been waiting for you." She pointed a tentacle at Dad. *"I had felt your presence almost from the beginning and knew you would find me. Those weak bastards would never have captured me if I wasn't betrayed by one of my kind."*

Those of us who could hear her gasped at this. A Fellat betraying their own kind was stunning. I quickly let everyone in on what Mira had revealed.

"I have a bone to pick with you later, naughty Nexi. You didn't tell me that I could communicate with your Fellat." Nathan smirked.

"We can discuss that later." I winked at him.

"What the fuck?" Grumpy growled.

I stared at him in shock because he rarely used that language.

Mom stood up from Dad's lap, and he reluctantly let her go. She walked over to Grumpy and took his hand.

"The Fellat that betrayed me had no choice in the matter, I forgave her immediately after it happened. They had taken her cub." Mira spoke to Grumpy in a soothing voice.

It was a testament to Damien's character that he hadn't become frustrated by all the interruptions. He continued his story, "We released the other captured Fellat before Mira formed the portal that brought us to you. Sly had no idea that you would be here. The joy it brings me to see him reunited with his Faction is immeasurable." Damien smiled gently at Mom.

"Damien, Jasmine is safe in an Aurathion town not too far from here," Pop said, realizing that Damien had no idea what had become of his own family. "We've kept in contact with her, making sure she's safe. Jasmine never wavered in her belief that you would return to her."

Damien fell to his knees and started sobbing. Mom

rushed to him, dropping to the ground and murmuring words of comfort. Dad joined them, laying a hand on his friend's shoulder, a look of absolute joy on his face.

"I'd gotten information that the Dark Factions were getting ready to attack, and we knew we had to return here as soon as possible." Damien wiped tears from his face. "Unfortunately, we didn't manage to leave without any issues. Selene, who was put in charge of the coliseum by the Brummond, had been closely monitoring Sly since his recapture. A member of Selene's faction, Beatrice, learned of our plan and was killed trying to prevent our escape."

Mom's gaze jerked to Dad, "Beatrice? Selene? The bitches that hated me at Emberhold?"

Dad hung his head, "Yes. Selene made me part of her Faction."

There was complete silence until Mom yelled, "I will murder that motherfucker!" We watched in awe when she levitated a foot in the air, her hair blowing behind her with the wind she was generating.

It looked like my mom was regaining her abilities. That bitch, Selene, better watch her back.

CHAPTER 9
REVERIE

We all looked at Mom, stunned by her outburst and the show of her power.

Well, everyone but me.

She was a passionate person, and I had always been aware that as much as my fathers worshiped her, she returned their feelings twofold.

After bonding with Nathan and Oren, I understood completely. I hadn't even bonded with the twins, and I had no doubt I'd kill for them, too. I wasn't ready to admit how I felt about Jet, even to myself.

Mom looked at Dad and demanded, "You will tell me everything she put you through. Do not try to keep anything from me, thinking that I can't handle it or that I would think less of you."

She lowered herself back to the ground and walked up to Dad, grabbing his face even as tears poured down hers. "I vow to you right now on all that I hold dear, I will kill her for you."

The smile that broke over Dad's face was unexpected. He

grabbed her and pulled her back into his lap. "Adelaide, I'm the one that's supposed to protect you." She started to protest, but Dad stopped her with a kiss. "Let me finish, " he admonished her gently.

She nodded her head.

Dad kissed her once more, slowly, then smiled against her lips, keeping his eyes closed. "I'd forgotten how fierce you can be." He took a deep breath, gathering his thoughts, then opened his eyes, meeting her gaze. "There are things I will never tell you. Not because I think you can't handle it, but because I vowed long ago not to let that bitch live in my head more than necessary. I lived for years feeling like I had betrayed you. Terrified that if you were alive, and I ever found my way back, you would reject me when you found out everything that had happened."

The thunderous frown on my mother's face was frightening.

She started to speak, but Dad interrupted her once again. "I know it was stupid, and being back in your presence, I realize just how ridiculous that was. I think losing our bond caused doubts to sneak in, and for that, I'm sorry." He brushed her hair back. "Now kiss me and help me forget that we were ever parted."

My mom's expression at his words was like seeing the sun break through the clouds.

"I love you." She raised her lips to his.

Grumpy stood and walked over to embrace them both. Pop immediately joined them. Seeing them together brought tears of joy to my face.

I watched for a few more moments, then motioned for everyone to follow me outside. My parents deserved a few minutes to have a private reunion, after everything they'd been through, before we continued our conversation.

When we gathered outside, Nathan pulled me into his arms.

"These months I've been gone have felt like forever."

I pulled back, "Months? Plural?"

He frowned, "Yes, why do you say it like that?"

"It feels like you've been gone for years, but it was just a little over a month for me." I was confused.

"Time can move differently from dimension to dimension. Initiation can be confusing because of this. Sometimes it seems like you've only been gone a matter of days, and when you get back, weeks have passed. Sometimes, for you it's been months and in this world, you've only been gone days," Damien explained.

"That is fascinating," Jet commented, standing right beside me.

I was a little startled that he was so close. That boy needed a bell around his neck. It was crazy that someone that big could move that quietly.

"Can you continue to fill us in?" Jet looked at Damien expectantly.

"Nathan can fill you in. I'm going to find out where my Nexus is and head there now. I'll be in contact so we can coordinate in a few days." He headed back into the barn, too impatient to see his family to give my parents any more time. I didn't blame him. It had been years since he'd seen them.

Nathan began to speak, squeezing me tightly, my back against his chest, both of us facing everyone.

"It was intense there. Aurathia is a mix of advanced technology and the ancient." He stopped, gathering his thoughts. "The battles I witnessed in the coliseum were brutal. Limbs torn off, blood and gore everywhere. I really hate that we left before I got to fight."

Why was I not surprised?

I hit his thigh, and he laughed, "The only thing that could have dragged me out of there was you, my sweet Nexi." He leaned down and whispered, "My existence depends on yours. Without you, there is no me."

I leaned my head back, and he kissed me; the kiss soon turned heated. He grabbed my hair, pulling my head back further to deepen the kiss. His taste consumed me as I turned in his arms, trying to climb inside him. This man and the other guys standing here with us were my soul.

A throat cleared, dragging me back to the present. Nathan reluctantly raised his head but kissed me softly before looking back at the guys.

"Hayes...dammit...Sly found out that an attack on my Nexi's parents might be imminent, so we moved our escape plan forward. Not that he told any of us before we left." Nathan frowned.

He looked down at me. "There were some complications that will probably cause us major trouble."

"What complications?" Zeke asked in concern. "The head bitch's bitch was killed, and I don't think she is going to take it well." The expression on Nathan's face was freaking me out. He was rarely serious, so I took notice when he was.

"Just to clarify, we are talking about Selene Ormand?" Oren asked. It sounded like he was really hoping he was wrong.

"Yes, and she's a fucking nutcase. I can't imagine being forced to become one of her Faction." Nathan shivered involuntarily.

"Fuck!" Oren ran his hands through his hair, then turned and jerked me away from Nathan, hugging me tightly.

"What the fuck, man? I'm the one that's been away from her for months." Nathan scowled at Oren. "Plus, we have some shit to deal with. I want details on how you made it into the Faction before the Wonder Twins."

Zane grinned at Zeke, "Finally, he gets it right."

"Wonder Twins, my ass," Chloe smirked. "More like two hanging nut sacks."

Zeke rolled his eyes at her and said to Nathan, "We can discuss all of that later. We need to figure out the best way to stay safe until we have a fully bonded Faction."

"I agree. We do need to have a discussion." He frowned at Nathan. "We will address it, but for now, we must decide our next move." He buried his nose in my hair and inhaled deeply, squeezing me tighter than before.

"Who is Selene, and why does she scare you?" I returned his hug.

This man didn't seem intimidated by much. Through our bond, I could feel the intensity of his worry.

"She is the third most powerful Aurathion and a vicious bitch. Beatrice has been her most loyal Faction, and if it's possible for a person like Selene to feel love, Beatrice would be it. They're both bloodthirsty psychopaths that love to torture and kill." Oren kissed the top of my head and then began pacing.

"We need to find out the extent of the damage here, then get back to the academy. There are only a few weeks before Christmas break. I need to learn everything I can from Kristine and my father." He frowned and then turned to me.

"What?" I asked when a few seconds passed, and he still hadn't spoken.

"We have to keep our bond secret. There is no way I can find out the information we need if my father learns of our connection." Oren spoke with regret in his voice.

I sighed, "Just one more secret in a long line of secrets." I knew he was right, but keeping my Faction a secret felt wrong and had from the beginning.

"It does suck, but I agree with the Shitstorm," Chloe said. "You'd have to be on alert twenty-four seven if Kristine knew."

"I'm not scared of that bitch." I glowered at her, annoyed that Kristine controlled my choices, even inadvertently.

She held up her hands, "I know that! I think you've proved that several times over. I just don't want you to have to deal with it."

My face softened, "I'm sorry, I just can't stand the thought of hiding my relationship with Oren because of her."

"I couldn't give a fuck about her. But we need information, and she definitely won't spill it if she knows about us." Oren reassured me.

I knew I was acting ridiculous, but our bond was so new that I didn't want to sneak around to be with him. Plus, the Nexus in me was pissed at the thought of other women not knowing he was mine, even if he was a giant dick most of the time.

"Guess who doesn't have to keep it secret, bitches?" Nathan crowed, "This motherfucker right here!" He pointed to himself and started twerking.

"What the fuck is wrong with you?" Jet looked at Nathan in disgust.

"All the things," Zane laughed. "But especially that twerking game. This is how it's done." Then he started twerking.

Damn, that boy had some moves. He could've starred in *Magic Mike*—my poor Nathan...not so much.

"Holy shit! My eyes! Please stop. I'll do anything." Chloe begged, covering her face with her hands. Oren closed his eyes and pinched the bridge of his nose.

"Okay, enough of this shit." He leveled a finger at Nathan and Zane. They both froze instantly. Their eyes were the only thing they could move.

I tried to contain my laughter, but it was impossible. They both had frozen mid-twerk, and it wasn't flattering at all.

Oren attempted to maintain a stern expression, but he was losing the battle. "Now the men can talk."

The grin fell off my face, and I teleported behind him, pinching his ass hard.

"The men.... hey!" I ended the sentence with a squeal when Oren swatted me firmly on the ass in retaliation.

"What the fuck, woman!" He frowned, rubbing the spot I'd pinched. Before I could respond, Jet had a huge knife at Oren's throat.

"Don't ever hit her again." He growled.

He wasn't fucking around because he was holding enough pressure that a drop of blood seeped out and slowly ran down Oren's neck, disappearing into his shirt.

Oren was so stunned he must have lost concentration, because Zane and Nathan were released from his hold.

I slowly raised my hand and gripped Jet's arm. He stopped glowering at Oren and transferred his gaze to me.

"I'm okay, Jet. It was nothing. Oren didn't mean anything by it and wasn't trying to hurt me."

Jet didn't comment and narrowed his eyes back at Oren. Briefly, I wondered if he was going to slit his throat no matter what I'd said. I didn't release my grip on his arm until he lowered the blade.

"I don't approve of men hitting women." Jet stepped back and leaned against the round bale of hay beside the barn. His face was expressionless, as if nothing had ever happened.

The rest of the guys were so shocked at his reaction that nobody said anything for a few minutes.

"Just a friend, huh?" Nathan smirked, breaking the silence.

Oren stared at Jet chillingly, "I would never hurt my Nexus. But since we both know it's not just 'any woman' you're worried about," he made finger quotations in the air. "I'll let you have this one." He narrowed his eyes, "But next time, I won't hold back. Passive or not."

Jet nodded his head, but his expression never changed. There wasn't even the tiniest bit of fear on his face at Oren's words. I got the impression that there was a lot more to Jet than any of us knew. He had no fear and seemed a lot older than Chloe and me. It felt like he had seen some shit.

What was he hiding?

"I would like to seal our bonds as soon as possible," Zane said, trying to ease the tension.

Zeke nodded his head in agreement. "It's time. I want to check on our parents and make sure everyone is okay. But I agree with Zane; it can only strengthen our Faction and help us in the long run."

Everyone looked at Oren to see what he thought. Me included. It was starting to feel like Oren was the leader of this Faction, and I was okay with this... to a point. I was secure enough in myself to know when I needed help, and this was one of those times.

Oren was more experienced than any of us and had been dealing with this evil for far longer than we had. We did need to have a discussion. It was time he filled us in on everything he knew. I didn't like being kept in the dark.

"Yes, let's check on our parents. If Reverie was attacked, it follows that the Aurathion towns would also be under threat." I could hear the concern in Chloe's voice.

I walked over to her and grabbed her hand. "Let's go and tell my parents we're leaving to check on your family. That needs to be done before anything else."

She squeezed my hand gratefully, and Zeke walked over, giving her a hug. "Let's do it."

When we walked back into the barn, my parents were deep in discussion, and Damien was nowhere to be seen. Grumpy looked up, then motioned us over. We joined them, and after a moment, I spoke up. "We need to see if any of the Aurathion towns were targeted, and my friends need to check on their families." I motioned to all the guys and Chloe.

"I don't give a fuck about my family, but I do need to get back to the academy as soon as possible. I don't want anyone to get suspicious, and I need to see if I can find out more about what the Dark Factions are planning." Oren ran a hand through his hair.

"Are you going to be in danger?" He had a lot of shit to make up for, but I couldn't stand the thought of him getting hurt.

Before he could reply, Pantar spoke. *"I will bring him back and make sure he is safe. There is no need for you to worry."*

"I appreciate the offer, but I can take care of myself. You need to stay with Reverie." Oren ordered.

It looks like Oren has gotten my ability, too. What the hell?

Pantar growled, *"You do not decide where I go. My Nexus is in capable hands with Mira and her family. You may need my assistance, so I will go."*

"Okay then, I guess we'll go." He sounded reluctant even though it was his idea. He continued to stare at me like he was waiting for something.

Before I could ask him what the problem was, Dad

growled, "She'll be back at the academy shortly. You can wait till then for your kiss. I don't think I could stomach it." Well then.

Oren scowled at him. Not in the least intimidated by my massive father. These men of mine were either stupid or extremely brave. I wasn't sure which. Truthfully, they wouldn't have any of my fathers' respect if they were ass-kissers.

Pantar created a portal, and they stepped through. Before he disappeared, Oren blew me a kiss.

He had a lot to atone for. I could feel the agony in my chest that he was experiencing due to our separation. Good. The dick deserved it. He had no right to force our union, even though I could admit it would have eventually happened. The bond between Faction members was a privilege, but sometimes, being able to feel their emotions was a real revenge killer. It was hard to plot payback when you constantly felt the love and devotion of your target.

Somehow, I would fight my way through it. I laughed internally at the thought. I'm sure I could find a couple of guys that would be willing to help me out.

CHAPTER 10
REVERIE

Mira returned shortly after delivering Damien to his Nexus and informed us that everything went well. I knew my dad would eventually want to check that out for himself.

"Can you tell us who attacked you?" I asked my parents.

Everything had been so chaotic since our arrival that the events leading to the fire had never been discussed—at least not in my presence.

"We filled your dad in on what happened. We need to confirm some information before we discuss things with your Faction." Pop said seriously.

I knew they probably wanted to confirm that Oren wasn't involved before discussing anything with me. Now that he was bonded to me and part of my Faction, it would be nearly impossible to keep anything from him. I could feel Oren's intentions, but my family couldn't. Even though I knew they trusted me implicitly, my fathers would never compromise on the safety of their Nexus.

"We're going to stay in our condo in Houston. I don't

believe our enemies would want to draw attention to themselves by attacking us there. Just know we're safe for now and concentrate on preparing for your initiation." Grumpy pulled me in for a hug.

"What about the animals?" I asked, laughing as Rubbish and Copper chased each other around my parents' feet.

"They will be taken care of. I plan on staying here to make sure of that. I'll pop in on your parents a few times a day." Mira swatted Rubbish playfully with her tail.

Rubbish wasn't amused, but after sharing his displeasure with Mira, both animals curled beside her for a nap.

Zeke and Nathan walked into the barn. Zeke had a phone in his hand. I hadn't even been aware they'd left. "Looks like we don't have to make a trip home after all, thanks to Nathan," Zeke smiled at Chloe.

"Nathan teleported to his house and picked up his phone. Mom and our dads are perfect. Nothing out of the ordinary has happened as far as they know." Zeke hugged Chloe when she let out a breath of relief.

"Tell me you didn't talk about everything that happened here on a cell phone." Jet frowned at Zeke.

"Hell no, I'm not an idiot," Zeke growled. "We have a code language that my parents developed for us all from a young age for situations like this."

Chloe narrowed her eyes. "Why would you know anything about that?"

Jet looked uncomfortable at Chloe's question, but only for a second. I would have missed it if I hadn't been watching him so closely.

"Anyone who watches crime dramas knows you shouldn't discuss anything important on a cell phone." He scoffed like she was an idiot for even asking that question.

Jet should be grateful he was pretty. His personality really left something to be desired.

"Well, if that issue is resolved, you better get back." Grumpy pulled me in for another hug.

Dad hesitantly approached me, "Could I get a hug from you, too?"

There was no need to answer that ridiculous question. Leaving Grumpy's arms, I headed straight for him. Dad met me halfway, hugging me tightly. I felt as safe in his arms as I ever had with Grumpy and Pop.

"I hate I've missed out on your life so far. Just know I don't plan on missing out on anything else." He kissed the top of my head.

"I'm looking forward to it." Dad held me for a few more moments until Pop became impatient.

"Give me my Tater Tot! You don't get to hog her just because you've been gone for years and years." Pop pulled me away from Dad and into his arms.

"I see you haven't changed, Jesse." Dad rolled his eyes but couldn't hide his grin.

"Let us know if you need anything. Don't worry about us, and concentrate on preparing for your initiation. We'll take care of things here. With Sly's return, we're stronger and regaining some of our lost abilities." He kissed my head, releasing me when Mom demanded her hug.

I was a lucky girl to have grown up with such loving parents. The things they'd been through were awful, and they could've let it affect everything in their lives. I was grateful every day that they somehow found the strength to be the parents I needed.

⁓☙⁓

M ira had opened a portal into mine and Chloe's dorm so no one would realize we'd been gone. It was late, so everyone except Nathan headed to their room to get some sleep. Tomorrow was Friday, and I was going to use the weekend to recover.

"My ass is dragging. I'm going to bed." Chloe groaned and staggered to her room.

"Finally!"

Nathan threw me over his shoulder and raced to my room.

"Slow down, psycho. I need a shower before this goes too far." I was covered in soot from the fire and wanted to be clean before bed.

"I can get on board with that." He waggled his eyebrows.

I wouldn't mind seeing his naked body glistening in the water, soap running down those perfect abs, as I licked... I grabbed Nathan and pulled him into the bathroom. I started the water as I got undressed. When I saw him standing there staring, I motioned to him to get on with it.

"Give me a moment to admire you, Nexi. It's been months since I've seen this stunning sight." Nathan's eyes blazed with heat.

I struck a pose and hit him with my "blue-steel" look.

"You're ridiculous," he laughed and started stripping.

Nathan began to hum "Slow Motion" by Juvenile, then slowly stripped out of his clothes. I almost hated to see the leather pants go. They did incredible things for his ass. Someone should start a petition for that to be mandatory wear for the guys at Emberhold.

When he pulled his shirt over his head with that one-handed grab that guys do, I felt my blood heat.

Nope, the pants needed to go.

The boy had an eight-pack now and was more sculpted

than when he'd been taken (I didn't think that was possible). I started panting.

Nathan removed his boots and socks, then gave me a smoldering look as he unbuttoned his pants, slowly peeling them off. He might not be able to twerk worth a damn, but this boy could put on a striptease like nobody's business.

When he was standing there completely nude, he struck a pose and blew me a kiss... and for some insane reason, I started to cry. Big gulping sobs that shook my whole body. Nathan looked horrified and discreetly glanced down at his dick. Apparently, deciding that everything looked normal, he pulled me into his arms.

"Nexi, what's wrong?"

"I...don't...know." I wailed in between sobs.

I knew snot and tears were all over his chest, but he didn't seem to care about that. He just held me, murmuring nonsense and trying to comfort me the best he could.

When my tears finally stopped, I remained in his arms for a moment longer, inhaling his scent, savoring the warmth of his body, and the feeling of his hand stroking my hair.

"Now that you've calmed down, tell me what's wrong? Because I have to tell you, no man wants his woman to break into hysterical sobs at the sight of his nude body. I've got more confidence than most, but I'm a little concerned about your reaction." He smirked, flashing that dimple.

I smacked his chest. "You know damn well your body is amazing. Angels would weep at the sight."

Nathan threw his head back and laughed, "Seems you've learned a thing or two from me over the years. I'll take the compliment, though." He grinned, "Was it the sight of my massive dick? You know I'll take it easy on you."

I'd missed this boy more than I thought was possible. I never wanted to be separated from him again. "I think everything just hit me all at once. I'm so glad you're back and that you're okay. I worried every second you were gone. Let's never do that again."

I knew that wasn't possible since I hadn't been sent to my initiation yet, but I really wished it was.

"I missed you too, my Nexi. But I'm a little insulted that you doubted me. Nothing, and no one could keep me from you."

He tipped my chin up with his finger and kissed me softly.

His hair had grown out, and now it touched his shoulders. I clutched it in both hands as he deepened the kiss. Nathan pulled back and ran his eyes over my face. I couldn't help but do the same. I'd been starved for the sight of this man for weeks.

Nathan was beautiful.

His hair and those gorgeous green eyes were a lethal combination. When joined with his fantastic body, no woman could resist him.

Nathan led me to the shower, and we both stepped inside. He tilted my head under the spray to wet my hair. Then he squirted some of my vanilla-scented shampoo into his hand. He applied the shampoo to my hair, massaged it thoroughly, and then rinsed and conditioned.

When he finished, I was so relaxed I'd almost fallen asleep. He took the soap, lathered his hands, and then began to wash me thoroughly.

That woke me up quickly.

My head fell back against the wall as he soaped my breasts, his thumbs rubbing back and forth gently on each nipple. He then lowered his head and kissed my mark, "I liked it better when I was the only one filling it." He lowered his head and kissed the dagger, then washed my stomach, and legs, skipping the part of me that was begging for his touch the most.

I held on to his shoulder as he picked up one foot, then the other, washing and massaging each one. He turned me and began washing my back, then dropped lower, gliding the soap over my ass, gently kneading my sore muscles as he went.

Nathan positioned me to face him again, then soaped his hands up and kneeled on the shower floor.

He parted my legs and began washing my pussy slowly with his soapy hands. He massaged me gently, circling my clit with one finger.

"*Please, Nathan.* I need you so much," I begged.

Nathan didn't answer me, continuing to play with me, not applying enough pressure to allow me to orgasm. He stopped suddenly and grabbed the detachable shower head, rinsing me gently.

He was going to drive me to violence. Nathan replaced the shower head and turned, staring at me with so much heat and adoration, it stunned me.

"You are so beautiful that it feels like I should be worshiping at your feet."

He kissed me gently, then bent, grabbing me under my thighs and lifting me until my legs were hanging off his shoulders.

Nuzzling my pussy with his nose, he inhaled deeply. "*God,* your scent makes my mouth water. Can I have a taste, my Nexi?"

I nodded my head. He stopped and looked at me, "I need your words."

"Yes! For the love of God, *yes!*" I'd reached my limit. I needed his mouth on me now.

Nathan smiled, flashing that dimple again, then dove in.

He sucked and licked every inch of me until my voice was hoarse from screaming his name.

Just when I didn't think I could take anymore he inserted two fingers in my pussy working them in and out and bit my clit gently.

I *exploded.*

I heard him moan and felt him orgasm soon after.

He continued gently thrusting his fingers until he'd rung every bit of pleasure out of me, then slowly lowered me down his body.

I kissed him gently several times before lowering myself to my knees.

"Nexi, you don't have to do that. Eating your sweet pussy and feeling your pleasure was enough to send me over the edge."

I glanced at his still hard dick, "Looks like you could handle a little more, my sweet psycho."

"I never stop craving you, Nexi. The moment I leave your warmth, I want more." He moaned as I ran my tongue up the length of his dick.

"Well, I'm hungry for the taste of you, so you're just going to have to suffer through this." I put just the head of his dick in my mouth and sucked gently, then rolled my tongue up and down his length.

"Fuuuuck!" Nathan dropped his head to watch me as I continued to lick and suck, never putting more than the head of his dick in my mouth.

I loved playing just-the-tip.

He started to gently thrust his hips, no longer able to stand my teasing. I took pity on him and sucked his entire length into my mouth until he hit the back of my throat, then began massaging his sack firmly.

He let out a deep growl, grabbed the back of my head, and started to thrust deeper.

"You dirty fucking girl, you just had to keep on until I lost control, didn't you...Fuuuck that feels good."

He began breathing harder, "I'm going to come and you're going to swallow every last drop." His eyes rolled back in his head, and his thrusts became erratic.

Tears were running down my face, but I reached around, grabbed his ass and forced him even deeper down my throat.

"Shiiiiiiit I'm coming— fuuuuck." He groaned, as cum erupted from his dick, and slid down my throat.

As soon as I felt his pleasure through our bond and tasted him on my tongue, I was thrown into my second orgasm.

We both collapsed on the shower floor, clinging to each other. Nathan kissed my lips, then stood up and retrieved a towel from the cabinet, drying me thoroughly before drying himself. He wrapped the towel around his waist and picked me up, carrying me to my bedroom. We both slipped under the covers, and Nathan pulled me back against him, tucking my head under his chin.

"I can't be separated from you again. I'm not sure I'd survive it."

"I love you, Nathan." I sighed, feeling myself drifting off to sleep.

"I love you too, my Nexi." He whispered, then followed me into my dreams.

CHAPTER II
JET

I lay there in my bed, watching the darkness through my window as the sun started to peak over the horizon. I don't think I slept more than four hours in total.

The events that transpired last night were disturbing, to say the least. Reverie's parents survived, but would the human race be as fortunate?

When we returned to the academy, I assumed Nathan would spend the night with Reverie.

I was right.

He never returned to our dorm room, and my feelings about the matter were confusing. I wasn't exactly jealous; it was more intense envy. He had the privilege of openly expressing his devotion... and I didn't.

Did I even want to?

I hated this war within myself. I was usually the kind of person who decided on a plan of action and stuck to it. If I embraced my feelings for Reverie, my life would irrevocably change.

I'd fought in horrible places and seen things most people

were fortunate enough never to experience. I did it in the name of my country, but I was honest enough to admit that I enjoyed it.

There was no one for me to worry about. I had no wife or children, which gave me the freedom to take chances I might not have otherwise. Most importantly, I was happy with the status quo. Then I found out I was Aurathion and met my Nexus.

My feelings for Reverie are complicated. The Aurathion in me wants her with no question.

That part of myself wanted to fuck her into the ground until no one could tell where she ended, and I began. I wanted to bite her until she bled and suck the very essence of her into my body, and eliminate all threats to her, taking on the Dark Factions entirely alone.

Then fuck her covered in their blood.

The other part of me didn't want any attachments. I wanted to continue my life exactly as it was, worrying only for myself and waiting on my next mission, not dealing with these messy emotions.

I suspected I was fighting a losing battle.

I got out of bed, showered and dressed in my workout clothes. Grabbing my knife, I strapped it around my waist, just under the waistband of my pants.

The only thing I could do to get my mind in the right place was put my body through an intense workout. Maybe it would help me concentrate on my mission and not the raven-haired beauty living rent-free in my mind.

I didn't see anyone on the way to the gym. It was still extremely early, and I was glad of it. I didn't want any interruptions this morning.

Jumping on the treadmill, I started slowly, gradually increasing my speed until I was at my preferred pace. After a few minutes, I was in the zone. My thoughts became clearer, and I felt some of the stress that had been weighing on me since last night disappear.

Before I returned to the academy, I had the opportunity to report to my contact. The information I received in return was concerning. Even though the Aurathion towns hadn't been attacked, the DF was in play and making serious moves on the board.

The Hawthornes were their first targets but wouldn't be their last. My contact even believed that there were several plants at Emberhold.

It was confirmed that the DF didn't learn about Reverie until recently. We weren't sure what their next move would be regarding her, but our intel suggested that kidnapping could be a possibility.

Over my dead fucking body.

I might be at war with myself and my feelings for Reverie, but I knew beyond a shadow of a doubt that she wouldn't be hurt or taken on my watch.

I had no problem with killing. I didn't go out of my way to do it, but if it needed doing, I wasn't bothered by it.

For her, I wouldn't blink.

After I finished ten miles, I stepped out of the room to take a piss and fill up my water bottle. When I was leaving the bathroom, I heard two sets of footsteps coming down the hallway.

I stepped into a small room used for ice baths and storing supplies. As passives, we weren't as immune to sore muscles as Aurathions with a Faction.

I didn't want to deal with anyone right now. My head wasn't in the right place to pretend I was an ordinary Aurathion looking for a Nexus.

Hearing the steps stop right before they passed the room

I was in, I looked through the tiny crack I'd left in the door to see who it was.

There were two guys I'd seen around. Both were mean bastards. They'd been in the group of people giving Cassandra hell on our first day of the obstacle courses.

The possibility of spies at the academy didn't come as a surprise; the way these two guys seemed to sneak around and whisper made them likely candidates.

The fact they were dicks made me hope they were.

They continued past the door, and I decided to follow them. I was curious about what had them out so early. I had to be careful because I didn't know their abilities. If they were DF, then they'd been taking injections for years.

Knowing this didn't scare me. It just meant I had to use more caution than I would with a *typical*. That's what my contact called humans with no Aurathion ancestry, and I'd adopted the practice.

The two men kept walking until they entered the workout room I'd previously been in. They both stopped at the weight station and began doing curls, looking around furtively before continuing their conversation.

I snuck closer, hiding in the shadows at the edge of the room until I was close enough to hear what they were saying.

"I think we should just grab the bitch. That fuckwit Nathan is gone, and if we're lucky, he won't be back."

The first guy to speak had dark hair and was almost as big as me—almost, but not quite. I'd seen him throw his weight around several times, but usually with people he knew were weaker than him.

"We can't grab her until we get the go-ahead. Do you want to explain to the Brummond that you decided to act without getting his permission if you fuck up this whole operation?"

This guy had to be the brains of the two. I'd seen him hanging out with Kristine. He had the look of someone with money; I think his name was Anthony.

"Hell no, but I'm also tired of being here." He frowned, then began smirking. "I say when we take her, we have some fun before bringing her to the Coliseum. She's strong, but without a Faction she's basically just a souped-up human. I know I wouldn't mind a taste of that. Have you checked out that ass?"

The *dead man* waggled his eyebrows.

"Torrence, that's positively fucked up. Surprisingly, I like it." Anthony, the other soon-to-be-corpse, agreed.

"We can stop right outside the city and bring her to Crispin. He'll be so pleased we might get double the money for this job." Torrence grinned, looking a little shocked that Anthony agreed with his idea.

I could understand his shock, as he seemed like the kind of guy who would need the instructions on a shampoo bottle.

"I'm proud of you." He seemed surprised that Torrence had an original thought in his head. "Crispin will pay us for any info he gets from her, and then we can bring what's left to the Coliseum."

Anthony smiled evilly. "If we're questioned, we can just say she gave us trouble, so we had to discipline her. No one will care as long as she gets there in one piece. She's just a tool to control her parents."

I felt my blood pressure rise, and rage began to take over my rational thought. The smart thing to do was to let them go and keep observing them, reporting the information I collected.

Unfortunately, hearing them talk about what they would do to Reverie interfered with my professionalism.

Torrence was getting excited just thinking about it. I could see the evidence in his shorts.

"I almost swallowed my tongue when she stripped down to run the obstacle course. The things I want to do to her would ruin her for life." He cupped his junk.

"I don't doubt that. That's exactly why I get my turn first. She needs a lesson from her betters. The bitch is a little too uppity for me."The smile Anthony had on his face was chilling.

"She's never been up against real Aurathions."

"You're going to use your ability on her, right?" Torrence looked intrigued at the idea. What the fuck was this guy's ability?

Anthony smirked, "Most assuredly. I never tire of using it to break people, and she's no exception. She'll be aware of everything we do to her but unable to stop it. I'll have complete control."

I gritted my teeth in rage.

These motherfuckers weren't long for this world.

The corpse continued, "I love seeing how they react when I allow them back in the driver's seat. Some people lose their minds, taking their own lives. Of course, she won't have that option."

"If the Brummond gives her to Selene, she'll wish she did. There won't be much of her left by the time her purpose has ended." Torrence grimaced, "especially when Beatrice gets involved."

I'd heard those names mentioned last night. Oren freaked when he realized they were involved in Nathan's ordeal. The death of Beatrice must not be common knowledge, at least by these two.

"Okay, fuck it. Now I'm horny. Let's wait until tonight and kill that redheaded roommate she has and just take the bitch. I need a taste, and I'm also getting sick of being here. These entitled shits need to die, and thankfully, it won't be long now." Anthony rubbed his hands together.

"I'm going to shower and rub one out before class." Torrence put the weight down and walked toward the locker room.

"TMI idiot." Anthony grimaced in distaste. "I'm going to finish up here. We can meet after lunch and finalize our plans."

"Sounds good," Torrence said over his shoulder, almost at a jog.

It looked like he was in a hurry to masturbate to my woman. I felt a blinding rage overtake me at the thought of these two men with Reverie at their mercy.

I wouldn't allow it.

Slipping the knife from its sheath, I moved closer.

Anthony had put in earbuds and increased the tempo of his workout. He had a small dumbbell in each hand and was going at a rhythm that was impossible for a typical.

When I put the blade to his throat, he had a moment of shock when his eyes met mine in the mirror. I saw the moment he started to use his ability on me and slit his throat from ear to ear.

The problem with Aurathions that had abilities was, in most cases, they relied on them too heavily, and all other training was neglected.

The cut was so deep that when I dropped his body, his head was almost completely severed, only hanging on by a bit of muscle and tendons.

I watched the blood pool at my feet for a moment, then bent and coated my fingers in the sticky fluid. I brought them to my face and painted two vertical lines down each cheek. Time to take care of the other motherfucker.

The locker room was quiet when I entered, except for the shower at the end of the row. I could hear grunts and groans as the *dead* motherfucker jacked off to the thought of what didn't belong to him.

I walked closer, not bothering to muffle my steps. When I was right outside of the shower curtain, I stopped.

"Keep walking if you value your life." He growled.

I didn't say anything.

I just waited.

"I'm not fucking with you. Move... the fuck... along."

Still getting no response, he pulled back the shower curtain and stuck his head out.

I was waiting for just this opportunity.

Torrence looked confused when he saw me standing there. It soon turned to alarm when he saw my knife heading toward his face. He threw up a hand to try to stop me, but my knife went through it and into his eye. When I pulled it out, there was a squelching noise but no resistance.

He screamed in agony and fell out of the shower, tangling up in the curtain before landing on his back.

"What the fuck?! Why did you do that?" He screamed.

Blood was everywhere, seeping between his fingers and running down his face.

I grabbed his flaccid dick (no hard-on in sight now) and cut it off with one swipe of my knife. When his screams became louder than I could tolerate, I wrapped the shower curtain tightly around his face. I knew he was dying, but I had a couple more cuts I needed to make.

Whether I decide to claim my Nexus or not, I'd never allow filth like this to touch her.

CHAPTER 12
OREN

I walked into the men's locker room just in time to see Jet hack Torrence Porter's hands off. What the actual hell?! After the shitty night of sleep I'd had, this was the last fucking thing I needed.

"What the fuck G.I. Joe?" I snarled at him.

Jet looked up, shocked to see me standing there. I bet he wasn't nearly as stunned as I was at seeing him holding two severed hands with war paint on his face that looked like.... Was that blood?

"Just taking care of a problem." He had the grace to look a little sheepish at being caught in this predicament.

"What kind of problem, exactly?" This guy was a dick, but I wasn't sure how he was a threat to Jet.

"The kind of problem that threatened our Nexus." He stood and dropped the hands he was holding onto Torrence's chest.

I glanced down when they fell and did a double-take. Was that a dick sticking out of Torrence's mouth?!

I looked back at Jet with a little more caution. "Threatened her how?"

"I overheard them saying they were going to kidnap her and take her to some guy named Crispin before bringing her to the Coliseum. They were sent here by the Brummond to kidnap her as leverage on her parents." He leaned over and spit on the body lying on the floor. "They were talking about raping her first, and this motherfucker was jacking off to the thought of it in the shower."

I walked over and kicked Torrence in the face, getting a small bit of satisfaction when his nose made a crunching sound.

I paused, running back over what he said. "Did you say they? As in more than one?"

"Yes." He didn't elaborate, and I couldn't say I was surprised.

The several sentences explaining what was going on probably maxed him out.

"Where's the second body? It's accurate to call the individual a body, I assume?" I raised my brows in question.

"Anthony is in the workout room. I slit his throat." Jet had no emotion on his face.

I sighed, "How were you planning to get rid of the bodies?" He just shrugged his shoulders.

"Really? This from a trained military man."

Jet lost his emotionless mask for a brief second. "You know?"

"Of course, I know. I know everything that goes on here." He must have missed the G.I. Joe comment in his bloodlust. "I've been keeping a close eye on the two lunatics in this Faction, but I thought you and Zeke both had level heads." I let some of the disappointment show in my voice.

"Why haven't you blown my cover?" Jet angled his head in question.

"Because whether you admit it or not, you'll eventually become my Faction brother." I decided to be frank. "Also, there may come a time when we can use your contacts to help protect our Nexus."

Jet nodded his head but didn't say anything else on the matter.

"Let's get this mess cleaned up." I raised my hand, and fire shot out, incinerating the disturbing scene I'd walked in on until all evidence was erased.

"That's convenient." Jet narrowed his eyes as if he were thinking of other ways my ability could be of service.

"Maybe, next time, come to me first, and we can come up with a plan that might be a little more subtle. Anyone could have walked in and reported this." I frowned at him.

"They would've had a bad day." He shrugged his shoulders. I could see this wasn't going anywhere.

"Take me to your first victim." I walked out, keeping Jet in my sights.

The guy did have a knife to my neck yesterday. Also, I felt like it was a good policy to be cautious around a guy that just cut off someone's dick and stuffed it in their mouth.

We entered the workout room, and I could already smell death.

It was a scent you never forgot.

"Damn, how sharp is the knife you used. It cut straight through the bone." This body was *almost* as disturbing as the other one. It was *hard* to beat a dick shoved in a mouth.

Pun intended.

I didn't think Jet would appreciate my sense of humor. Too bad it wasn't Nathan who had done it. He would get it.

"Sharp," He grunted.

The big guy was a fantastic conversationalist.

I incinerated this body, too.

"Follow me to my office. I'll send for Nathan and the twins and see how we want to deal with this. These guys were friends with Kristine and her crew, so they'll be missed. Not to mention the Brummond will send someone to look for them."

He grunted in agreement.

"You know you fucked up, right. Now he's going to recruit someone new. We could've gotten more information out of these two." I opened my office door and took a seat behind the desk.

Jet sat down in one of the chairs. He was so big that I was scared the chair wouldn't be able to hold him.

"After I heard what they'd planned, I couldn't allow them to keep breathing." He ran his hand down his face.

Finally, he appeared to realize that he'd fucked up.

I got up, went into my small bathroom, and wet some paper towels.

"Nathan, find the twins, and get your ass to my office asap."

"Wipe the blood off your face. There can't be any evidence leading back to you or Reverie."

Jet took the paper towel and cleaned his face. He threw it in the garbage can, and I sent a few sparks to burn it.

"Reverie had nothing to do with it." He said gruffly.

"I know she didn't, but if the evidence leads back to you and you're in her Faction…you can see the problem." I leaned back in my chair.

"I'm not in her Faction. You act like it's a done deal. It's not."

He looked at me in aggravation.

"You keep telling yourself that," I frowned, shaking my head at the hard-headed bastard.

"If you know everything about me, you know I can't be part of her Faction. I've got a duty to my country." Jet ran a hand through his hair.

"After the mess I just cleaned up, it looks like your loyalty to Reverie supersedes any other obligations you have," I smirked. Jet snorted but didn't comment.

My door swung open, startling us both. Nathan and the twins entered.

"You can't fucking knock before entering my office?" I growled.

Nathan's hair was in disarray, and his clothes looked like they had been thrown on haphazardly.

"Fuck no! You had the balls to speak in my head uninvited and order me here. I'll be damned if I 'knock before entering' asshole." The last part was spoken in a mockery of my voice as he knocked papers off my desk to sit on the corner.

Zeke sat in the other chair in front of my desk. "Why are we here?"

He and Zane weren't much smaller than Jet. I didn't know if my chairs would survive this meeting. I guess I needed to get larger furniture for my Faction brothers.

I leaned back in my *large,* comfy chair. "Jet, would you like to explain why they're here?"

Zane walked forward and sat facing Jet on the other corner of my desk. "What did you do, Jolly?"

Nathan leaned over and fist-bumped Zane, then turned to Jet, "Yes, what did you do, Jolly? And it better be good to pull me out of bed with my Nexi. I'd made plans for how I was going to wake her up." He smirked.

The dick was happy to throw it in our faces. No matter, I'd have my time with Reverie tonight. I may not be able to claim her openly, but I would be with her every chance I got. She was everything to me now.

And like Jet, I'd kill to keep her.

We also needed to discuss her unique mark. I'd seen it when we made love but didn't mention it. Only a fool would want to start a discussion when buried deep in Reverie. I was many things, a fool wasn't one of them.

"I took care of a couple of problems," Jet said, not really explaining anything.

The three guys looked at me in question, "Jet killed two guys that were apparently spies for the Brummond."

"Why would you kill them instead of capturing and questioning them?" Zeke frowned at Jet.

This guy was going to be pivotal in the success of this Faction. I'd known him for years, and he could be just as much of a killer as Jet, but he used reason before he acted. I hoped he retained this skill when the situation involved Reverie.

Jet looked over at Zeke, "They planned on raping Reverie."

The room erupted.

"What the fuck?" Nathan shouted and pulled a knife from his boot.

Zeke had shoved his chair back and stood towering over Jet, who had remained seated.

"Explain."

Zane stood, also glaring down at Jet. He and Zeke looked like large matching bookends.

Jet sighed, not the least bit intimidated. "I came into the gym early and overheard them planning on taking Reverie back to

Aurathia. The things they talked about doing to her pissed me off."

Zane smirked, "You sure are protective of your *friends*."

"I am." Jet narrowed his eyes at Zane, daring him to make something of it.

"I hope you fucked them up good before you killed the bastards," Nathan growled, obviously pissed he didn't get to participate in their deaths.

I scoffed, "He damn near cut Anthony's head off. Then he *did* cut Torrence's hands and dick off, stuffing Torrence's dick in his mouth." I smirked at their stunned expressions, "I'd say he fucked them up good."

"Torrence and Anthony?" Zeke asked, "Kristine's friends?"

"Those two guys were dicks. When we used to hang with Kristine, there were several times I almost beat their ass." Zane growled.

"I would've been happy to give you a hand," Nathan smirked, slipping his knife back into his boot, content that the guys were killed with the proper amount of blood and gore.

I smiled slightly; I knew he had my macabre sense of humor.

The other three just stared at him.

"Too soon?" Nathan asked innocently.

"Because Jet acted so impulsively, we need to be on the lookout for other students whom the Dark Factions may have planted. They're after leverage over Reverie's parents; lucky for us, they have no idea how powerful Reverie is, or she would be their focus."

I turned to Nathan. "I can't openly claim Reverie, but you just might be able to get away with it. We need to get you into the housing for new Factions sooner rather than later. It'll be easier to keep track of the people trying to get close to her. When we can't be with her, Pantar can, and no one will get by him."

"I thought we 'needed to wait until after we were all initiated, to be officially bonded?'" Nathan made air quotes.

"I think this incident calls for drastic measures. I'll see if I can put a bug in the Dean's ear. Let him know that I think Reverie has found her first Faction, and maybe we should let her do the ritual."

I was already pondering ways to make this happen.

"I'm on board. I can't wait to play house with my Nexi." He rubbed his hands together in anticipation.

"Don't get too comfortable having her all to yourself." Zane nodded his head at Zeke.

Zeke nodded back and cleared his throat. "We're going to ask Reverie if she wants to have a private bonding ceremony with us over winter break."

"She didn't get to do any of the special stuff with you two punks, so we've decided to make sure she gets to experience it all when she bonds with us." Zane smiled in satisfaction at Nathan.

"Hey, our bonding was an accident! I've made sure to make her feel special every day since." He began muttering under his breath. "Fucking soulless gingers trying to make me look bad."

Suddenly, he raised his head and looked at me, "How did your bonding come about? I don't think anybody ever told me."

I sighed. I knew he was going to want an explanation. Nathan narrowed his eyes, "She couldn't stand you, so it seems like a large leap to think in the short time I was gone, you both fell in love and completed the bond."

"Yeah, Storm, you should explain to Nathan how you bonded his Nexi." Zane smiled evilly.

Zeke cuffed him in the head, "Stop instigating. We have enough going on."

Zane pouted, "I was just advocating for an open, healthy dialogue."

"Riiight." I flipped him off.

He smiled so big I could see his molars.

"Let's head out to the Arena and settle this once and for all."

I stood up and headed for the door. I knew it would come to this, and I might as well get it over with now. I knew I deserved it on some level, and Nathan, as Reverie's only other bonded, had the right to dole out the punishment. Reverie's safety needed to be our only focus.

Hopefully, after we resolve this, we can get back on track.

CHAPTER 13
REVERIE

I woke to an empty bed and a full bladder. I got up to head to the bathroom and paused, noticing the small black feline curled up on Nathan's pillow.

Was that Pantar?

"Yes, my Nexus, it is me. With the crazy one here, this was the only way I would fit on your bed." He yawned, jumped from the bed, and expanded to the size of a cheetah in a weird popping and cracking of bones.

I just continued to stare at him in amazement.

"This size will make it easier to follow you through the hallways. I didn't want to minimize my size until all of your classmates understood the threat I posed." He yawned once more and then stretched.

"I know you told me you could do it. It's just a little shocking when I'm used to you being the size of a rhino." I smirked, "Maybe when you're in your cat size, I could get you a selection of collars with bells and tie pretty ribbons on your tentacles. You'd look so precious!"

Pantar looked at me and blinked slowly.

"I think not Nexus."

He disappeared.

I fell back on the bed laughing, but my Pantar wasn't amused in the least bit.

Rolling over, I grabbed Nathan's pillow and inhaled deeply. That man smelled like bad decisions and long nights. I was here for it. I got out of bed, clutching the pillow, and twirled around the room like a Disney princess. I was expecting some birds to fly in and assist me in dressing.

Nathan was back, and the world was right again.

I now had some revenge to plan for my Shitstorm. I was ready to forgive him and get on with things, but he had to be taught that I wasn't going to put up with his bulldozing shit.

Zeke may be willing to help. Nathan was out because I didn't want Oren killed. Zane was a no-go because I'd noticed that he and Nathan had bonded last night, so he might be tempted to tell him. Zeke was level-headed and would respect my right to plan this. He was my most patient Faction and would be perfect in this situation.

Chloe would definitely be brought in. That girl was diabolical. This would be epic with the three of us working together.

I walked over to my vanity and decided to rock some high pigtails today. I was feeling "little monster" vibes, thinking about my revenge plot.

I slipped into my black cargo pants and a snug red shirt, revealing just a hint of skin. Pulling on my black combat boots, I strapped on my ankle sheath and slid my knife in. Then swiped on some mascara and deep red lipstick.

I looked in the mirror once more. Yep, the lipstick was perfect for my inner Harley Quinn. Satisfied with my appearance, I headed into our tiny kitchen for coffee.

Chloe was already up and making two cups.

"I hope one of those is for me." I put as much desperation in my voice as I could.

She looked up and smiled, "Of course, who else would it be for? What's with the Harley Quinn vibes this morning?"

"I started thinking about what I was going to do to get Shitstorm back, and I felt like the outfit would inspire me."

"I know you're going to let me in on that. No one fucks with my bestie." Chloe narrowed her eyes.

"Hell, yes, nobody else has an evil mind like you do. I have a few ideas, but it's got to be epic. Maybe something permanent on his body that he can see; remind him not to make decisions for me." I caught my breath. Making eye contact, we both smiled evilly.

"Let me make arrangements. You can work out a time."

Chloe smirked, "This is most assuredly going to be epic!"

Yes... yes, it was!

Chloe handed me a cup, and the conversation paused as we both took a sip.

"Damn, that's good." I closed my eyes and savored the feel of caffeine hitting my system.

"Sounded like you had a great time last night," Chloe smirked.

"I'm not the least bit embarrassed. I've missed that boy." I waggled both brows. "Nathan can make you change your religion."

"If a man could make me scream like that, I wouldn't give a tinker's damn in hell who heard me." Chloe laughed.

"Right?" I started laughing with her.

"How are you feeling after being reunited with your dad?" She took another sip of her coffee.

"I think I'm still in shock. I'm positively overjoyed, but it doesn't seem real yet." I smiled softly, thinking of the happiness I'd felt seeing my mom reunited with him.

"I can imagine." She took her cup into our living room, and I followed.

We both sat on the couch. "It's crazy that he's been in Aurathia all this time. But what I can't get out of my head is that he's been part of another Faction."

Chloe frowned, "You don't blame him, do you?"

"Hell no! I just meant that it must have been horrible for him. I can't imagine how I would feel knowing my bonds were here, and I was forced to join with another." Tears began welling in my eyes.

"He was raped emotionally, Chloe. I can't even think about what he went through physically." I wiped a tear that had run down my face.

Chloe grabbed my free hand and squeezed. "Reverie, you have to put faith in your mom and their love for each other."

"I do. I noticed him flinching away from Pop when he grabbed his shoulders, but he was more than fine with Mom in his lap." I tried to smile.

"It's just going to take time. But my money is on him." She smirked. "This Selene chick better hope your mom doesn't get hands on her anytime soon." Chloe's eyes gleamed maliciously at the thought.

A genuine grin broke free. "That's for sure. With Dad returning and their bond reinstated, Mom seems to be gaining her abilities back."

"I hope we get the chance to be there for that." Chloe finished her coffee and stood. "I'm heading to the cafeteria to meet Sarah and Joan for breakfast. Do you want to come?"

"No, I'm going to see if I can find any of my men. It seems strange that none of them were here this morning." I went into the kitchen and rinsed my cup in the sink.

"Okay, I'll see you in class." She saluted me, then headed out the door.

I grabbed my bag and started out when Pantar appeared in front of me.

"What the hell?!" I grabbed my chest. "You scared the shit out of me!"

"Sorry, Nexus, but I thought you would be interested in what your Faction is doing." He sat and began grooming himself.

"Yes, if you think it's important for me to know."

I waited, but he continued to lick his paws and fluff his tail.

"Well, aren't you going to tell me?" I was confused by his actions.

"Maybe I feel like I'm owed an apology from earlier." He blinked innocently, mid-lick.

Now I was really confused, "An apology? For what?"

Pantar narrowed his eyes, *"The collar incident."*

"The collar incident? Are you talking about the joke I made?" Was my Fellat serious right now?

"Exactly that." He said sternly.

"I'm sorry for teasing you about wearing a collar." I tried to hide my exasperation.

"You did not sound sincere, Nexus." He started grooming himself again.

I reached deep and channeled my inner Nathan. "Dearest Pantar, I sincerely apologize for any emotional damage I may have caused when I mentioned buying you a collar with a bell." I got on my knees. "Please forgive me, exalted one. I promise to never do it again. If you feel this promise is broken in any way, I vow to never wear pink again in any form."

Pantar stood and nodded in acceptance, *"Nathan and Oren are in the arena fighting. The others are there observing."*

"Those idiots! If it's over Oren and me bonding, it's my

prerogative to punish him, not Nathan's." I growled in aggravation.

I should have expected this. I knew when Nathan found out, he would be pissed. It wouldn't surprise me if Oren took it upon himself to inform him of what happened. His actions suggested he had no honor, but he followed his own set of rules. Oren wouldn't have hidden what he did from Nathan because he was equally proud and ashamed. I could feel this through our bond.

"Are you coming?" I asked Pantar.

"No, I believe that my Nexus will set them straight." Then he disappeared once again.

I teleported outside the cafeteria soon after because I'd never been to the arena. You could teleport places you hadn't been to, but a risk was always involved. I had no problem finding the arena because of the roars and screams of encouragement from what sounded like a massive crowd.

After pushing my way to the front to see what was happening (short girl problems), I finally got my first view of the arena.

It was simply a pit dug in the ground with seats carved into the rock, rising in curved rows around the open space. Basically, it resembled an ancient amphitheater.

Shirtless and circling each other were two of my men. And what men they were. I felt my temperature rise at the sight they made.

Nathan's hair was pulled back out of his eyes and touched his shoulders with a hint of wave; those broad shoulders tapered down to a slim waist; his stomach was a series of muscles that made up the eight-pack he was rocking. All that smooth, golden skin was unblemished, and his only tattoo was located where no one could see.

On the other hand, Oren's skin gleamed bronze in the

sun. His longer hair was pulled up in a man bun; the only thing they had in common was that mouthwatering eight-pack. He had his beautiful lightning tattoo on full display, which covered his entire left arm from shoulder to wrist.

As they circled one another, Nathan unexpectedly threw a punch, hitting Oren in the face. Oren staggered but remained on his feet. It felt as if he had momentarily lowered his guard, almost allowing Nathan to land that blow.

I saw Zeke, Zane, and Jet sitting on the first bench near the floor at the very bottom of the arena. I pushed and shoved my way down until I slid into the space between the twins.

"What in the hell is going on?" I leaned over to speak into Zane's ear since it was so loud here. Zane was startled, his focus entirely on the men fighting.

"Hey, sweet girl, I wondered when you would show up."

I eyed him in annoyance, "I would've been here sooner if I'd gotten a heads up on what was going on."

He gave me a sheepish look, "Honestly, in all the excitement, I forgot. You can't be mad at me, though. Zeke is the responsible one, and he didn't warn you either."

He had a point.

I turned to Zeke and elbowed him. "Why didn't you let me know what was going on?"

Zeke looked as surprised to see me as Zane had. Pulling me onto his lap, he spoke into my ear. "I was going to, but I wanted to give you time to eat breakfast first. These two idiots shouldn't cause you to go to class on an empty stomach." I kissed him softly.

"What was that for? Not that I'm complaining." He smiled.

"For always having my health and well-being in mind." I kissed him once more.

I felt like sometimes my sweet Zeke didn't get enough attention. He was almost as quiet as Jet and caused the least friction out of anyone in the group.

"Why are they fighting?" I asked, returning my attention to the men in the arena. I was sure I knew the cause, but I wanted to confirm it.

It looked like Nathan had gotten a few more shots in on Oren yet he was still untouched.

"Over you, of course." He moved his lips against my ear as he talked, causing me to shiver uncontrollably.

That's what I thought. I needed to have a talk with Nathan about my capabilities. "Nathan found out about how Oren became Faction."

Zeke nodded, "Yep. I'll give Oren credit. When Nathan asked him about it, he led him here. He didn't give Nathan an answer until they arrived, and you can see what happened next."

I watched as Nathan continued to pummel Oren. He was now bleeding from his mouth and nose and hadn't thrown any punches at Nathan so far.

"Are you going to stop it?" Zeke asked his attention back on the guys.

I thought about it for a minute before answering. "No, not at the moment. Apparently, Oren thinks he deserves punishment, and my psycho needs to dole some out. It's a win, win."

About that time, Chloe forced her way between me and Zane.

"What the fuck, Chloe?" Zane yelled when her elbow caught him in the ribs.

"Well, move your fat ass, Moon. My bestie needs me to comfort her during this time of turmoil!" She stuck her tongue out at him.

"You take that back! My ass is perfect. Just the right amount of lift and roundness." He said, outraged.

Chloe stared at him briefly, shaking her head, then turned to me. "What the hell is going on with these two?" She waved her hand at the two morons currently bleeding. Well, the one moron bleeding and the idiot handing out the punishment.

"Seems like Nathan found out how Oren became Faction," I rolled my eyes.

"That makes sense. Are you going to stop it?" She cocked one eyebrow.

"Nope. Not yet, at least. They're both grown-ass men and need to work it out."

I heard the crowd give out a collective "AWWW" and saw that Oren had started fighting back. He gave a roundhouse kick to Nathan's face, which rocked him back on his heels.

"What are the rules?" I asked Zeke.

"Usually, there aren't any. But before they started fighting, Oren and Nathan agreed not to use their abilities. Neither are supposed to have any, so at least they're keeping a cool head."

I could hear in his voice that he agreed and was proud of them for keeping my safety at the forefront. I sighed in relief. I wasn't planning on stopping them unless it got out of hand. But their decision not to use their abilities pleased me. Nathan was strong, but Oren had abilities we weren't even aware of yet.

I winced when Oren struck out with a punch Nathan could not defend against. It was a direct hit to his nose, and I could hear the crunch from here. Nathan came back with a punch to Oren's gut that had the breath whooshing out of him.

It seemed like Nathan had learned a thing or two since he'd been gone.

While Oren was bent over, Nathan punched him in the chin, snapping his head back and causing him to stumble. He chose that moment to look over at me in triumph.

Unfortunately, that was his downfall. The minute he turned his head, Oren swept his legs out from under him and took him to the ground. Then he straddled him and delivered punch after punch until Nathan tapped out.

I didn't realize I'd stood, but Zeke grabbed my hand and pulled me back into his lap.

"He's fine, Nexus. Watch."

When I looked back at my guys, Oren was helping Nathan up, and they were both smiling, blood covering their teeth.

"I'll never understand men if I live to be a thousand years old." Chloe shook her head.

"Me and you both, sister." I nodded my head in agreement. Zeke and Zane started laughing.

"We're more straightforward than women. We disagree, fight it out, and then continue our lives." Zane chuckled.

"Women, on the other hand, will pretend to work it out, then make plans to destroy the other in a feud that can go on for generations." He raised a brow at Chloe and me, daring us to contradict him.

Chloe shrugged her shoulders, "That's fair."

He might just understand women more than any of my other men.

CHAPTER 14
REVERIE

Nathan walked over while Oren cleaned the blood off his face.

"Hey, my Nexi, how are you this fine morning?"

He leaned over and plucked me out of Zeke's lap. I automatically wrapped my legs around his waist, "I'm fine. How are you, Rocky Balboa?"

"I'm more like Clubber Lang. I kicked ass in the beginning but lost in the end." He grinned.

"You look weirdly happy about that." I gave him a puzzled look. He carried me toward Oren, who stood in the arena watching us approach. "That's because I know Storm is capable of defending the most important thing to us both. You." He kissed me deeply.

I licked the blood from his mouth, savoring the taste. Why was that a thing for me now? I wasn't craving a taste from anyone but my Faction, so there was that, at least.

Nathan moaned, "You better stop that, Nexi, or we won't be going to class today at all."

"You'll be going to class, no matter what. Appearances must be kept." Oren scolded Nathan, but the heat in his eyes softened his words.

I smirked at Oren. "Yes, sir!" I saluted, then lowered my voice. "Just because you two worked things out doesn't mean I'm not still planning my own form of payback."

He gave me a slow, sexy grin. "I'm looking forward to it."

Then he leaned closer, ensuring no one could hear him, "I'll see you tonight. You're bunking with me."

I nodded my head in agreement, then felt a warm kiss of air on my lips and a hand on my ass. When I jumped in surprise, I saw Oren smiling.

That was going to take some getting used to.

Nathan started to protest, and Oren rolled his eyes, "I guess you're invited too."

He then left the arena to get ready for class. Nathan kissed me again and carried me out to join our friends who were headed to the cafeteria.

When we caught up with them, Zeke, Zane, and Chloe were laughing and joking. I had no idea where Jet had gone. He needed a collar with a bell way more than Pantar did.

"What a waste of prime man meat." I heard a whiny voice say from my left.

"True story, I'm surprised he can lift her with all that ass she's packing." Sophie sneered.

I saw her and Kristine walking near us on their way to the cafeteria. Sophie was practically drooling at the sight of Nathan's muscles gleaming with a light sheen of sweat. They walked closer, and she reached out to touch his back with her grubby hand.

I completely lost it.

He...

was...

mine!

I executed a backflip out of Nathan's arms, and he released me in surprise. I quickly stood up, catching the bitch's hand before it could make contact.

"Damn, bestie!" Chloe yelled. "That's some next-level shit right there!"

I grinned but didn't look away from Sophie. She tried to jerk her wrist out of my grip, but I didn't let go.

"Why don't we head back to the arena? Seems like you need a lesson in not touching things that don't belong to you."

Sophie blanched, "I'm not going to fight you just because you're a jealous cow."

I smiled evilly, "Are you sure that's the reason? Or is it because you're all mouth and no substance?"

Zane started bouncing up and down, holding up his hand. "I know the answer to that one! Call on me, teach!" Chloe and Zeke started laughing.

"Come, Nexi mine, she's not worth it. As much as I would enjoy watching you kick her ass, I'd rather get something to eat. You can always beat her 'fat ass' later." Nathan grabbed my shoulders and kissed the top of my head.

I squeezed her wrist for a few moments more and then released her. "You better watch yourself. I'm at my limit with y'all's bullshit."

She narrowed her eyes at me but didn't say anything. Maybe she was smarter than her friend Kristine.

Nathan weaved his fingers through mine. "Damn, Nexi, just when I think it would be impossible for you to get any sexier, you do shit like this. Now I'm going to be in pain all day."

"You and me both." Zane licked his lips and adjusted his pants.

"You and me, three." Chloe licked her lips and adjusted her pants, mocking Zane.

Zane narrowed his eyes on Chloe as we roared in laughter.

"I worry about you, Chloe. I really do." Zane curled his lip in disgust.

That made us laugh harder as we entered the cafeteria and found a table near the back.

"I'll get your food. Any special requests?" Zeke asked.

"I'd like some pancakes with extra syrup and keep them coming." Nathan shrugged his shirt back on. "I worked up an appetite getting my ass kicked."

"Then I suggest you take that 'kicked ass' up to the buffet and get them." Zeke rumbled, then winked at me and headed for the line.

Nathan pouted, "Well, Zane, it looks like you and I have to get our own food."

"Let's get to it. I want pancakes, too, and I see Oliver heading that way. You know he'll eat every single one of them."

Zane jumped to his feet with Nathan right behind him.

"Who's Oliver?" I eyed the massive guy. He was almost as big as Jet, and that was saying something.

"He was on track to play starting center for the Bengals right before his Aurathion ancestry was determined." She leaned over to get a look at his ass.

"That's bad luck." I shook my head in sympathy.

She smirked, "After meeting me, I don't think he would agree." At that moment, Oliver saw Chloe eyeing him and winked.

"I bet." I laughed.

Chloe's expression became serious. "That fight was

brutal. Are you really okay after seeing your men throwing fists?"

I considered it momentarily, "Yes, with our connection, I would sense any genuine malice. Oren exhibited no anger, while Nathan's anger seemed righteous, not lethal."

"I've never heard of Factions members killing each other," Chloe pondered.

"If it's a true connection, I think it would be nearly impossible. It's hard to hold a grudge when you can feel the emotion behind the actions taken." I shrugged.

"Then why do you still want to punish Storm?" She looked confused.

"Because I can feel that he needs it to move on from everything that happened. And if I'm being honest, I do too." I shrugged.

"I can understand that." Chloe nodded, then eyed me briefly,

"Out with it, bestie. I can see you're wrestling with something else."

I wiped imaginary crumbs off the table to avoid eye contact.

"A part of me feels ashamed that I'm not more outraged by his actions, but the Nexus in me revels in the deviousness and cunning of my new bonded. It's like, I know what the human world expects me to feel, but as an Aurathion, I don't."

Chloe made a weird buzzing noise, and I jerked my head up to look at her. "That's a strike."

"What's a strike?" I was confused.

"No one has the right to tell you how you should feel. You don't have to justify yourself to anyone, human or Aurathion." She pulled me in for a hug. "If you're happy, that's all that matters."

I squeezed her tight, "I agree with you, in theory, but sometimes it's hard to convince myself."

She pulled back and grinned, "And that's why you have me. I'm a great convincer!"

"Hey, what's with all the serious faces?" Zane plopped down on my lap, holding his plate up high.

"Can't... speak... I'm being crushed." I groaned out.

"Get the fuck off her." Zeke snapped at his brother as he put a massive plate of food before me.

"Just giving my baby some love," Zane kissed me with plush lips.

"Well, give her some love from your own seat." Zeke sat down on my other side.

Zane looked at Chloe with puppy dog eyes.

"That shit doesn't work on me." She laughed, pulling her beautiful red hair in a ponytail with the scrunchie on her wrist.

"What if I promise to bring you Java and Jam tomorrow morning?" Zane bargained.

"Now you're talking. How about you bring me Java and Jam three mornings?" Chloe smirked.

"One morning and a late-night ice cream run." Zane threw back.

"Deal!" Chloe stood, and they shook hands on it.

Just when Zane started to lower himself into the chair, it was jerked out from under him, and Nathan sat.

"What the hell, man? Get your ass up, I paid for that chair." Zane growled.

Nathan leaned over and kissed me, his eyes never leaving mine as he spoke to Zane. "I'm feeling generous this morning, so let's make a deal?"

"What kind of deal?" Zane eyed Nathan with suspicion.

Nathan kissed me once more, then stood. "I'm going to

let you have this seat in exchange for a little help with a project I have going on."

"Color me intrigued." Zane's eyes lit up. "I'm in."

Lord, what was Nathan getting up to now? It could be anything from pranking an instructor to cold-blooded murder.

Nathan held the chair out for Zane. He sat, then dug into his plate piled high with breakfast, not worried in the least about what he'd volunteered for.

Zeke grabbed my chin, turning me to face him, as Nathan took the chair across from us.

"You need to eat, my treasure. Our first class starts soon, and I don't want you to have to function on an empty stomach until lunch." His sapphire eyes sparkled. "Now open up." I was mesmerized by the deep rumble of his voice and opened my mouth at his command without a thought.

He popped a forkful of pancake dripping with syrup into my mouth. "Good girl."

It was delicious. Some of the syrup ran down my chin from the large bite. I grabbed my napkin, but before I could bring it to my face, Zeke leaned forward and kissed my sticky lips, licking the syrup that had dribbled down my chin.

Zeke continually took me by surprise; his brand of sexy was lethal. I was going to have to start carrying extra panties in my backpack at the rate these men were going.

"Damn, Zeke's got game. Why the hell am I turned on by another man kissing my woman?" Nathan asked no one in particular.

"Treasure?" Zane asked, puzzled. "What kind of nickname is that?"

I couldn't take my focus off Zeke long enough to acknowledge them. He continued to stare into my eyes,

"That's what she is to me, a treasure. More valuable than any fortune found here or on any other world."

I swallowed hard, this guy and the things he made me feel.

"Now eat, treasure," Zeke told me once again.

So… I ate.

CHAPTER 15
REVERIE

After leaving the cafeteria, we headed to our first class of the day... Aurathion History.

My parents taught me a lot about our people, but this class still intrigued me. I smiled ironically, especially when Oren decided to hijack it. Learning was always easier with a little eye candy added, not to mention the life-changing information being dropped.

Jet had already arrived and was surrounded by women, as usual. I couldn't blame them because the tight black shirt he had on molded to his body, showing off all of those beautiful muscles.

I wanted to unwrap him like a candy bar and then lick every delectable inch.

For some reason, I assumed his involvement last night would change things. I guess I was wrong.

Sophie sat beside him, chatting animatedly. Jet didn't engage in the conversation and seemed oblivious to the blonde on his left, who was rubbing her hand along his massive biceps. I could feel my blood pressure rising and couldn't take my eyes off her hand.

Going up.

Then down his arm.

Chloe cleared her throat, and it snapped me out of my trance before I could embarrass myself.

Jet wasn't mine, and clearly didn't want to be. There would be no licking or unwrapping of the gorgeous man, at least by me. That thought wasn't helping my blood pressure.

"Let's take a seat before you maul Alice." Chloe smiled knowingly.

Nathan smirked and grabbed my hand as Chloe put her arm through mine on the other side. Apparently, they thought it might take both of them to hold me back. I was afraid they were right.

They steered me to seats in the back corner, where it would be hard to see Jet when the seats filled. For his part, he hadn't even looked up when we entered the room. He'd appeared lost in thought. He was probably trying to decide which girl he was going to pick.

Professor Austin entered the room, "Okay, class, let's get started. We have much to cover before winter break in the next few weeks."

He shuffled some papers on his desk and then approached the podium.

"I heard that Instructor Storm gave quite the lecture the other day. Are there any questions before I move on?"

Damn it, with everything going on, I didn't get to ask my parents about a shortage of D's wine. We needed to have another meeting this weekend to discuss everything.

I was surprised to see Jet raise his hand.

"Yes, Mr. Lockley?" Professor Austin asked.

"Is it true that there's a shortage of Dionysus's wine?" he narrowed his eyes.

Great minds, I thought, rolling my eyes.

"Yes, it is," Sophie butted in, "My friend Kristine confirmed what Instructor Storm told us. There won't be any more made unless a solution is found."

Everyone gasped, panicking all over again at her words.

"This is the first I've heard of it, but I'm sure the Council would tell us if it were true. There is no need to panic." Professor Austin mumbled, not meeting the eyes of the class.

I wondered if it was from guilt or if he genuinely didn't know. I'd bet it was the former if I had to guess.

Sophie mumbled something under her breath but didn't say anything loud enough for the class to hear.

I tended to believe Oren, especially since our bonding. The Council didn't want our people to know. I could understand it to a degree because I knew it would cause widespread panic.

"Everything will go on as usual. Initiation first, then groups petitioning to become a Faction." He said in a calm voice.

"Nothing changes."

The blonde, Alice, spoke, "I can't wait. Those who expect to be Nexus will begin choosing the best, strongest Passives to join our Faction." She smiled at Jet, who looked at her with his usual blank expression.

Sophie leaned up from Jet's other side to address her. "You better start looking somewhere else because he's already spoken for. When I'm Nexus-" Sophie's voice died off as Jet slowly turned and narrowed his eyes.

"I don't belong to you or anyone else."

Well damn. I didn't get scared easily, but that look he gave her caused the hair on my neck to stand up. That man was deadly without any abilities. I couldn't imagine how he'd be with them.

"I didn't mean it like that. I just... I meant... I know how *amazing* we would be together." Sophie stumbled over her words, trying to save face.

Jet stared at her until she dropped her eyes and faced the front of the class.

"Dumbass." Chloe coughed out.

Sophie turned and gave her a hateful glare.

"Maybe my Nexi will want to grab him... *up*." Nathan wheezed out the last part when I gave him an elbow to the gut.

"*Your* Nexi?" Sophie frowned.

"Yes, mine." Nathan clarified.

"Just because she knows her status already doesn't mean she's the best choice," Sophie gritted out. Suddenly, she smiled and fluttered her lashes, "I could be your Nexi."

A throat cleared toward the doorway, and Sophie blanched when she saw Kristine standing there.

"Ahh, Kristine, there you are." Professor Austin looked relieved at the interruption. "Class, Kristine is going to be my teaching assistant.

She smiled at him sweetly, then sashayed to the desk in the corner. "Please, Sophie, don't let me interrupt what you were saying."

Today, she wore skin-tight jeans, a blue sweater, and knee-high boots. I couldn't stand her, but I knew, objectively, that she was beautiful. It was her personality that was unappealing. Her momma probably had to tie a pork chop to her ass to get her dog to play with her.

Sophie tried desperately to cover her tracks. "I was saying that just because Reverie knows she's Nexus doesn't mean she's the only choice. Everyone knows you'll be Nexus and you're way superior to her."

"That's correct. Nathan might call me his Nexi in the next few weeks." Kristine winked at him, "Stranger things have happened."

Now, it was my turn to hold Nathan back. I understood how he felt. I wanted to get up and punch the bitch in the nose again myself. A reckoning was coming between Kristine and me. It was inevitable.

"The fuck you will. I'm already hers in every way that matters." He narrowed his eyes.

I could feel his blood pressure rise, and the hand I was holding started to get hot.

Shit!

I had to do something fast, or he would expose his ability. If that happened, everyone would know he was already bonded.

Unable to think of anything else, I grabbed his face and kissed him with everything I had.

I heard whistles and catcalls from the class. I knew it looked like I was staking a claim, and make no mistake, I was. But if it also saved Nathan and me from questions we couldn't answer, I would make the sacrifice. I began to pull away from the kiss, but Nathan wasn't having it. He grabbed my head with his large hands, deepening the kiss until I forgot why I even started it in the first place. He finally drew back, and I couldn't tear my hungry gaze away from his face. Nathan smiled sweetly and leaned in for one more gentle kiss.

"That's why I know I'm hers." He stared at my face, smiling in satisfaction at what he saw.

I blinked, unable to look away from his beautiful green eyes.

He turned to Kristine, "You'll never be anything to me because she's the only thing I see. You don't even exist in our world."

Kristine was fuming, her face red. "We'll just see about that."

The professor cleared his throat, "I feel like that took a turn. Let's get back on track. Everyone, open your books to chapter twenty-four."

～&～

The class continued without any more incidents. When the bell rang, we headed to Biology. Zane was waiting outside the classroom and wrapped around me like a boa constrictor.

"There's daddy's little monster." He whispered, kissing my ear.

I chuckled, "I wondered when one of you would make the connection."

"I'd like to make a connection, alright." He said, then moaned. "Especially when you slap my ass like that."

I was confused, "You have both of my hands wrapped up."

Now *he* was confused, "Then who slapped my ass?"

We glanced around and saw Chloe laughing.

"What the actual fuck?" Zane released me quickly when he started gagging.

Nathan pulled me into his arms, and we laughed so hard that the only thing keeping us upright was the wall.

"You're a teaching assistant, so you need to show some decorum." Chloe lectured him, grinning.

"Because of you, that might be all I can show. I think my dick just ran up my asshole." He shivered in disgust.

At his words, Nathan and I lost it again. Never a dull moment.

How did I survive without the Moons in my life?

~ ⚜ ~

B iology went off without a hitch, except my jealousy was growing at an alarming rate where Jet was concerned. In every class, beautiful women surrounded him. As we took our seats in Battle Tactics, it was no different.

I needed to control this feeling. I felt jealous of the other four, but it was never this bad. The *why* of that wasn't hard to figure out. I was confident in their feelings, but Jet ran hot and cold. If I weren't Aurathion, I'd kick him to the curb and move on, but my Nexus wasn't quite ready to give up.

Jet just wanted to be friends...maybe. I wasn't entirely sure where I stood with the impassive giant. But I wasn't the kind of girl to dwell on shit like this, Nexus or not.

I had four beautiful men I was sure of, and every single one of them wanted to become a member of my Faction. Two of them hadn't taken no for an answer. I wouldn't chase after one man who blew hot and cold, even if I had to fight myself every step of the way.

I'd have to learn to be his friend and keep the stronger emotions to myself. It wouldn't be easy because my Nexus wanted Jet with a passion. I knew our bond would be true, just like with my other men. That's why it was so hard to control my emotions.

I glanced at Zane, who winked at me from the desk in the corner. We'd previously had another student teacher, but with the higher threat level we now faced, the guys wanted to make sure at least one of them was with me in every class. Two of them, if they could manage it, were even better.

Nathan pulled me out of my thoughts. "Don't worry so much about Jet. He'll come around." He squeezed my thigh.

"I hope I'm not that obvious." I frowned.

"You wouldn't be to anyone else, but I have a master's degree in Reverie Hawthorne." He smiled.

I stared into his beautiful green eyes and whispered, "I love you. I feel like I don't say it enough."

Nathan looked taken aback, and then his face lit up. "I'll never get tired of hearing it." He smiled tenderly, "There aren't words to describe what you are to me."

I threaded our fingers together, brought his hand to my face, and kissed his knuckles, dropping it immediately when I felt a sudden burst of heat in my chest. My eyes fell closed, and I could see the source of my Nexus abilities and the strand that represented my bond with Nathan.

Typically, it was a beautiful, glowing emerald green, like his eyes, surrounding my vibrant center of power. The color remained unchanged, but now amber flames mixed with green, appearing to merge and leaving the red ring, representing Oren, to encircle the larger orb.

Nathan grabbed my shoulders in alarm when I opened my eyes, staring at my face in concern.

"What?" I asked, my voice sounding slurred.

I didn't feel so good. The lights were too bright, and everything was blurry. Before he could answer, Nathan grabbed his left peck and hunched over, moaning in pain.

"Nathan! What's wrong?" I rubbed my eyes, trying to focus. I squinted toward Zane's desk, hoping to get his attention. I didn't know what was happening, but we needed to get out of here before everyone noticed.

Thankfully, the blur I assumed was Zane got up and headed our way.

Before he reached us, Nathan raised his head slightly. "Your eyes are back to normal." He whispered, obviously still in pain.

"What the hell was wrong with my eyes, and why are you clutching your chest?" I knew he had no more answers than I did, but I was starting to freak out.

"My chest was burning like I was being branded from the inside out." He looked as confused as I felt.

"What's going on?" Zane asked when he reached us, his eyes narrowed in concern.

"We need to get out of here because something strange is happening. Can you make an excuse to Professor Lee?" Nathan asked urgently.

"Shit," Zane mumbled.

"What?" I couldn't tear my gaze away from Nathan.

It was like our connection had grown ten times over. The ball of amber light in my chest was going crazy, and it seemed to expand. Suddenly, I felt a burst of power spreading throughout my body.

"Professor Lee is heading this way," Nathan whispered. He hadn't taken his eyes off me, so I had no idea how he knew that.

"What's going on?" Chloe demanded. She had paused to talk with Joan on her way into class and hadn't been nearby when whatever this was happened.

Just then, Professor Lee arrived. "Get both of them to Oren now. I'll make an excuse to the class for her departure."

I was unable to speak or move at that moment. The power flooding my body felt as if it was changing me on a cellular level.

A tingling sensation spread from my head to the tips of

my toes, making me feel invincible. Slowly, the power began to fade, and exhaustion started to set in.

Nathan stood and took my arm, urging me to my feet, not taking his gaze off me.

"We need to get to Oren."

Chloe laid her hand on my other arm, and as soon as her flesh met mine, two things happened simultaneously: Nathan let out a vicious growl, and I felt a surge of power where she touched.

Chloe yelped and fell back, "Shit!" She cradled her hand.

Zane grabbed her wrist and turned her palm, where we could see that it was red and looked like she had a second-degree burn.

He looked at me in astonishment, "What the hell just happened?"

Nathan was still staring at Chloe like he might jump her at any minute. When I started to go to her, he snarled and wrapped his body around me protectively. I jerked away from him, desperate to check on my friend. I was surprised at the ease with which I could accomplish this. I narrowed my eyes at him when he reached to pull me back into his arms again.

"Chloe, I'm so sorry! I have no idea what the hell is going on!" I approached, careful not to touch her.

"Don't worry about me, bestie, just get to Oren and find out what's going on." She gritted out, obviously in pain.

"Get them out of here, now! I'll take care of your sister." Professor Lee ordered Zane in a gruff voice.

He nodded, "Let's go." Though reluctant to leave Chloe, he knew we needed to go before people noticed what was happening.

I grabbed Nathan's hand, desperately wanting a physical connection. I was acting like a crazy person, throwing him off one minute, then pulling him back the next. When we got to the door, Jet stood there waiting for us.

"Why are you coming?" I wasn't trying to be a bitch, but I just didn't understand why he kept inserting himself into our group. This man's actions confused me to no end.

"He can come," Nathan growled out. Still sounding like he'd gargled with glass.

I was momentarily stunned by Nathan's defense of Jet. He didn't want Chloe near me and *knew* she wasn't dangerous. Why was he okay with Jet? This day couldn't end soon enough.

None of that mattered now. I needed to get to Oren. Usually, Nathan was my safe place, but right now, I wanted Oren like I needed air to breathe. Instinctively, I felt he would know what was going on.

"Where are they going?" Kristine demanded.

"You're here to assist me. What they're doing is none of your business." The Professor said in a no-nonsense voice.

She replied to him, but I couldn't hear what was said as Jet closed the door behind us.

"Contact Oren and tell him to meet us in his apartment."

Zane was staring at Nathan in concern.

He'd wrapped himself around me again and was looking around the dark hallway like we were going to be attacked at any moment.

"Oren, can you meet us at your apartment? Something happened to Nathan and me. We need your help figuring out what's going on."

"What the fuck happened?" He sounded frantic.

"I wish I knew. Nathan is acting more psycho than usual, and Chloe burned her hand just touching my arm."

"Tell him to teleport there now. I'm on my way."

"Can you teleport us there? Jet and Zane can walk over."

We needed to get behind closed doors before something else happened. Nathan didn't say anything. He just led us to an alcove hidden in the shadows. He picked me up, and I wrapped my legs around his waist.

"Grab my hands." He told Jet and Zane.

Was he going to teleport us all? What the fuck? They glanced at each other, but did as he asked. I felt my stomach bottom out, and I closed my eyes. When I opened them again, we were all standing in Oren's apartment; Zeke and Oren were already there waiting for us.

There was complete silence for a moment as we all processed the fact that Nathan had teleported us all at the same time.

"What happened?" Oren asked as I dropped my legs from Nathan's waist and stood.

Ignoring his question, I slowly raised Nathan's shirt. I needed to see if I had injured him somehow, too.

A dagger that perfectly matched the one inside my Nexus mark was now on Nathan's chest. The green lines were interposed with amber and glowed slightly.

Nathan slowly raised his head to look at me. His eyes glowed with love and amazement.

"You marked me, my Nexi."

I couldn't argue with that. I just wish I knew how I did it.

CHAPTER 16

OREN

I couldn't believe it. Reverie had done something I'd only read about in my research.

An ability that was thought to have been lost thousands of years ago.

An ability that gave her Faction members all the powers of a Nexus.

"What the fuck is that?" Zane asked no one in particular.

"That is something that hasn't happened in thousands of years." I was still staring at Nathan's chest in amazement and a dash of envy. I wanted to wear Reverie's brand. Nathan shouldn't be the only bond to have one.

Unfortunately, if I was right about this ability, Reverie had to be willing to use it... I couldn't trick her into giving me one.

Not that I would. I was turning over a new leaf.

Maybe.

Probably.

Fuck it. It was too late for that. I wanted her so wrapped up in me she couldn't tell where I ended and she began.

Nathan, for his part, was smiling like the lunatic he was. I'm sure he was in heaven, sporting a brand that let everyone know who he belonged to. I was more than a little salty about it.

"What do you mean it hasn't happened for thousands of years?" Reverie looked panicked and headed right for my arms. I liked this. I always wanted to make her feel safe. If she needed answers, I would find them, no matter what I had to do to get them. My angel was so precious to me. I loved it when she got that little crinkle between those gorgeous amber eyes.

"The last time it was mentioned in my research was before Dionysus was born. Once upon a time, Faction members were marked when it was a true bond by their Nexus." I let them digest this for a few minutes, relishing the moments when I had Reverie's full attention.

"So, is this a new ability she's gained?" Zeke questioned.

Reverie turned to look at him, and I narrowed my eyes at the prick. Leave it up to the ginger to fuck it up.

"It would seem so." I turned to Nathan. "What exactly happened with Reverie's eyes?"

He was still looking at his chest, not paying attention to anything being said. If he weren't my Faction brother, I'd ruin him.

"Nathan!" Zane yelled.

"What?" He didn't even raise his head.

He was fucking annoying, and if he kept up his shit, I would cut the mark off him at my earliest convenience. I'd noticed the others giving him hateful looks, too. Even Jet. This morning's incident proved he was just as unhinged as the rest of us. No doubt he'd fit right in.

"What happened with Reverie's eyes?" I repeated slowly.

Nathan looked at me in annoyance, irritated that he had to glance away from his new mark.

"Her pupil was replaced with a green flame. I've never seen anything like it."

Reverie shook her head in denial at his words. I'd noticed that she looked exhausted. The last few days have been hectic for all of us. This new development was just one more thing she had to deal with. My poor angel needed her rest, and I would ensure she got it.

Preferably while my face was between her legs.

"I felt a heat in my chest, and my vision blurred. When I checked the source of my power, Nathan's ring of green had merged with my Nexus ability." She looked at me imploringly, "Please tell me you know what this means."

She tucked her head under my chin, and I felt her breathing in my scent.

I was gone for her.

I had been since the first time I'd seen her.

"I know the ability, but I don't understand why it's reappeared now." I kissed her head. "I have some theories, but I need to dig deeper before I have a solid lead." She snuggled deeper into my embrace.

"How dangerous is this for her?" Jet spoke up from his position by the door.

I could hear the worry in his voice. The time was coming when he'd have to come to terms with all of this. He couldn't split his loyalty between his Nexus and his career in the military. The Aurathion in him wouldn't allow it.

Neither would I.

After seeing the lengths he was willing to go for her, I knew it was only a matter of time. The issue was that we needed to come together sooner rather than later. Reverie's new ability would be difficult to hide for long. We needed her Faction to be complete.

There was no other option.

I'd do whatever was necessary to make it happen.

She was my priority.

All the guys were waiting for my answer.

"On a scale of one to ten, I'd say a twenty."

"Fuck!" Zeke stood and started pacing. "Do we need to leave the academy?"

I thought about it as I cuddled my Nexus in my arms. Having her this close was distracting. Feeling her breasts pressed against my chest, smelling her sweet scent, those things combined had my dick standing at attention.

I took a deep breath, "No, that would be the worst thing we could do. She has to finish her initiation so that her bonds can be revealed. We *need* to complete this Faction." I narrowed my eyes at the three guys who were yet to bond with Reverie. "You're all going to need abilities to help defend our Nexus. As it stands now, you're less than useless."

"Fuck you, Oren." Zeke bit out. "I would die for her."

"That's not what she needs. She needs you to live for her." I growled, frustrated with the whole situation.

Zane didn't speak but was watching Reverie with a gleam in his eyes. He was planning something.

I smiled with approval. It's about time the Moons got off their ass and made something happen. The bonding ceremony was a good idea, but keeping her safe was more important. I was starting to wonder where the guys who had been my friends were.

They'd never denied themselves something they wanted. Now would be a perfect time for them to make a reappearance.

Jet started to speak but I cut him off. "Yes, even you."

That dumbass was going to dig a hole he couldn't get out of with my Nexus if he didn't figure his shit out. Any other time, I'd enjoy watching him suffer, but I needed her Faction whole, so I would have to push him. Reverie raised her head.

"Not him. He doesn't feel that way about me, and unlike you two," she raised an eyebrow at Nathan and me. "I refuse to force anyone."

Rolling my eyes, I kissed the top of her head. She hadn't let go of that yet?

Sigh... I suppose I needed to work a little harder to earn her forgiveness.

"I know it was wrong to do that. Will me eating your sweet pussy for a few hours earn my forgiveness?"

Reverie raised her head again, giving me a wide-eyed look.

Then, much to my surprise, she smiled slightly.

"Maybe."

Fuck, my dick jerked painfully. Was it hot in here?

I was so deeply in love with this girl. She was the perfect mix of innocence and temptress, and most importantly, she was mine. I sighed. It was time to get back on the subject.

"Nexus, you know he will be a true bond, and you'll need his strength in the coming days."

"Speak where the rest of us can hear. It's rude to flaunt your ability to communicate with her in front of us poor fucks who aren't bonded to her yet." Zane spit out.

I flipped him off.

Reverie narrowed her eyes, "I won't bond with anyone who doesn't need or want me. I'm plenty strong enough with you four."

She turned to Jet, "I value your friendship, but I don't expect anything else."

Jet moved closer, "It's not that I don't want you. Any man

with a brain in his head would want to be with you. I have other commitments that I have to fulfill." His voice sounded almost pleading.

I was stunned that he'd put that many sentences together. Jet wasn't known for his prose.

"I think it's time we talk about those commitments." I raised a brow at the big idiot.

Jet's eyes widened the smallest amount, and if I hadn't been watching him so closely, I would have missed it. He couldn't have thought I would keep this from Reverie. She deserved to know what was holding him back.

"What commitments are we talking about? Do you already have a Nexus you're involved with?" Reverie sounded hurt.

I *knew* she was already feeling the need to bond with him. It was going to suck when I had to kill him for hurting her.

"His ties to the human military." Nathan blurted out.

What...the...fuck?

I need to keep a closer eye on my Faction brother. It seems that I'd underestimated him.

"What?" Reverie yelled.

"You son of a bitch. If you tell them anything about Reverie, I'll kill you!" Zeke started in his direction.

"Fuck you. I haven't told anyone anything about her. I'd never put her in danger." Jet clenched his massive fists and motioned for Zeke to bring it on.

I raised my hands and froze them both where they stood.

"None of that nonsense. He hasn't said anything to anyone. I've been monitoring his communications, and after his actions this morning, I don't think his loyalty can be questioned."

"What actions?" Reverie asked me, frowning at Zeke and

Jet. I let them both go, and Jet slowly turned his head toward me.

"If you ever do that to me again, you'll regret it."

I smiled, "Don't make it necessary."

He had a lot to learn. Those men he'd dealt with this morning were nothing compared to me. I wasn't anything he'd seen before. That would also need to be addressed before long.

"This crazy bastard tore two men apart for threatening you. I've seen some fucked up shit, but the brutality of it shocked even me." Zane shivered.

"Why would you do that?" Reverie looked honestly confused. He just shrugged his shoulders and looked away.

"I don't like violence against women. I would've done it no matter what. It wasn't specifically because it was you they threatened."

When I saw the hurt again in Reverie's eyes, I couldn't let that go unpunished. Making a fist with one of my hands, Jet's eyes widened, and he grabbed his throat.

He looked around desperately, not knowing where the threat was coming from. Seeing my fist raised in the air, he realized it was me.

The big guy headed in my direction, thinking he could use his strength to make me let go. I didn't even move, knowing he would never reach me.

Jet fell to his knees before he made it halfway. No matter how tough a person was, they couldn't function without oxygen.

"Let him go, Oren!" Reverie punched me in the chest.

"He must understand he can't say things like that to hurt you." I kept the pressure on his neck until his lips turned a beautiful blue.

"Fuck him. He doesn't deserve you anyway." Nathan came

up behind her, so she was cradled between us. He was not upset in the least by my actions.

I leaned back and took her chin, raising her eyes to meet mine. "None of us deserves you. Me, least of all, but I would destroy the world to keep you from being hurt. I love you, Nexus."

Suddenly, a red flame took the place of her pupil, and I felt a terrible burning pain under my right shoulder blade.

"Fuck!" I let go of her and fell forward, holding my head in my hands. I lost my grip on my ability and heard Jet gasping for breath.

When the pain stopped, I stumbled to my feet and went into the bathroom to look in the mirror. Sure enough, there was a mark on my back. It was a bolt of lightning lined with red and amber.

My mark was fucking gorgeous.

I closed my eyes and checked on my nucleus of power. It had been a ball of deep red, and after I bonded with Reverie, an amber thread had surrounded it. Now, it was one big ball of amber and red flames.

I'd been keeping secrets, too.

Because my father had been injecting me from a young age, I'd become a Nexus in my own right. I knew I wouldn't take that route from the moment I met Reverie.

My love for her would always come before power. That's why I allowed myself to have her. I chose Reverie instead of forming my own Faction. That was unheard of in our world, but I'd give up anything: family, status, and power

…for her.

CHAPTER 17
REVERIE

This was now my life. Unexpected abilities and stubborn men.

Jet remained on the ground, trying to take in as much oxygen as possible. The guys watched him warily as if they expected him to erupt into a murderous rage. Apparently, their caution was justified, as tearing people limb from limb was well within his wheelhouse.

Oren was in the bathroom, looking at the results of my new ability, which seemed to have its own agenda.

As for me, I was stuck somewhere between exhausted and horny.

It was sexy as hell to see Oren and Nathan defending me like that. I understood now how the guys felt seeing me put Sophie in her place. If I had a penis, I'd be adjusting myself too.

Unfortunately, doing anything about it wouldn't happen until I could close my eyes for a few minutes. I sighed and hoisted myself off the couch to check on Oren while the guys were occupied. There would be no rest for me if I didn't make sure my Shitstorm was okay with everything that had happened. If this is how regular humans feel daily, then don't sign me up.

He was admiring his new mark in the mirror.

"It's beautiful." I couldn't help but feel a small amount of pride at the sight, even if it wasn't done deliberately.

Oren turned and took me into his arms. "You know that bonding with you saved my life, but I never explained how."

Indeed, he hadn't. Since it occurred, we've been racing from zero to sixty and haven't had the opportunity to simply exist.

I yawned and turned my head, trying to cover it up. All of this was exciting, but I was drained. I could barely keep my eyes open after marking Nathan and Oren. This new ability took all of my energy. I needed to find out everything about it as soon as possible. Well, maybe in a few hours.

"My angel looks tired. Why don't I get you something to eat, and then you can lie in my bed and nap?" Oren tugged on a pigtail. "I can explain things later when you're not about to drop from exhaustion."

I wanted to protest, but I was just so tired. "Okay, that sounds good."

"I made you some soup and a sandwich," Zeke said, startling us both.

"You really can't stand for anyone else to feed her, can you?" Oren asked, smirking.

"No one knows how she likes it but me." Zeke grabbed my hand and led me to the bar.

"That's what she said." Zane joked, taking the seat beside me.

Zeke just rolled his eyes and fixed me a glass of sweet tea, clearly used to his brother's jokes.

"Where did you get that?" Oren looked at it in distaste. "Tea is supposed to be served hot."

"I may have to rethink your mark." I narrowed my eyes.

He smiled indulgently, "For you, I'll make an exception."

"My crazy brother ran to our apartment to get it. He made sure to have a supply ready after your Pop told him it was your favorite beverage." Zane stole a chip from my plate and popped it in his mouth.

Zeke growled at him, and Zane held up both hands. "I promise not to take another bite. Damn, I'm your twin, and you're just going to let me starve to death."

I tuned them out and looked around the room. When I didn't see Jet, I assumed he had returned to class.

You know what they say about assuming, I thought, as Nathan and Jet walked through the door. Nathan was carrying a pizza, and Jet had a twelve-pack of beer in his arms.

"Where did you get the beer?" Zane raised a brow.

"Jolly and I blinked to a store and picked some up. With those muscles and that height, no one asked for ID." Nathan waved a hand to showcase Jet like a model on *The Price Is Right*, presenting a new car.

Jet hadn't taken his eyes off Oren since he entered the room. I just thought he was intimidating before. The look of death in his eyes upped his badass factor by several levels.

"No need to be pissed, Jet." Oren grinned, "I can't let you say things that could harm Reverie, even if you think it's for a noble cause. I believe you're just postponing the inevitable and perhaps creating a hole you won't escape from."

"Storm is correct." Nathan set the beer on the kitchen counter and handed each guy one. "My Nexi can hold a grudge, and once she gets something in her head, getting her to change her mind is a monumental task. Believe me, if not for my superior skills of persuasion, I wouldn't be here."

"No beer for Reverie?" Zane asked, nodding his head in my direction.

Nathan smirked, "When the choice is sweet tea or beer, my Nexi always chooses tea. Maybe there's a good reason she hasn't bonded with you yet."

"Fuck off, I know the important things, like how she sounds when she cums." Zane flipped him off.

I choked on my grilled cheese and took a large gulp of my sweet tea.

"What the hell, Zane?" I said, my eyes watering.

He walked over and hugged me. "It was the best moment of my life. Nathan may have known you longer than the rest of us, but I know who you are to me and my brother."

I was mesmerized by his sincerity. He played around a lot, but when he focused all his attention on me, it was devastating.

"You're our life, past, present, and future. We have all the time in the world to learn the rest." He rubbed his nose against mine.

Zeke came up behind me, "He's not wrong. Every moment in your presence is a gift." He hugged me and laid his chin on my head.

Suddenly, they both moaned in agony and dropped to their knees.

I jumped to my feet.

It's happening again!

What the fuck was going on? I hadn't bonded with either man. Surely, this new ability couldn't bypass the ritual or blood exchange.

Zeke clutched the left side of his stomach, while Zane clutched his right.

After a few moments, both men stood up and raised their shirts. Zane was marked with a yellow and amber sun that looked so realistic I could almost feel the heat coming off it.

Zeke's mark was a purple crescent moon with a scattering of amber stars. They both stared at me in shock, but before I could comment, I felt an intense burn between my breasts where my mark was.

What the fuck was happening right now?

When I raised my shirt, I saw a sun directly below Nathan's dagger, followed by a crescent moon at the bottom of my mark, opposite the ash tree representing a Nexus.

Every vacant spot was filled except for one.

My eyes rolled back in my head, and for the second time in my life, I fainted.

CHAPTER 18
ZEKE

I caught Reverie in my arms before she could hit the floor, which was a true miracle because I felt a little woozy myself. I wasn't sure what the hell was going on here, but I could feel Reverie inside me.

It felt like we had bonded.

"What the fuck?" Zane was nearly hysterical. Looking at his mark, then at me, like I had answers. Spoiler alert... I didn't.

Oren was pacing the room and muttering to himself. He suddenly disappeared, only to reappear a few seconds later, holding several books and scrolls.

He used his arm and swiped everything off the table, not paying the least attention to the mess he'd made. However, I noticed Jet's eye twitching at the disorder.

I gently picked up Reverie and placed her on the couch, covering her with a throw. She had noticeable dark circles under her eyes and appeared extremely tired. This girl was a powerhouse. I'd never seen her like this before.

Although I'd never mentioned it, in all my stalking of her,

I'd witnessed her abilities energizing her. Typically, when most Aurathions used our abilities, we needed to rest to regain our strength, not my treasure.

Nathan sat at the end of the couch and put her feet in his lap. "She never ceases to amaze. I've known her for most of my life, and she still surprises me." We all agreed on that. I was grateful to be along for the ride.

All I wanted was to take care of Reverie and protect her as much as I could. My brother and I had calmed down over the last year or so, but there was no doubt that I'd become whatever I needed to be to keep her safe.

I edged over to my brother, "Are you okay?"

"I'm more than okay. I feel powerful," Zane had removed his shirt and was running a hand over his sun mark, smiling like crazy.

I closed my eyes and breathed deeply. My body felt changed as well. Reverie had filled all the empty spaces inside me with pure power. I felt invincible, and there was a strange coldness to my core that was invigorating.

Zane inhaled loudly when I opened my eyes, "Zeke, your pupils!"

"What about them?" I blinked rapidly. Freaking out a little at his tone.

Before he could answer, Oren rose from the table and started pacing the floor with his nose stuck in one of the books.

"I knew it!" He went over to the couch and sat on the coffee table, laying the book beside him.

"What do you know?" Jet asked as we all gathered closer.

I was surprised he hadn't left after what had occurred between him and Oren. Maybe Jet stayed because he knew he deserved what Oren had done... and perhaps he didn't want to be away from Reverie. The big dumbass better get with the program because I had a feeling we were going to need all of us to protect this amazing creature.

"I thought Reverie had gained a new ability until she marked Zeke and Zane. I was wrong." Oren lovingly ran a hand down Reverie's face with an expression of awe, "It's more of a lost trait than an ability. Most Aurathions scholars consider it a myth. Now her unique Nexus mark makes complete sense."

"I've never seen anything like her mark. I knew she'd have one since she bonded Pantar, but it looks nothing like the ones in any textbooks we've studied." I looked at Oren, hoping that he had answers.

We all drew as close to Reverie as we could, feeling the need to protect our Nexus when she was this vulnerable.

"I thought the same until I witnessed it with my own eyes," He muttered, ignoring my comment. "This, combined with her mark, confirms it." Oren was obviously thrown by everything that had happened.

This concerned me more than anything. I'd never seen Oren behave anything but confidently in any situation he was involved in.

"What is it?" I spoke in a whisper, feeling the weight of the moment.

"It's called Amalgamate," he said reverently.

"Amalgamate," Jet repeated in his deep voice, then moved even closer to Reverie, edging me out the slightest bit.

I growled low and felt a strange pressure building in my throat. Before I could unleash it, Oren distracted me, continuing his explanation. Reverie was more important than Jet's serial-killer-want-to-be-ass, so I pushed my rage down and tuned back in.

"Yes, it's the power to unite or combine a group into a single unit... or a Faction." Oren put his head in his hands.

"Without a ritual or blood exchange?" I asked in disbelief, my voice sounding huskier than it usually did.

Oren raised his head, "Yes."

The look in his eyes was starting to worry me.

"How much danger is she in if this gets out?" Nathan narrowed his eyes, asking the question we all had on our minds.

"More than you can conceive," Oren said, locking eyes with each of us, seemingly assessing our capability to safe-guard our Nexus.

Jet snarled, standing up and positioning himself in front of the door as if someone were going to burst in at any moment. I understood how he felt. The need to rip and tear to protect her was riding me hard.

"It'll take all five of us and our abilities to protect her." He leaned over and gently kissed her lips. "And even then, it might not be enough. The Council and the Dark Factions would love nothing better than to get their hands on her."

No one spoke after that statement.

From the first instant I met her, I instinctively sensed that she was extraordinary. At this moment, I vowed to dedicate myself to honing the new skills my treasure had bestowed upon me, to protect her, and to defend her against anyone who made the grave mistake of threatening her.

I didn't know what the rest of my Faction brothers were thinking, but as for me, I knew that my heart now lived outside my body, and I would burn the world down to keep it safe.

CHAPTER 19
REVERIE

I woke up slowly, hearing the soft murmur of the guys' voices close by. I reluctantly opened my eyes and stretched, feeling incredibly well-rested.

Realizing I wasn't in my bed, I panicked before remembering what had occurred earlier. Sitting up abruptly, I raised my shirt.

Except for one, every empty place on my mark was filled. It wasn't a dream, it really did happen.

How in the hell did I bond with the twins without a blood exchange?

I didn't regret it. If possible, I would have bonded with them just days after we met. All the guys, even Jet, felt like they belonged to me from the beginning.

I took a moment to close my eyes and check on my well of power. My breath caught at the sight. It was simply beautiful: my usual amber blended with vibrant green, enchanting purple, bright yellow, and the deepest red, creating a mesmerizing ball of fire. It was ever-changing, with the power ebbing and flowing as the flames danced sinuously.

I noticed Pantar curled up at my feet in his smallest form.

"Busy day, Nexus?" He grinned, showing all of his sharp teeth.

"Yes, you could say that." I blinked rapidly, trying to hold in tears. The surprises kept coming, and I'd really appreciate a moment to process before the next one occurred.

Pantar walked up my legs and nuzzled the side of my face.

"You will be fine. There is a reason for everything happening."

I knew he was right and took a deep breath. I was stronger than this. With all these amazing men bonded to me, I could deal with anything.

"Not to mention the amazing Fellat you have by your side." Pantar licked my cheek before springing off the couch, enlarging to the size of a large leopard mid-leap. *"I will be back, Nexus. Your men will take care of you."*

He disappeared before I could ask where he was off to. Pantar's comings and goings were a mystery to me most of the time.

Zeke must have heard me moving around because he walked over from the kitchen. "Hello, my treasure. Are you hungry?" he smiled warmly. "And I didn't hear you. I felt your hunger like it was my own. That's going to help tremendously with taking care of you."

That's going to take some getting used to. "How are you doing with everything that happened?" I could feel his emotions, but I wanted to hear him say it out loud. Before he could answer, my stomach let out a deep growl.

"You know how I feel. I would have bonded with you when you entered the room on the first day we met." He leaned down and kissed me softly, lingering for a short moment. "Let me get you something to eat, then we can all talk."

Zeke kissed me again and returned to the kitchen.

When he entered, I saw Nathan and Zane turn my way. I didn't see Jet or Oren and was a little disappointed.

"I wouldn't have left if it wasn't important for your safety. It's imperative that my routine not change, especially now. Eat and rest. I'll return as soon as possible, and we'll discuss everything."

"Okay, stay safe." I felt a kiss on my forehead. How the hell did he do that? That man was still keeping secrets. Lucky for him, I knew whatever they were, he meant no harm. I'd trust that he'd tell us everything when he was ready.

I closed my eyes and dozed off again.

⚓

"Hey, my Nexi, open those beautiful eyes so the ginger can feed you. He's going to lose his shit if your stomach makes one more noise." Nathan kissed the tip of my nose.

I smiled and opened my eyes to three of the most beautiful men on the planet... with three of the firmest, most bite-worthy asses I'd ever seen.

Where did that thought come from? It was true, but why was I thinking about their asses... and those abs.

Damn, was it hot in here? Did I have drool running down my face?

"Aww, precious girl, I know I'm handsome, but your eyes deceive you concerning these other two." Zane's smile was as cocky as ever. "And my ass is, without doubt, exquisite."

I smirked, loving his sass... ass... no, definitely his sass, and then my eyes widened, "Are y'all hearing my thoughts?"

"Some of them." Zeke rubbed the back of his neck and ducked his head, trying to hide his grin.

"More like all of them." Nathan laughed. "I think you'd be more truthful if you'd ended with ass. Though, I think mine is better."

"The hell you say? I can crack walnuts with mine." Zane smiled brilliantly. "Tell him, Zeke."

"We promised never to discuss that night, ever again." Zeke narrowed his eyes at Zane.

Zane pouted, "You're right. What happens at camp stays at camp." Then he looked at me and whispered, "I'll tell you later why my brother wants that night to be kept quiet. It involves a clothespin, a rooster, peanut butter, and plastic wrap."

Zeke started for him, and Zane leaped over the couch, almost hitting the ceiling.

"What the fuck?" Nathan said, as stunned as the rest of us.

Talented Aurathions created these apartments and everything else in this pocket dimension. This meant that everything was much larger than should be possible, including the height of the ceilings.

They were nearly twenty feet.

Zane stood from the crouch he'd landed in, just as stunned as the rest of us. "Damn, that's going to come in handy."

"The surprises just keep coming." Zeke shook his head and grinned.

These boys were something else, and I was here for it.

"You better be here for it. There's no going back now."

Nathan smirked, raising his shirt and pointing to his mark.

"Y'all really can hear my thoughts?" I covered my face with my hands.

"We really can," Nathan smirked.

"Thanks for not sugarcoating it, asshole." I slapped Nathan's arm.

"Hey, why am I getting hit for being honest? Thing One is acting like you can't handle the truth so hit him. I know you for the bad bitch you are." Nathan growled playfully.

Zeke closed his eyes and shook his head. "I know she's a badass. I'm just trying to save her some embarrassment."

"What's to be embarrassed about? She's one lucky woman."

Nathan began to hum "Pony" by Ginuwine and dancing around the room, shaking his ass.

I felt myself overheating again. What the hell was going on?

He was one sexy guy, but his dancing skills needed improvement.

I wouldn't usually get this turned on by his antics. Who am I kidding? I most definitely would, but maybe not this quickly.

"It's the bonds. Completing so many at once has your hormones on the fritz. Usually, they're consummated shortly after being formed." Zeke blushed.

Zane waggled his eyebrows, "Want to do a little consummating?"

Zeke slapped him on the back of the head.

"Damn, asshole, I was just kidding." He frowned at his brother.

Why didn't Zeke want to consummate things with me? Maybe he didn't find me as attractive as I saw him.

I heard a deep growl, and then I was being picked up.

"Don't think for a single second I don't want to lay you down and bury myself in your sweet pussy for hours." Zeke narrowed his eyes, holding me up effortlessly so we were eye to eye.

"Damn, Nexi, you made a ginger snap." Nathan laughed, still dancing around the room. Was he drunk?

"Eyes on me." Zeke snapped when my attention wandered.

I immediately turned back to him, astonished by the authority in his voice. He sat on the couch, positioning me so I straddled his lap.

"I know you can feel how much I want you." He flexed his hips.

I nodded.

"Give me your words," Zeke said.

"I do. It's obvious unless you carry a log around in your pants," I snarked at him.

He grabbed my chin, "I want you to understand the level of desire I have for you."

Zane came and sat beside us, grabbing my hand and placing it over the prominent bulge in his pants.

"We want nothing more than to worship your beautiful body for hours. Believe that."

My panties were so damp at this point that there was probably a wet spot on Zeke's pants. These two together were lethal.

"We discussed it, and if you're willing, we would like to take you home for a bonding ceremony." Zeke ran his hand down the length of my pigtail, then tugged on the end.

I didn't know what to say.

Thinking I was upset, Zane started speaking rapidly, "We were going to ask you much more elaborately, but that was before you decided to mark us immediately... Not that we're upset about that. I couldn't possibly be happier."

"Calm down, brother, and feel her emotions." Zeke closed his eyes and breathed deeply, "She's happy."

I blinked the tears away, "She's so happy." I leaned over and kissed Zane.

"Only our parents and Faction brothers will be able to attend. We must keep our bonding secret, but we want to give you this." Zeke kissed me softly.

"And I'm going to perform the ceremony." Nathan casually dropped that bomb as he sat on the coffee table in front of us.

"The hell you are." Zane frowned.

"It's either that or this isn't happening. I refuse to be left out."

He crossed his arms over his chest and pouted.

"Let him," Zeke smirked. "If nothing else, it'll be memorable."

"That's what I'm afraid of." Zane grumbled.

Nathan rubbed his hands together.

"Just wait and see. It'll be the best bonding ceremony anyone's ever seen."

"Okay, now that's settled, let's get you fed." Zeke smiled.

He grabbed the plate he'd prepared and hand-fed me until I couldn't eat another bite.

"Can we talk now about what this all means?" I patted my full belly.

"I would prefer you wait until I return." Oren sounded out of breath.

"Are you okay?" I was worried.

"Yes, my angel, I'm just trying to run off some of this excess energy all the bonding has caused. I'll be back as soon as my classes are over. Can you wait for explanations until then?"

I sighed, *"I guess so."*

"That's my girl. See you soon."

"I guess that answers your question. Let's clean up and put on a movie until Oren gets back. You still look exhausted, and I don't like it." Zeke rose and took the dishes into the kitchen.

"Sounds like a plan." Nathan scooted in behind me.

Zane picked up my feet and put them in his lap. Zeke returned to the room and put on a movie. He sat on the floor in front of me, and I ran my fingers through his hair. I relaxed immediately, feeling a sense of contentment by our connection.

Now, if Oren and Jet were here, it would be perfect. Damn it, I'd told myself not to think of Jet like that anymore.

"He'll come around. What he did for you this morning proves that." Nathan murmured.

Feeling soothed by his words, I drifted back to sleep.

⌒☖〜

When I woke, the apartment was quiet, and I seemed to be alone. Stretching, I stood up, noticing a trail of rose petals leading into Oren's room. I smiled, followed them into the bedroom, and somewhat disappointed, on into the bathroom.

I'd been expecting Oren to be waiting for me in the bedroom, ready to consummate his new mark. My disappointment was short-lived, seeing what was awaiting me in the bathroom.

I grinned. I could get used to this.

The beautiful tub I'd noticed before was filled with steaming water, and the bathroom was filled with the scent of honeysuckle.

This gorgeous man must have stocked my favorite bath bombs.

I stripped and lowered myself slowly into the hot water. Damn, that felt nice. My body was strangely sore like I'd been working out twenty-four hours straight.

I leaned back and closed my eyes, deciding to take inventory of how I felt. I took a deep breath and realized I felt fabulous—stronger than I'd ever been.

The minor soreness in my limbs dissipated quickly in the steaming water.

The source of my power was raging. Bands of color no longer surrounded the nucleus. They'd all completely merged, forming one massive sphere. All the colors representing my men had mixed and were continuously moving, the colors fighting for dominance.

Continuing to take stock of the changes inside, I tried connecting with my Faction.

I smiled, feeling Oren and Nathan together somewhere nearby.

Zane and Zeke were also together, so serene that I was positive they were asleep.

I could even tell that Pantar was hunting in the forest.

"Do you require me, Nexus?"

Of course, he sensed me lurking.

"No, just testing out the limits of my abilities." I grinned and slid down, submerging my head underwater.

"Yes, they seem to be coming along nicely, though you're still incomplete. As I'm sure you are aware."

I felt his concern for me. But honestly, I was too content to care right now.

"Enjoy these moments. Bring your Faction closer together. I will continue to build my strength and prepare for things to come."

In my mind's eye, I saw him sniff the air and bound off, giving chase to whatever prey he was hunting.

I sat up, thoroughly washed my hair and body, rose from the bath, and dried off. I didn't see any clothes to put on, so I grabbed Oren's fluffy bathrobe and returned to the living room.

The door opened, and Oren and Nathan walked in, murmuring softly to each other. Both had two bags over-flowing with food.

"I see you're awake and took advantage of the bath we filled for you." Oren smiled as he walked past and set his bag down.

"I told you she wouldn't be able to resist," Nathan smirked and kissed me softly, following Oren into the kitchen.

I was eager to question Oren about everything, but my stomach picked that moment to show its appreciation for the delicious smells permeating the room.

"Come sit down, my Nexi." Nathan pulled out a chair at the bar. "Let me fix you a plate."

I felt like I was starving, even though it hadn't been long since Zeke fed me, so I eagerly did what he said.

"Where are Zeke and Zane?"

"They didn't want to stick around, scared that the temptation you represent would be too much for them." He smiled slightly, heat building in his eyes when my robe parted, exposing my leg to the top of my thigh as I sat at the bar.

"You *are* quite the temptation," Oren smirked as he put a generous helping of fried rice and teriyaki chicken on a plate and slid it in front of me. He ran his finger lightly over my hand before returning to the kitchen.

I didn't feel the need to reply as I began stuffing my face.

Nathan set a glass of water near my elbow, and I stopped eating long enough to take a long sip of the cold water.

The guys fixed a plate, sat near me, and ate almost as hungrily as I was.

When we finished, Oren cleared the plates and put them in the sink while Nathan took my hand and led me to the couch.

Oren joined us and sat on my other side. The guys were so close that I was almost in both of their laps, surrounded by the heat from their bodies.

I almost moaned in pleasure at the feel of it.

Nathan turned slightly and pulled me to him. "I think it's time we consummated the Amalgamate joining, don't you?"

"What joining?" I asked, ending my question in a moan as Oren ran his hand up my thigh.

"The new circumstance that marked us so beautifully as yours," Oren whispered in my ear before biting it gently.

I had so many questions, but I couldn't remember a single one as both guys stood, each taking a hand and leading me into the bedroom.

Somehow, while we were eating, candles had been lit, and rose petals were scattered over the bed.

"I love it when I can use my abilities to spoil my Nexus instead of just defending her." Oren smiled.

Nathan laid me gently on the bed, "We know that our start wasn't what it should have been, and before the twins dazzle you with a ceremony, we wanted to show you the advantages that we monsters can contribute."

Oren laughed, "I've never thought of myself as such, but I guess I am." He grew serious, "I'll embrace that title if it keeps you safe and brings an end to the danger that's coming."

CHAPTER 20
NATHAN

Reverie looked so beautiful on display before us. Oren had used his ability to spread her robe and expose her body to our gazes. She met my eyes, and I could see the concern there.

I was a possessive fuck, to be sure. She had every right to be concerned. The only explanation was that my connection with Reverie extended to my Faction brothers. Not in the same way as it did with Reverie, but with a brotherly bond.

I could feel Oren's need to fuck her, and it turned my own need into a blazing inferno.

No one was more surprised than I was at that fact.

Knowing his love for her was as deep and never-ending as mine comforted me. Also, the ability to feel that Reverie truly loved each of us equally allowed me to be grateful I'd have my brothers to help protect her.

Reverie would be *our* Nexus, but she'd forever be my Nexi *only*. She'd been right. There was no jealousy.

I walked closer, pushed Oren aside, grabbed a handful of her inky black hair, and pressed my lips fiercely to hers.

"What the fuck, Nathan?" Oren grumbled as he sat on the other side of Reverie.

I didn't answer him as I tried to devour her with my mouth. I'd committed to sharing, but I never claimed to be anything other than selfish.

~⚜~

REVERIE-

I was nervous because I had zero experience pleasing two men simultaneously. The hallway incident between me and the twins was mainly about them pleasing me, so it didn't count.

I wasn't expecting to feel such intense desire at being admired by two of my men. Lying here naked while both of them were fully clothed felt forbidden and decadent.

Now, with Nathan kissing me like he wanted to devour me whole, any nerves I might have had were forgotten.

Oren jerked me away from Nathan and pressed his mouth to mine, kissing me as hungrily as his Faction brother. Desperation came through our bond like he hadn't just fucked me yesterday.

I could feel Nathan's annoyance, but instead of the explosion I expected, he turned his attention to my breasts. I moaned as he sucked gently on my hard nipple, laving the tip with his tongue.

I squirmed with irritation, wanting his tongue between my legs more than I wanted my next breath. He took my pointed nipple between his teeth and bit down hard in punishment.

"I won't be rushed, my Nexi. Let your men tend to you properly." Nathan growled before putting his mouth back on my breast, soothing the ache he had caused.

I felt wetness gush between my legs and dampen the bed underneath me. Oren moved his fingers between my legs and ran his hand through my dampness. He ended our kiss, then brought his fingers to his mouth and licked them clean.

"Taste how sweet you are on my tongue." Oren kissed me again, licking the inside of my mouth. I could taste the honeysuckle and cookie flavor on his tongue and could feel my dampness increase, soaking the bed beneath me even further.

I felt almost crazed with desire. I could feel them both through our bond, and the intensity of their want was driving mine even higher.

Nathen moved to my other breast, sucking and kneading it until I was writhing once more. Then I felt his hand trail down my side, then between my legs. He began circling his large finger around and around my clit, never giving me the pressure I needed to find my release.

Oren released my mouth, looking into my eyes adoringly. I felt him trail his hand down my hip, ever so slowly, then he shoved two of his fingers into my tight opening with no warning.

He thrust them in and out at such a speed that it caused me to arch off the bed completely.

The twin stimulation of Nathan's finger circling my clit paired with Oren thrusting in and out of my pussy caused my orgasm to hit me like a tsunami.

I stiffened my legs and arched my back as the pleasure rolled over me, and just when I thought it would cease, I felt a mouth on my clit, sucking gently. The fingers in my pussy continued their motion, and another wave of pleasure hit me.

When I'd gained enough sanity to open my eyes, I saw that both men were stepping away to remove their clothes. Their eyes were blazing with desire.

I felt my arousal returning quickly at the sight of Nathan licking my juices from his lips. Not to mention the male perfection both had on display.

Oren's body had muscles in all the right places and was sculpted perfectly.

He didn't look real. His penis was long and beautiful, if a penis could even be such a thing.

Nathan had a magnificent eight-pack, and his skin had a golden sheen in the lamplight. His dick wasn't as long as Oren's, but he had more girth.

Both men were well above average, and my nerves returned slightly as I wondered how this would work.

Before I could get too worried about the logistics, I felt two fingers gently thrust between my legs once more. I closed my eyes in pleasure but then opened them abruptly in shock at an intense pulse of heat.

Neither man had approached me, so I realized Oren was using his power.

I closed my eyes as the heat became more intense and felt the brush of silky skin slide across my lips.

"Open that beautiful mouth, Nexus, and take me in." Oren was holding his gorgeous cock out to me like an offering.

I opened my lips and licked the crown like it was my favorite treat. Then I rolled to my knees in one smooth motion and took his entire length in at once. Oren gave a filthy moan at my abrupt action, then began gently thrusting in and out of my mouth.

I felt Nathan slide his head between my legs, grasp the

back of my thighs and bury his face in my pussy, licking and sucking until I couldn't contain my whimpers of pleasure.

Oren pulled out of my mouth, "Enough of that, or I'm going to embarrass myself."

Nathan had continued to eat me like I was his last meal, and all I could do was send Oren a pleading look.

"Nathan, I think our Nexus wants us to fuck her. Do you think we should give her what she wants?" Oren brushed my hair back gently.

"I've never been able to deny her anything. I'm not going to start today." Nathan sat up, and I rose to my knees.

I gripped Oren's hard length, pumping my hand slowly.

Nathan stood and came to my other side, and I grabbed his cock too. I ran my thumb over his silky head and the precum covering it. Raising my eyes to meet his, I brought my thumb to my mouth and licked it clean.

He groaned at my action, and what restraint he was holding onto snapped.

Both men reached for me at once. Oren fell back on the bed, holding me under my arms above his cock, then slowly lowered me down until he filled me completely. He spread his legs so Nathan had room to kneel behind me.

Nathan took the tip of his dick and coated my ass in his precum and my wetness, then gently inserted one of his fingers, preparing me for his entrance. I felt my nerves start up again, even with the distraction of Oren's dick moving in and out of my pussy.

He tunneled his hand in my hair and pushed my face into his neck. I had the intense desire to bite him, and I jerked my head back, scared of the feeling.

"It's alright, Nexus. Trust your instincts." Oren cooed as he gently tugged my face back to his neck.

I felt my incisors lengthen slightly and my mouth water before I struck.

Nathan entered me at precisely the same time. They paused, giving me the chance to adjust to the fullness of having them both inside me. Nothing in my life thus far could compare to being filled by my men.

"Nexi, you feel so fucking good." Nathan groaned, "I don't know how long I'm going to last."

I raised my head from Oren's neck. "Move, I need you to move!"

I'd barely spoken when the two of them started to fuck me, slowly at first, then quickening their pace until the pleasure became so intense it bordered on pain.

The feel of them driving in and out of my body, combined with the taste of Oren's blood, created the most powerful orgasm I'd ever experienced.

When Oren and Nathan felt my pleasure through our connection, they both followed right behind me, shouting and growling their completion. The intensity of their pleasure threw me into another orgasm, this time causing me to pass out.

When I awoke, Nathan was gently cleaning me with a warm rag as Oren held me close to his body.

"There you are, my sweet Nexi. I missed having those beautiful eyes looking at me." He threw the rag in the bathroom and lay on my other side. I turned slightly to lay my head on Nathan's chest, and Oren cuddled behind me.

"Get some rest, Nexus." He kissed my shoulder, "We have a lot to deal with and many decisions to make."

I acknowledged the truth in his words, but I felt a sense of satisfaction in this moment. Tomorrow and its challenges would come soon enough.

For now, I would relish this feeling.

I smiled as I drifted off. Had any other Nexus ever been as lucky as I was?

Nathan whispered, "I love you, my Nexi."

Then I heard nothing more.

CHAPTER 21
JET

I entered my dorm and slammed the door.

What the fuck was my life turning into? I sat on the couch and buried my head in my hands.

The jealousy I felt was so intense that I felt sick to my stomach. Seeing the marks on the guys made me so angry that I became a danger to everyone around me. I thought it was best to isolate myself in my dorm until I regained control.

I knew that Oren believed he was more powerful than me since he had abilities, and I didn't.

I wasn't so sure.

It wasn't my arrogance speaking either. I couldn't shake his grip on me, but I sensed it weakening before he let go. I didn't know the reason, but it was true. I was sure it had something to do with Reverie. I even looked for a mark but found nothing.

I got up and headed into the kitchen for a beer. Twisting the top off, I turned it up, finishing it in one swallow. I threw the bottle into the trash and headed into my room to shower.

Stripping down, I stepped in and ducked my head under the warm spray. I had decisions to make that couldn't be put off any longer.

My feelings for Reverie were unmistakable, and I was tired of denying them. Watching the other guys hold her while I couldn't drove me crazy with envy.

I hated seeing her upset. What I had done this morning was merely the beginning of how far I would go to keep her safe from harm.

Seeing her lying there on the couch, upset and not understanding what was happening, drove me crazy. Those beautiful eyes should never be filled with worry. If I could snap my fingers and get rid of all of my obligations, I'd take her tiny body in my arms and dare someone to fuck with her.

Every time I said something that caused her pain, I wanted to vomit. It felt unnatural and disgusting to utter words that hurt her, but I had to do it. I could see her looking at me with more affection than she should, and I needed to kill it.

I thought pushing her away would lessen her pain when she found out about my betrayal. Imagine my astonishment when I found out that Nathan and Oren already knew. I really shouldn't be surprised.

They skulked in the shadows, looking for any danger that might get close to Reverie. Vetting every guy who was a potential Faction member was probably Oren's first action.

It was time I figured out a way to escape my obligations. Would Oren be willing to help with that? Maybe it was time to swallow my pride and ask him. I had a feeling he'd do just about anything to complete our Faction.

I'd owe him a debt I could never repay. Being able to touch Reverie and give in to my feelings was everything I wished for. The ability to touch her satin skin and kiss those plump red lips would be worth everything. I groaned thinking about the pigtails she'd worn today and what they'd feel like held in my fists as I drove my dick deep into her throat.

I groaned as I reached for my cock, gliding my hand up and down the shaft. I had to squeeze below the head when my thoughts of Reverie almost caused me to come instantly. I wanted this to last.

Fantasizing about her was all that I had.

I'd let her suck me for a few minutes before I'd use her pigtails to hold her still while I fucked her face. She'd willingly open her throat and let me go deep while tears poured down her cheeks.

I resumed stroking my dick, unable to resist, as my fantasies built. I'd pick her up and put her legs over my shoulders to bring her pussy close to my face. Then I'd grip that luscious ass while I ate her sweet cunt until she came all over me.

It only took a few more pumps of my hand, and I couldn't hold back any longer, "Reverie... fuuuck!" I came, spraying the shower as I felt my legs grow weak.

Fuck, if using my hand and fantasizing about her made me come this hard, the real thing might kill me.

I stepped out of the shower and dried off, feeling better about things. And a hell of a lot lighter.

I had made my decision. I would approach Oren tomorrow.

I was done fighting.

Hearing a knock on the door, I threw on some grey sweatpants and a T-shirt.

When I got to the door, I heard giggling that stopped abruptly when I opened it.

"Hey, Jet, we didn't see you at dinner and thought we'd bring you something to eat," Sophie batted her eyes.

Kristine stood next to her, smiling. "We brought plenty for you and Nathan." She held up two bags of food.

"Nathan's not here, and I'm not hungry." I started to shut the door.

Kristine extended her hand to stop it from closing and looked me in the eye.

"A great big man like you probably has an insatiable appetite."

The next thing I knew, we were all sitting on the couch, and I was between them. My head hurt, and I massaged my temples to relieve the pain.

"Take another bite. I know you want to." I automatically opened my mouth to accept the food Sophie put in my mouth.

What the fuck was going on? I didn't remember sitting down or them coming in.

"I bet there's something he'd like you to put in your mouth,"

Kristine smirked before both girls started giggling. Sophie ran her hand up my leg and grasped me through my pants. "My, that is quite the weapon you seem to be packing."

Why didn't I stop her? I didn't want her hands anywhere on me. It was like I was a puppet, and they were pulling my strings.

"I can't wait to feel that inside of me." She pulled the waist of my sweatpants down, exposing my dick, then leaned down and took me in her mouth.

I wanted to vomit, but all I could do was sit there, staring into space like nothing was wrong. I was screaming inside, but on the outside, I wasn't making a sound.

After a few minutes, she raised her head and whined, "He's not getting hard."

"He probably has a thing for brunettes. Let me try," Kristine smirked at her.

"No, he's mine. You said you were here for Nathan." Sophie lowered her head to my dick once more.

I knew her efforts were pointless because Reverie was all I saw. No other girl interested me in the least.

"Well, I have to build a Faction, and a strong man like this would fit perfectly." Kristine laughed and jerked Sophie back by her hair.

Sophie let out a screech as she fell on the floor, bumping her head on the coffee table on her way down.

"That wasn't the deal, Kristine!" Sophie stomped her foot as she stood.

"Deals are made to be broken." She laughed as Sophie stomped toward the door.

"Whatever! I'll be back in our room." She slammed the door so hard that the wall shook.

"Now that the whiny brat is gone, we can have some real fun." Kristine pulled a syringe out of her pocket and stuck it in my thigh.

I felt my dick get hard, and Kristine smiled evilly as she started to strip.

I would kill this bitch if she went through with this.

⤿⚜⤾

REVERIE-

I woke abruptly, anxiety pulling me out of my dreams. My men were asleep, Nathan gently snoring in my ear. Rising slowly to avoid waking them, I went into the bathroom to pee. After washing my hands, I quietly put on my clothes and headed for the living room.

I began to sit down, but then jerked back up and started pacing. I felt nauseous and couldn't shake the thought that something was wrong.

I closed my eyes, *"Zeke, can you hear me?"*

For a moment, I heard nothing.

"Reverie?" Zane answered me hesitantly.

I guess they were on the same wavelength.

"Are you both okay?"

"Yes. Why wouldn't we be?" he said, then spoke again hurriedly before I could answer. *"Are you okay?"*

"I'm fine. I feel like something is wrong, but I don't know what."

"We're watching a movie with Chloe in your dorm, and everything is fine here. Do you need me?" I could feel his worry through our bond.

"No. I'm sure it's nothing. I'll see you in the morning."

"Okay, if you're sure. I'm going to sleep in your bed. I don't think I can sleep any other way but with your scent surrounding me." I felt his desire.

"He'll do no such thing. The last thing you need is him loping his mule in your sheets." Zeke entered the conversation.

"What the hell does that mean?" I was confused.

"Fuck off, brother. I refuse to even touch myself. It'd feel like I was cheating." Zane sounded crazy...but sweet.

"I don't care if you both sleep in my bed and... lope your mule?" I was reasonably sure I'd guessed the correct meaning.

I could hear their laughter, *"Neither of us will be doing that. Get some rest, and we'll see you in the morning."* Zeke sent feelings of love and affection through our bond.

Well, if they were okay, maybe it was Pantar.

"Pantar, where are you?" Maybe the big Fellat had hurt

himself hunting or something. I thought it was unlikely, but who knew what he got into when he disappeared for long periods?

"At this moment, I'm taking a nap. Do you need me?" Pantar yawned.

"Not really. I can't shake the feeling that something's wrong."

"Never ignore that feeling, Nexus. Trust your instincts. I'll check around the campus and see if I can sense anything." He abruptly left the conversation.

Even knowing Pantar was scouting for trouble, I couldn't settle. I stopped and closed my eyes, tapping into that ball of power inside me that had grown since this morning.

Suddenly, my eyes sprang open, and I raced out of the dorm toward Jet and Nathan's room. I ran faster than should have been possible, even for me. Everything around me blurred as I moved at such an incredible speed, and it was only when I stopped in front of the door that I realized I could have teleported.

I felt silly now that I was here, but I could swear that Jet was in extreme distress. How I was able to determine that, given we weren't bonded, was a mystery to me.

I knocked softly on the door, "Jet, are you in there?"

I didn't hear anything, so I knocked a little louder. I put my ear to the door. Was that a female's voice?

My heart throbbed in pain. How fucking embarrassing. Jet's getting his dick wet, and I'm interrupting. Desperate much, Reverie? I turned and started to walk away, but then felt another pulse of distress. Frowning, I turned back to the door.

Fuck it, I could get over my embarrassment for interrupting. I'd *never* forgive myself if something happened to him and I didn't do anything about it.

Turning the knob and finding it unlocked, I slowly

opened the door. My jaw dropped when I saw Kristine lowering herself onto Jet's massive dick.

I started to leave, disgusted, but Jet turned his head toward me with some apparent difficulty. His eyes were distraught, and he looked at me as if he were imploring for help.

Was this happening without his consent? I was so confused. He was obviously hard, but I could still feel his distress in my chest.

Fuck it.

I let rage overtake my body as I stormed into the room and grabbed Kristine by the hair, pulling her off of him.

"What the fuck? Let me go, you crazy bitch!" She screeched.

I didn't even bother answering as I punched the bitch so hard I felt her nose crack and her eyes rolled back in her head. I pulled back to hit her again, but Jet pulled me into his massive body, holding me so tightly that I was having trouble breathing.

"Thank you, my Nexus, but your precious hands should never have to touch such filth." He breathed deeply into my hair, and his voice shook. "Can you ever forgive me for this? I wasn't willing. She injected me with something."

"I…"

He interrupted, "I swear on my life, I wouldn't betray you like that. Please forgive me."

"I…"

Jet interrupted again, "I'll kill her if she costs me a place in your Faction. Please tell me that hasn't happened!"

I put my hand over his mouth, "I believe you."

He fell back on the couch and pulled me into his lap, rocking me back and forth. He was so large that my head was buried between his massive pecks, not reaching his shoulder.

Once more, I struggled to breathe, but sensing his need, I turned my head slightly and wrapped my arms around him as best I could, providing as much comfort as possible.

Just then, the door burst open, and all my men piled into the room, followed closely by Pantar.

"What the fuck is going on?" Oren growled, grabbing Kristine's upper arm and jerking her to her feet.

She was still unconscious, her body sagging in his hold. Jet didn't answer him and never stopped rocking.

"Reverie?" Zeke hesitantly approached.

"I'm the one that knocked the bitch out. She gave Jet something that made him hard and was in the process of raping him when I came in."

"What the fuck? Why didn't he throw the bitch out?" Zane said in disbelief.

"I couldn't fucking move. She did something to my head." Jet growled, holding me even tighter, fearful that the guys would take me away from him.

Oren threw her onto the floor, and her head bounced from the force. Too bad she'd probably be healed when she woke up; the least she deserved was a headache.

"That's what the cunt gets. Who the fuck does something like that?" Nathan asked, with zero sympathy for Kristine.

"The kind of cunt that's been given anything she wanted since she was born and the abilities to get it." Oren curled his lip in disgust.

"Let me guess, she was injected too," Zane said between gritted teeth.

"Yes, but she's been cautious about concealing most of her abilities around me. Although now I have an inkling."

Oren frowned. "This is not a good situation. She's the last person who should possess the power to manipulate some-one's mind."

"It wasn't strong, I felt like she was losing her grip on me right before Reverie entered the room." Jet murmured.

"That may be true, but as she gains Faction, her ability will strengthen." Oren was eyeing her like he might dispose of her right now.

Kristine started moving around and slowly cracked her eyes open. She sat up and rubbed the back of her head, still in pain.

"What happened?" She narrowed her eyes at me in Jet's arms.

No one answered, and she hesitantly stood. I tapped Jet's arm, and he reluctantly dropped his hold and let me get to my feet.

I walked over to Kristine, and she took a step back.

"I challenge you to a fight in the arena."

"No!" Jet growled.

I turned and gave him a look.

"Dude, I'd advise you to shut your mouth. I've had that look leveled at me, and the consequences of ignoring it aren't worth

the pain." Nathan smirked, "Well, sometimes they are."

I now transferred the look to him, and he motioned, zipping his lips.

Kristine laughed, "Why are you challenging me? He obviously wanted me." She gestured to Jet's still-hard dick, displayed prominently in his sweatpants.

"I didn't want you bitch! You injected me with something." He balled up his fists and headed in her direction.

"Are you going to let him talk to me like that?" She turned to Oren.

"I'm not getting involved. I heard the commotion and came to see what was going on." Oren said, not wanting

Kristine to know about our connection. "I did hear her challenge you, though."

"I did," I sneered. "But I guess she's scared. The bitch hasn't accepted yet."

"That's ridiculous! No true Storm would be scared of a challenge." He smirked at Kristine.

"I'm not scared of this weak bitch. I accept!" She fell right into Oren's trap.

"Good, the fight will happen the last Friday before winter break." He grabbed Kristine and led her out of the room, turning to wink at me right before he closed the door.

I waited in resignation for the yelling to begin.

CHAPTER 22
ZANE

After Storm left with the cunt, you could've heard a pin drop. The silence didn't last long.

"No." Jet stated, staring at Reverie.

Even I knew that was a bad move. Nathan tried to warn him, but he didn't listen.

"No?" Reverie raised a single eyebrow.

"We don't know what her abilities are. I won't have you put in that kind of situation." Jet stood and ran a hand through his hair.

"*You* won't?" Reverie asked, raising both brows this time.

"Abort the mission, soldier." Nathan cupped a hand over his mouth but didn't attempt to lower his voice in the least. Jet narrowed his eyes at Nathan and flipped him off.

"Let me get this straight. You've been spying on us for the military, never intending to become Faction or embrace your Aurathion heritage. You've followed us when it suited you, even blackmailed me into taking you with me to see my parents. You've insulted me at every turn and let other women touch what's mi-"

The fool didn't have the sense not to interrupt.

"This wasn't my choice."

"*This* isn't what I'm talking about, and you know it." Reverie motioned to the couch, where I assumed she'd found him and Kristine. Jet hung his head, but Reverie continued showing no sympathy.

"As I was saying, before you interrupted, letting women touch you, knowing you were meant to be mine. Implying that I was nothing special to you. *Now*, you want to tell me what to do?" She put both hands on her hips and tapped her foot.

Was it weird that I was strangely turned on by her dressing down Jet like he was a student, and she was a schoolmarm, ooh, or maybe a librarian...no, the principal? Now, I was adjusting myself. Maybe after our bonding ceremony, we could use Storm's office to play this out again, only this time she's wearing a pencil skirt and glasses...

"-and furthermore, you have no right..."

I'd be shirtless and glistening with sweat—because why not?

"-I will not tolerate..."

I'd bend her over my knee...wait, that's not right...she'd bend me... no. I needed to put a little more thought into this.

"...and Zane will agree. Won't you, Zane?" Reverie turned to me.

What? And Zane will agree with *what*? Don't panic, you've got this.

"Of course I will." I nodded. "There isn't a shadow of a doubt... I'm in." Stop talking, idiot! "You can count on me! I'm here for whatever you need." Finally, I stopped with the verbal diarrhea.

The guys looked at me like I'd lost my mind, but Reverie smiled so big that both dimples were visible.

"I knew he'd be okay with Luke joining this Faction. I'll talk to him as soon as possible." Reverie headed towards the door.

"Fuck no, that douche isn't getting anywhere near you!" I stepped in front of her.

She looked at me and winked, "Stop thinking about role-playing and pay attention when I'm talking." Reverie thumped my nose, "The reading the thoughts thing goes both ways, asshole."

My Nexus motioned, dropping a mic, then sashayed to the couch and took a seat.

Could she be any more perfect? I followed right behind her and bundled Ms. Hawthorne, I mean Reverie, into my lap.

"Okay, you have my full attention. Continue to tell Jet what a tremendous wanker he's been." I looked at the guys, "That's British for dick, in case you morons didn't know that." I kissed

Reverie on the nose. "I'm bilingual."

Take that! Now, it was me dropping the mic on my Faction brothers.

Zeke covered his face with his hands, "I'm so embarrassed. Maybe our resemblance wouldn't be obvious if I dyed my hair."

"Don't even think about golden brown. You'd never be able to pull it off with that skin," Nathan said, tossing his hair and looking at Zeke haughtily.

Pantar turned up his nose in disgust.

"If I were unaware of how loyal and strong your Faction members are, I'd advise you to break these bonds and start over."

"Hey! That's a bad kitty." I stuck my tongue out at the Fellat.

"Wait! Did I just hear you?"

"Welcome to the Faction. Now I'm done here. Nexus, if you want me to eat the disgusting excuse for an Aurathion, I will do it. If not, I will watch you pummel her in a few days. Tell the dishonest one to have more faith in his future Nexus." He blinked out.

"Jet, I understand you're worried about me, but have some faith. What she did was wrong, and I refuse to let it stand."

Reverie looked at Jet pleadingly.

"I have complete trust in your ability to fight. I've seen you in the gym, but people like that never fight fair, and I don't want to see you get hurt." Jet sat beside her and took her small hand into his. The size difference between the two was ridiculous. She almost disappeared beside his bulk.

"Who says I fight fair?" Reverie smirked.

There she went, making me hard again. This girl was the total package.

Reverie rolled her eyes at me and then began speaking to Jet again.

"I'll be ready for whatever she throws at me. I only challenged her to fight in the arena because girls like her are more susceptible to the influence of status and public opinion. This will damage her reputation so badly that she won't be able to beg someone to join her Faction."

Oren appeared at that moment, "Reverie is right."

Jet growled, "You shouldn't have baited Kristine into accepting the challenge."

"It's the only way she doesn't get away with this." Oren walked into the kitchen and grabbed a beer out of the fridge.

"Help yourself," Nathan mumbled, with no real heat.

"Look, I'm more powerful than ever, thanks to whatever this new ability is. The only thing I'm afraid of is accidentally killing the rapist whore for what she did." Reverie leaned into Jet, instinctively trying to give him comfort.

"I think it's time we talked about that." Oren sat beside Reverie on the couch but didn't pull her away from Jet.

"Finally!" Reverie turned toward Oren, and I noticed Jet shift, so she leaned back onto his chest.

"I have some theories, but I want to reiterate that they are only theories. I believe you've gained the trait of Amalgamate." He paused, clearly waiting for the questions to begin.

"Trait? Not an ability." Reverie wrinkled that cute little nose in confusion.

"Yes, trait. From everything I've read, most Aurathions consider Amalgamation a myth. I, on the other hand, was able to get my hands on one very ancient scroll that mentioned Queen Lilibet-"

"Who was that?" I interrupted, "Our people have never had a queen." I played around a lot, but I'd taken my studies seriously, and I'd never heard of a queen.

"That's where you're wrong. The Council has been around for millennia, but our people were once ruled by a monarchy, and the title was passed down through the female line." Oren smiled smugly.

And that was why nobody liked him, he was a know-it-all. He flipped me off. We really needed to get a handle on this mind-reading thing.

"We were once a matriarchal society?" Reverie looked as stunned as I was by all this.

"Yes. But I'm talking millions of years ago. Back before most recorded records." Oren tucked a long piece of Reverie's midnight hair behind her ear.

The smug bastard was eating this up, having Reverie's attention trained solely on him. The corners of his mouth turned up, clearly amused at my thoughts.

"How can this be unknown when we are so long-lived?" Zeke questioned.

"How can it not be? Do you think the Council wants any of our people to be aware of this? They don't want their power questioned," Oren stated.

"But there are females who have been Council members throughout the years. I've never thought that our culture had a problem with women being in power." Reverie snuggled back deeper into Jet's chest, unaware of her actions.

"The issue wasn't about that. It was about the same families retaining control. Over the years, we've experienced both effective and ineffective Councils, yet the same seven families have maintained their influence." Oren leaned in closer, "I've always thought it odd that the Hawthornes, despite their strong abilities, have never been on the Council."

"I find all of this completely fascinating, but back to the topic of Amalgamate. What is it, and how does it work?" Reverie asked.

"The trait lets you mark your potential faction when they've earned your trust and affection. The exact definition is: to combine or unite to form one structure." Oren was in his element. Reverie looked horrified.

"So, I could just start marking people willy-nilly if I like and trust them *against their will?*"

Oren held her hand and said, "No, my love. While it's true, the queen marked many individuals, *most* were outside her Faction. Those became trusted court members and loyal guards." He leaned in for a kiss and continued, "None of those positions were romantic. The mark was different from the one given to her Faction. I need to seek out additional sources, but I'm sure the candidate also had to be willing to make the mark possible. Let's focus on what's in front of us and avoid worrying about things beyond our control."

Reverie sighed in relief, "Okay, the truth is I can't really handle any of that right now. I trust you to find any information you think might be relevant to our situation."

Oren's chest puffed out, and he looked ready to slay a dragon for our queen. I knew he was on to something; Reverie had seemed like *more* right from the beginning. Nathan walked over and tugged Reverie to her feet.

"Let's all get some rest. Tomorrow will be a long and demanding day, and we all need to regroup." Jet started to protest, but Nathan interrupted.

"I'm not suggesting anyone leave. Let's clear the living room and pull both of our mattresses in here. I don't think my Nexi is eager to leave you, and none of us wants to leave her."

"I agree. I can ward the room so no one can enter without our permission." Oren stood and walked toward the door.

"You're just full of surprises, old friend." I narrowed my eyes at him.

"That's true, but now you benefit from the many abilities I've kept secret." He held his hand palm up and followed the seam of the door all the way around, and for just a moment, I could see a red light emanating from the door before it was abruptly sucked into the wood.

"What if Pantar wants to come back?" Reverie walked to the door, running her hand over it in amazement.

If the asshole's head got any bigger, his neck wouldn't be able to hold it up.

Oren grinned at me as he pulled Reverie into his arms. "Anyone you've bonded can enter at will. I'd never keep Pantar away from you. He'd kill me. Literally." Oren actually shuddered.

Reverie smiled, "Well, let's get this slumber party started."

That's what I'm talking about. I wonder if Reverie would be willing to pillow fight in the nude?

"NO!" She laughed, surprising me with her sudden shout.

"The first order of business is finding out how to shield our thoughts." I narrowed my eyes.

"I second that." Nathan agreed.

"That's because you two will never be in our Nexus's good graces if she knows how your minds work." Zeke laughed.

"We can start tomorrow. For now, let's get some sleep."

Oren smiled when Reverie let out a cute little yawn. He was right, and for now, it was enough that we were all together. There were numerous things to figure out, but for the present, this was all that mattered.

CHAPTER 23
JET

Oren and Zeke sorted night clothes while Nathan and Zane cleared the living room and brought in the mattresses. I slipped off to the shower. I'd taken one earlier before the bitch showed up at my door, but I had to wash the feel of her hands and cunt from my body. I cranked the shower to scalding and stepped under the spray.

Grabbing my soap and loofah, I scoured my skin until it was red and raw. I didn't care as long as every trace of her was gone from me. I swore I could still smell her perfume, so I started the process all over again. After the fifth scrubbing, I finally began to feel clean, and I ducked my head under the spray, letting the water run over my body.

Even though this experience was fucked for someone who had always been able to defend himself, I appreciated that it helped solidify my earlier decision regarding Reverie and our relationship. I knew I had a long way to go before she accepted me, but once I committed to a course, I was all in.

My determination was legendary, and Reverie was about to become my focus.

Tomorrow, I'd begin to show her how much she meant to me and what I could bring to her Faction.

Tonight, I had to deal with this sickness in my gut that Kristine caused so I could focus on my soon-to-be Nexus. I felt deep disgust for myself. It was intolerable that I had been so powerless. It was sheer arrogance to be completely unguarded when the girls arrived at the door. Having been here long enough, I should have remembered that havoc and harm can be caused without physical strength. I'd over-looked one of the vital lessons I'd learned through the years: evil takes on many forms.

I stepped out of the shower and brushed my teeth, then slipped on grey warm-ups and a white t-shirt. I'd heard that grey warm-ups were like sexy lingerie to women. I needed to take advantage of everything I could at this point.

As I reentered the room, the mattresses were pushed together, made up in sheets and fluffy blankets. Nathan lay on one side of Reverie while Zeke and Zane were on the edge of the mattress on the opposite side. Oren lay next to them. I noticed he had shifted over, creating a space for me beside Reverie.

I must have stood there staring for a moment too long because Reverie patted the space beside her. The days of hesitating to come when she called were over, so I walked directly to her and got under the blanket. I pulled her into my arms and tucked her head under my chin.

She was asleep in seconds.

"I hope you're ready to commit fully to this Faction and her," Oren spoke softly.

"I am."

I inhaled deeply, pulling her scent into my lungs. How

could this tiny body contain such strength and determination?

"It's about damn time," Zane said before rolling over and closing his eyes. Nathan raised up to look at me over Reverie's shoulder.

"You better not hurt her again."

"I won't." He held my gaze for a few seconds before whatever he saw in my eyes must have satisfied him, and he lay back down.

Zeke stared at me for a full minute, the intensity of his gaze needing no words, before nodding his head and lying down to sleep.

Ten minutes later, everyone was asleep. It didn't come as easy to me because I was fighting the urge to sneak into Kristine's room and slit her throat. My respect for Reverie was the only thing stopping me.

Apparently, it was important for her to fight the crazy bitch after what she'd done. The guys would've been shocked if they could see the grin on my face at the thought. I'd protested Reverie facing her in the arena, but a piece of me was a little smug that she cared about me that much.

Afterward, if I still felt the need to kill her, I would. I'm sure Oren wouldn't be opposed to helping me get rid of the body. That flame power of his really came in handy.

～⚜～

I woke slowly, and unlike every other day, I felt a contentment that stemmed solely from the beautiful woman lying still in my arms, snoring softly. Could she be any more adorable?

Usually, I'd be up and headed to work out, but nothing

could make me move from this spot. I'd dreamed of holding her like this, and now that it was a reality, it was even better than I'd imagined.

I smelled the delicious aroma of coffee, and simultaneously, Reverie began to stir. Her love of the hot brew may surpass her feelings about her Faction. Zeke walked into the room holding two steaming mugs.

"Wake, my treasure, we have lots to do today, starting with a visit to see your parents."

Reverie stretched and cracked one eye open.

"That's the best sleep I've had in my life." Nathan popped up from her other side.

"How could it not be? You had that cute butt snuggled up against Big John."

Reverie jack-knifed into a sitting position, grabbed Nathan, then blinked out of the room.

Before any of us even had time to panic, she was back.

Without Nathan.

"Where is Nathan?" Oren asked, looking as stunned as we all felt.

"Sitting in the pigpen on our farm," she said with a smug smile. "I warned him. Let this be a lesson to everyone: don't mess with a Hawthorne, or you'll end up in deep shit. Literally."

At that exact moment, Nathan appeared in the room covered in mud and shit. "That was harsh, Nexi. Expect retaliation."

"Bring it on, psycho." Reverie grinned.

I, along with my Faction brothers, was laughing so hard at this point that we could barely breathe. Zane was cackling one moment; the next, he was trying to fend off a hug from Nathan.

"Get the fuck off of me!"

Nathan swiped his hand down his shirt and then rubbed the gunk he'd collected in Zane's hair. Zane started gagging and punched Nathan in the stomach. Nathan's breath whooshed out, and he bent over from the force of it. I was expecting him to be pissed, but he surprised me by laughing hysterically. The man was obviously just the slightest bit unhinged.

"Okay, that's enough. Both of you get cleaned up, then let's take our Nexus to breakfast before we visit her parents." Oren's voice was filled with authority.

If he was going to be the leader of this Faction, then I planned on being the enforcer. I think for this to work, we all had to carry our weight, no one role was more critical than the other.

Nathan and Zane turned to him and started his way; both now covered in mud and shit.

"Touch me with that shit, and you'll both be sporting new hairstyles." His hands sparked with electricity.

This motherfucker had lots of secrets. Exactly how many abilities did he have? Both guys wisely decided to heed his warning and went to get cleaned up.

"I'm going to get dressed. Do y'all want to meet me in my dorm?" Reverie was headed toward the door.

I jumped to my feet, "I'll walk you."

"You need to get dressed. I don't need an escort." She put her hand on her hip.

Pantar appeared suddenly, and even though I couldn't hear him when Reverie rolled her eyes, I took it to mean he'd agreed with me.

"*Fine!* I guess I do need an escort," Reverie said, reaching out to scratch under the giant Fellat's chin.

Oren walked over and pulled Reverie into his arms.

"I'll meet you 'accidentally' at Java and Jam," he said. "Then, after, we'll teleport to your parents' apartment."

"Sounds like a plan." Reverie leaned up and whispered something in his ear.

Oren grinned, the action looking out of place on his face.

"That sounds like an even better plan."

"You know we can hear what you're thinking, and I call bullshit," Zane smirked. "There is no sex before the bonding ceremony."

"It's *your* bonding ceremony, not mine. My ceremony is going to involve silk ties and hours of worshiping her body with my mouth." Oren leaned down and bit her ear. Reverie blushed a beautiful pink, then cleared her throat.

"And on that note, I'm out."

She and Pantar disappeared, and Oren turned to us, his expression growing serious.

"Everyone, be on guard. If Kristine can find a way out of Reverie's challenge, she will, by fair means or foul. She knows that Reverie will annihilate her, and she won't want my father to learn of it."

"I figured as much. Kristine has abilities that we weren't aware of, and it's come back to bite us. We need to try to find out what else she's hiding." Zeke ran a hand through his hair, obviously stressed at the situation.

Nathan entered the room, and Oren said, "It's time for you and Reverie to go to the dean to discuss Faction housing. I know we can sleep in her dorm, but I can ensure her safety more easily in one of the houses."

"Should Zane and I go with him?" Zeke asked, taking a sip of his coffee. "We can present ourselves as potentials, and our third-year status might help the process along."

Oren looked thoughtful, "That might be a good idea. You

won't be allowed to move in until after her initiation and the ritual, but it may expedite things."

"We'll go first thing Monday morning. You know our Nexus isn't going to be happy about leaving Chloe." He raised a brow at Oren.

"That's true, but if you talk to Chloe, I bet she'd help convince her."

Oren pointed his palm at our pallet, and the mattress rose into the air, landing in the correct rooms on the beds, with the sheets and blankets intact.

"What the fuck, dude?" Nathan growled out. "Why in the hell didn't you do that when we brought them out here?"

"I don't want my Faction brothers getting lazy," he smirked and then disappeared from the room.

"That guy has a lot of secrets he needs to share with us."

Nathan narrowed his eyes at the place Oren had been standing.

He wasn't wrong.

"Are you alright, man?" Zeke moved closer to me and asked in a soft voice.

"I will be."

He nodded and clapped me on the back, not pressing me any further.

I could see us growing close. He was a man of few words, like me, and he clearly took care of the people he considered friends. I could respect that.

"Is everyone ready? I don't want her out of my sight for too long." Nathan pulled on his boots.

None of us had anything to say about that because we all felt the same way.

CHAPTER 24
REVERIE

We materialized in my room, and Pantar curled up on my bed, shrinking to his smallest size as I headed toward the shower.

I was anxious to see my parents and discuss this new marking thing I'd done. Honestly, I also wanted to check in on my dad. I couldn't imagine the things he'd been through, and I just wanted to be with him. I was overjoyed that my mom had him back in her life, and I prayed that Rue would also be returned to her. She deserved all the things, and if I had anything to say about it, she'd get them.

Stepping out of the shower, I dried myself, my thoughts drifting back to what I'd walked in on in Jet's dorm. I thanked every deity I could think of for listening to my instincts and checking on him—the thought of what might have occurred if I hadn't terrified me.

I was going to wipe the floor with that rapist bitch. Smirking, I thought of how silly the boys were for worrying about Kristine fighting dirty. Apparently, they were under the impression that I was naive and wouldn't know how to fight someone who didn't stick to the rules.

I rolled my eyes at the thought. Nathan knew just how ruthless I could be. It seemed the rest of my men would soon find out. My parents had taught me that there was no such thing as a fair fight. You did what you had to do to survive.

No matter what it took.

I wrapped the towel around me and went back into my bedroom. Since I was leaving the academy, there was no need to dress in preparation for initiation. I pulled on some jeans, a Chris Stapleton concert tee, and my boots. After applying some mascara and lip gloss, I brushed my hair and braided it, so it hung over my shoulder, then headed out of my room.

Pantar followed closely behind, expanding to his largest size and placing himself in front of our door. I could defend myself, but it was nice knowing the big Fellat had my back.

Chloe was lounging in the living room. "Where are you headed this morning?"

I plonked down beside her, "Hey, bestie. I'm going to breakfast with the guys, then to visit my parents."

"What's wrong?" she narrowed her eyes.

"How do you know something's wrong?" I tried my best to look innocent.

"I just do. So, spill it!"

There was no point in resisting, so I told her everything that had happened the previous night.

"'I feel like I'm in the galaxy of This-Sucks-Camel-Dick'!" Chloe growled.

I looked at her, momentarily stunned, then burst out laughing.

"That's better," she smiled. "Nothing like a *Step Brother*'s quote to put a smile on your face." Her smile dropped, "I'm glad you challenged that bitch. What she did was disgusting. I'm surprised Jet let her walk out with her head attached."

"I think he was in shock. I don't imagine he ever thought something like that could happen to him."

I'd never forget the look of helplessness on his face when I walked into the room. I could barely fight the instinct to hunt down that bitch and beat her face in right now.

"No one I know has ever deserved a beat down like that bitch does." She shook her head in disgust.

We were truly simpatico.

"True that, bestie. True that," I said, leaning over and hugging her. "So, do you want to come with us?"

"I think I will. Your house is filled with lots of eye candy, not to mention your amazing mother."

"Whatever." I gave her the side-eye, slightly grossed out, and changed the subject. "I may also have forgotten to mention that Zeke and Zane want to have a bonding cere-mony during winter break." I braced for her reaction.

"Shut the front door!" Chloe jerked me to my feet and started jumping up and down.

"I knew you'd be excited." I laughed.

"Excited? That doesn't even begin to cover it! We'll be real sisters!" She stopped jumping and pulled me in for a tight hug.

"Don't tell your brothers, but that's my favorite part," I whispered. The smile on her face was dazzling, and I'm sure mine mirrored it.

"Nexus, I hate to interrupt, but your men are getting impatient. The lying one is going to break the door down if you don't come out soon." Pantar yawned, not looking that concerned at the prospect.

"Pantar said Jet's here," I told Chloe as I went to open the door.

Sure enough, there he was with his usual scowl in place.

"I've only been out of your eyesight for thirty minutes tops!"

"Seemed like forever." He pulled me into his arms and kissed the top of my head.

"This is new," Chloe grinned, with a twinkle in her eye.

"Get used to it." Jet grumbled.

I was more than happy to get used to it. We had a lot of things to work out, but he was finally where he belonged. I wondered when my Nexus would decide to mark him. Referring to the power inside me as a separate entity felt appropriate. I didn't consciously mark my other Faction. It felt like the decision was taken out of my hands.

"It's about damn time. I thought I was going to have to give you a beat-down." Chloe narrowed her eyes, "There was this one time I wrestled a giraffe to the ground with my bare hands, so I know I could do it."

Jet smiled. My bestie was at least a foot shorter than the big man, and her intimidation factor was practically nonexistent.

"That was definitely one of the deciding factors." Jet smiled, "I would never want to experience that. Did you acquire that skill from watching *Step Brothers*?"

I knew this guy belonged to me. There wasn't a single doubt.

"Did he just say two whole sentences?" Chloe glanced at me for confirmation.

Jet rolled his eyes, "Yes, *he* did."

"He's on a roll," I smirked and kissed his peck. There was no world in which I could reach his cheek without a ladder. "Let's head to Java and Jam, I'm starving."

Jet grabbed my hand as we walked out the door. He paused to ensure that the door had shut completely.

"Aww, he does care." Chloe fluttered her lashes.

"I take my future Nexus's safety seriously," Jet told her, falling into step behind Pantar.

We'd barely made it out the front door of the building when I saw Kristine and Sophie heading in our direction. I felt Jet stiffen beside me just as Nathan appeared from around the corner to stand in front of us both—Pantar at his side.

"Really? I'm so dangerous, you need to protect the giant?" Kristine tried for an innocent look. "You need to talk to someone other than Reverie. She's turned out to be quite the liar. Jet and I were trying to have a romantic tryst when she busted in and made horrible accusations toward me." She fluttered her lashes, "Isn't that true, Jet?"

"Fuck you!" Jet lunged toward her.

Thankfully, Pantar prevented him from getting to her. I didn't know what would happen if he attacked her openly without apparent provocation. Her father would probably have him removed from Emberhold.

Kristine smiled widely, "That's what I was trying to accomplish when we were so rudely interrupted."

Sophie laughed, but it sounded forced. Maybe there was a chink in their friendship that could be exploited.

I stepped in front of Nathan and Jet, "That's enough. There's no need to give this rapist bitch another moment of our time. I'll teach her a lesson in a few days she won't soon forget."

"Damn right, you will." Chloe moved to stand beside me and glared at Kristine.

"Maybe, but I doubt it. I'm way out of your league, little girl. You'd do well to rethink your challenge before it's too late." Kristine gave me an evil smile.

She thought we were unaware of the injections she'd been

given that had unleashed her abilities. But I *knew* she was unaware of my bonds, and my abilities were natural, not the result of an injection.

"We'll see." I was done giving this bitch the time of day. She'd find out soon enough that I was not to be fucked with. I doubted her intelligence because I'd thought it had already been demonstrated.

I walked up to Jet and grabbed his hand, pulling him away from the two women. Nathan and Pantar placed themselves between Kristine and Jet as we passed by, primarily for Kristine's safety. Jet's expression was murderous, and I could actually feel him vibrating with rage.

He'd calmed down somewhat by the time we reached the café. The twins were waiting for us, but Oren hadn't arrived yet.

Zeke pulled out my chair, "Sit. I've already ordered your breakfast, and it should be out soon."

I pulled him down for a kiss, "Thank you, kind sir."

He actually blushed before sitting beside me. Pantar shoved his way beside our table, causing the nearby students at the neighboring tables to evacuate quickly. The lady behind the counter frowned, but she wasn't about to tell a Fellat he wasn't welcome inside.

It wasn't long before our doughnuts and coffee arrived, and we fell on the food like locusts. I always had a healthy appetite, but this morning it seemed bigger than usual.

"That's because the markings you gave us yesterday took a toll on you physically. You're not used to being depleted like normal Aurathions are after using an ability," Oren spoke in my head.

Looking around, I spotted him sitting at a table near the door, drinking his usual cup of tea with an old book lying on the table in front of him. He winked at me and then turned his attention back to the book. That man was sneaky. I hadn't seen him come in.

"Eat, baby." Jet put another doughnut on my plate.

Zeke nodded with approval, then motioned for my cup to be refilled. The lady behind the counter came over immediately with a fresh pot of coffee.

"Girl, I need to get a Faction sooner rather than later. These guys are on it." Chloe smiled.

"How do you know you're going to be Nexus?" Zane grinned at his sister.

"Isn't it obvious?" I winked at Zane, "This girl was made to be the center of attention."

"We are well aware. She's been like this since birth." Zeke rolled his eyes but smiled affectionately at Chloe.

We heard a throat clear near our table, and I turned to see Oliver standing there. I'd seen him for the first time in the cafeteria, and I assumed from Chloe's comments that they had a little flirtation going on.

He was a massive guy, only the slightest bit shorter than Jet. His Samoan heritage was obvious: bronze skin, dark brown hair, and gorgeous dark eyes.

"Chloe, I wondered if you'd like to go on a walk with me?" He said in a beautiful, deep voice.

"Is that what the kids are calling it these days?" Nathan laughed.

Chloe stuck her tongue out at him, "No, we're still calling it fucking."

Coffee sprayed out of Zeke's mouth and all over Nathan's shirt.

"What the hell, ginger?" Nathan scowled at him.

Jet started laughing silently at first, then his laughter grew progressively louder until the room was filled with the sound.

Everyone paused what they were doing and just stared.

"Well, my work here is done." Chloe grinned, "I think I'll take you up on that offer, Oliver. Reverie, give your parents my regards. We'll catch up when you get back."

Oliver held out his arm, and Chloe grabbed it. "We really are just going for a walk. There will be no fucking until Chloe puts a ring on it." He spoke to Zeke and Zane, then kissed Chloe on the lips when she pouted.

She gave him a sweet smile as they both turned and sashayed out of the café. They made a striking couple, and more than one eye turned in their direction in appreciation.

"I think he might be perfect for her." Jet smiled.

I thought he might be right.

CHAPTER 25
REVERIE

We left soon after, with Oren and Nathan teleporting all of us. I wanted to visit our farm first to see the animals and Mira. I knew the Fellat would keep them safe, but after the attack, I needed to check on them myself.

As we reached the barn, tears welled up in my eyes at the sight of the charred remains of my home. It was the only house I'd ever known. Even though the people in it mattered most, the place held countless cherished memories.

"It's alright, baby." Jet crooned, pulling me into his arms. "I'm going to kill them all."

Getting accustomed to this new *all-in* Jet would take time, but I was here for it. The venom in his voice made me shiver, in the best way.

"*We're* going to kill them all." Nathan corrected, leaning in and kissing my cheek.

Mira came from around the corner of the barn, followed closely by a miniature donkey.

"*Hello, Cub. Is everything well?*"

"Yes, I just wanted to check on things before I visited my parents in the city." I smiled, "Who is our new friend?"

"This is Alfonso. He showed up last night looking for John."

She used one of her tentacles to pat his head. *"I let him know that John would be around this evening, and he could introduce himself then."*

Alfonso pranced directly to Oren and bowed. Oren looked a little taken aback by the little donkey's action, but hesitantly rubbed his head. The precious animal jumped up and pranced around as if that was the best thing that had ever happened to him.

"Seems like one jackass recognizes another." Zane quipped.

I smothered a giggle as Oren stared at him, not amused in the least. He turned his attention to Mira.

"Has there been any more trouble?"

"Not here. Another Aurathion town in Oklahoma was attacked. I don't know all the details, but my Faction will have more information for you." Mira tilted her head toward the barn.

"Would you like to visit with the others before you go to your parents?"

"Yes, please," I grabbed the handle to pull the big door back when Zeke appeared by my side and gently removed my hand so he could open it. I rolled my eyes.

"Thank you, Zeke, but I'm more than capable of opening this door. I've done it a hundred times."

"Just because you can do it doesn't mean you should have to." He pulled me into his arms and kissed me so thoroughly I forgot where I was for a moment.

Before I could fully recover, Zane grabbed me and kissed me as intensely as his brother. When he ended the kiss, the heat in his gaze made me take a step back.

"I told you that I wouldn't be left out," Zane said, kissing the tip of my nose before releasing me and joining his brother at the far end of the barn, near the large back entrance. I fanned my face.

Damn! Those Moon boys could kiss.

Oren laughingly threaded his fingers through mine.

"Those two are going to keep you on your toes. When they fully accept the fact that they're bonded and you're not going anywhere, their true selves will start to shine through. You better buckle up because it's going to be a wild ride."

Nathan approached and intertwined his fingers with mine on the other side. "She can manage them. After all, she tamed me, and that was no easy feat."

"Did I, though?" I questioned. I was reasonably sure he was far from tamed.

We all went into the cool interior of the barn, and Rubbish ran straight to Jet. He tried his best to avoid him, but Rubbish wasn't having any of it. He ran up Jet's leg and perched on his shoulder, chattering away.

"What's he saying?" Jet leaned his head as far away from the raccoon as he could. I started giggling.

"He says there's some fresh chicken shit in the yard if you're interested."

Jet grabbed Rubbish quickly and sat him on the ground with a frown.

"I'm just messing with you. He said hi." The guys burst out laughing, and even Jet cracked a smile.

"Very naughty, baby girl. Payback is a bitch." He smirked at me.

It might very well be, but seeing the smile on his face was worth whatever he came up with. After the incident yesterday, I was glad to know that he would be able to move past the trauma of it. When he got to see me kick Kristine's ass in the arena, it would heal him even further.

If I were honest with myself, I needed that too.

Jack started braying, and Alfonso trotted over to his stall to greet him, along with Nathan.

Nathan had always loved the big jackass. It was probably because they were both so hard-headed. I knew that if Nathan had a spirit animal, it was Jack.

"I wonder if Oliver knows he has competition for Chloe's affection?" Nathan scratched behind the big donkey's ear.

"Not funny. My bestie isn't here to defend herself." I narrowed my eyes at him.

Before he could answer, I felt a body materialize behind me and a muscled arm clamp around my neck in a choke-hold. Oren raised a hand, and sparks flew, but before he could do anything, the person behind me spoke.

"I wouldn't do that if I were you, Storm. I can snap her neck before you can hit me." The man behind me said. "Selene just wants to talk to her. She'll be returned alive."

His play on words was interesting. A lot of damage could be inflicted on a person without causing their death. I didn't see Pantar or Mira, and Zeke and Zane seemed to have disappeared as well.

"Calvin, there is no chance you're taking her anywhere. I won't allow it." Oren growled.

"Nexus, Jet, and Nathan have made their way near you. One is to your left, and one is above. The twins are going to distract him, and that's when you'll have your chance." Oren sounded worried with a good dash of rage mixed in.

"We'll see about that." The man, Calvin, said in a rather whiny voice. I don't think Selene sent her most high-level Faction member. Was it weird that I was a little insulted?

I felt his arms tighten around me, preparing to teleport

me who knows where, just before Mira and Pantar raced in with a Moon twin on each of their backs. Both men were screaming an Aurathion war cry that hurt my ears.

Calvin loosened his hold on my neck for a split second, and that's all it took. I grabbed his nuts and squeezed with all the strength I had. He screamed and then struck me on the side of my head, trying to make me release him. I saw stars, but I didn't let go; my hand began to heat with my ability.

Suddenly, his nuts were ripped out of my grip when Jet dropped from somewhere above him. He punched Calvin in the kidney, causing him to stagger and fall to his knees. Nathan appeared and grabbed his hair, pulling his head back, and slit his throat.

"That was my kill, motherfucker." Jet growled, blood covering his face from the spray that had erupted from Calvin's throat.

Nathan used his shirt to wipe the blood from his knife.

"She's my Nexi, *motherfucker*. You've just seen fit to pull your gigantic head out of your ass. Until she trusts you fully, you're just a *friend* and nothing more. I get the privilege of killing for her."

Zeke and Oren had rushed to my side to check my head while Zane stood between the two hotheads, trying to keep them from killing each other.

I pushed the two men away. "Enough! That's enough," I yelled, then grabbed the side of my head from the pain. "We have enough threats out there to let who-got-to-kill-who divide us."

Zeke pulled me into his arms and laid his hand on my head where I had been injured, and I felt a soothing coolness. When he removed his hand from my face, all the pain was gone.

"Did you just heal her?" Zane asked incredulously.

"Did I?" Zeke turned me in his arms so he could examine my head. I felt him reverently glide his fingers down my face. "I did. I healed her." He whispered in disbelief, then pulled me tightly against his body.

Oren walked over, and I was sandwiched between the two men. There were zero complaints from me because I could use the comfort. For all my training, I had never faced any real danger. I can't say I was afraid exactly, but for a second, I forgot about my abilities in the heat of the moment. I needed to work on that; a war was coming, and I refused to be the weak link in this Faction.

Oren reluctantly released me, "This is bad. I knew who he was because I've intercepted communication between Selene's

Faction and my father over the years." He rubbed his temples, "Between the death of Beatrice and now him, she's going to be enraged."

Nathan paled a little at his remark, and that scared me more than anything. "That woman is true evil. She needs to be destroyed sooner rather than later." He walked over and pulled me from Zeke, holding me and swaying from side to side.

"There is no argument there, but for all her wickedness, the real danger lies with the Brummond. If she embodies Lilith, then he represents Lucifer in the flesh." Oren met each of our eyes, "And we have to get through my uncle first to destroy him."

"Nothing will ever happen to you as long as I draw breath," Nathan whispered, still rocking me in his arms.

"*A tremendous malevolence resides within Ubel Brummond. He is the chief architect of all that has transpired. He must be destroyed to restore our world to its former greatness,*" Mira said, approaching our group.

"You should let me go to Aurathia and destroy them all."

Pantar prowled over and nuzzled my temple.

Mira chuffed, *"I admire your bravery, but you're not ready for such action yet. If there is any lesson to be learned from my Faction, it's that staying together is essential. A pack is at its strongest when it attacks together."*

I knew Mira spoke the truth and was relieved when Pantar nodded in agreement.

"I thought your Uncle Trent was the strongest of the Dark Faction?" I asked Oren, confused by his and Mira's comments.

"He is. But Ubel controls him through lies and manipulations. That's why Trent doesn't have a Faction. There is no way Ubel would take the chance of losing his influence over Trent. Unfortunately, my father helps with this." Oren hung his head in shame. I approached him and took his face in my hands.

"None of that. I can feel your intent inside me. You want the best for our people." I kissed him gently, "Even if you won't admit it out loud."

I knew he was ruthless. His actions proved that. Even so, there was a nobleness inside him that couldn't be denied. Oren hugged me, then, shaking off his self-blame, took charge of the situation.

"I'll get rid of the body. Then we need to go to your parents and inform them of what's happened here."

"We now know that Reverie is in even more danger than we thought." Zeke ran a hand through his hair.

"When this guy..." Zeke kicked the body, "-doesn't return with Reverie, she's going to send someone else."

"I'll kill them." I thought Jet had calmed down, but apparently, I was wrong. The heat in that statement was blazing with hate.

"Let's not forget you didn't kill this one." Nathan taunted him, always ready to throw gasoline on a fire.

Jet's face turned red, and he pulled a knife from his boot. I screamed, thinking he was going to stab Nathan, but instead, he threw the knife, and it hit Calvin directly in his dead eye.

"Now we've both drawn blood." Jet walked to me, much calmer than just seconds before, and kissed the corner of my mouth.

All of my men watched him with varying degrees of alarm, and even Nathan kept his mouth shut for once. Jet was as insane as the rest of them. Why was I not surprised?

Oren lifted his hand and incinerated the body, likely saving us from having to watch anyone else decide to take a stab at it. The thought made me laugh, and everyone looked at me as if I were the crazy one. I noticed Zane and Nathan adjusting themselves.

I suppose crazy attracted crazy.

CHAPTER 26
ZEKE

W e teleported into the living room of Reverie's parents, where Oren took on the task of explaining the situation to them.

Mira and Pantar had stayed behind to comfort the animals and do some scouting. Mira was pissed that her bond's cub had been in danger on her watch.

"What the hell is that bitch up to?" Sly/Hayes paced around the room, pulling at his hair. The thought of his tormentor trying to take his daughter had sent him into a rage.

Adelaide approached him and started rubbing his back soothingly. "I don't know, but we'll stop her. No one messes with my baby." The expression on her face was chilling. Now that Adelaide had regained the use of most of her abilities, she was a force to be reckoned with once again.

John stood and walked to the bar, poured a glass half full of whiskey, and downed it in one shot.

"You can bet your ass on that. We'll camp out at the academy if we have to."

"There's something else I need to tell you." Reverie wrung her hands, nervous at the prospect of upsetting her parents even more.

I resisted the urge to go to her because seeing her in distress fucked with me hard. I understood she hated to worry them, but anyone could see how deeply they loved her. I knew they'd want to help her shoulder her burdens, as did the rest of us. That surety was the only thing that stopped me from dragging her into my arms.

"What is it, Tater Tot?" Jesse asked.

Before Reverie could answer him, Zane took matters into his own hands.

"How about we just show you?" My dumbass twin raised his shirt so they could see the blazing yellow sun that Reverie had gifted him.

Of course, Nathan didn't want Zane to get all the attention, so he raised his shirt, too.

Oren and I exchanged glances, and he shrugged. If we couldn't beat them, we might as well join them. We both took off our shirts, and he turned to show his back, displaying a bolt of lightning that raced down his spine.

At the sight of our marks: Adelaide gasped, Jesse shook his head in disbelief, Hayes punched the wall, and John dropped down in a chair, the whiskey glass shattering on the floor.

I'm guessing this wasn't going to be the relaxing weekend I was hoping for.

~⚜~

J esse and John each grabbed another glass of whiskey, both shaken by this latest development. Adelaide suggested that we prepare some lunch and continue our discussions on a full stomach, probably hoping her two Faction members would take the hint and lay off the booze.

I agreed because it was my mission in life to ensure my Nexus was fed. I'm sure Reverie's parents could use a moment to digest everything we had told them.

"Zeke, why don't you, Oren, and Zane help me in the kitchen while you three get cleaned up?" She directed the last part to Reverie, Jet, and Nathan, who were still wearing bloodstained clothes from their earlier encounter. "Sly, find some clothes for Jet. You're the only one with anything that might fit him."

"I can blink to the academy and grab some clean clothes for us," Nathan said, starting to teleport out.

"No!" Adelaide yelled, then winced. "Sorry, I don't want anyone going anywhere alone until we hash this all out. Jesse will get something for you to wear."

I was the only one to follow Adelaide into the kitchen. Oren and Zane were delayed by Reverie's fathers, who wanted more information about everything that had taken place, too anxious to wait until after lunch.

"So, Zeke, Reverie tells me you like to cook," Adelaide inquired, retrieving a large skillet from the cabinet. Trying to keep the conversation light and away from the bomb we just dropped.

"I do. And it helps with the driving need I have to keep my Nexus fed." I smiled sheepishly, more than willing to play along.

Adelaide pulled out bell peppers, onions, celery, and a large package of chicken breasts from the refrigerator.

"Can you dice these vegetables for me?"

"Yes, ma'am, no problem." She handed me a knife, and I got started.

Adelaide placed the skillet on the burner over low heat and added a stick of butter along with some olive oil. She then seasoned the chicken breast and placed it in a large pan, which she put in the oven.

"Do you mind if I ask what you're making?" I asked curiously.

She smiled at me, and for a second, she resembled her daughter so much that it took me aback.

"I'm making Chicken Creole," she said. "It's a favorite of Sly's. I can't resist spoiling him after everything he's been through."

"I don't think I've ever tried it." I finished dicing the celery and then started on the bell pepper.

Adelaide walked over and checked my work.

"Good job. Reverie was right. You do know your way around the kitchen."

"My mother loves to cook, and I enjoyed spending time with her. Zane loved working on anything with a motor, so he was always in the shop with my fathers." I finished the bell pepper and started on the onion.

Adelaide pulled out a bag of rice and began preparing it, then made a pitcher of sweet tea.

"I can't wait to meet them. Have you talked to them about your relationship with Reverie?"

"I haven't told them about our mark. I think we should keep that as quiet as possible for now. But my brother and I asked Reverie to bond with us in a small private ceremony in our hometown." I wanted the mother of my Nexus to know how much we cherished her daughter.

Adelaide gave an excited squeal, then pulled me into her arms for a hug.

"That would be amazing! I'm going to need your mother's number before y'all leave. We have so much planning to do."

Sly rushed into the kitchen and pulled her into his arms.

"Adelaide, is everything all right? I heard you screaming!" He began checking her over, looking for injuries.

She brushed him off, "Sly, our baby is going to have a bonding ceremony with the twins. Isn't that exciting?"

Sly abruptly straightened.

"No! That would be the perfect opportunity for Selene to get access to Reverie or our family."

Adelaide's face fell at his words, and I could see the regret he felt at having to disappoint her.

"Respectfully, sir, we only want a small private ceremony, nothing that would draw attention. The only guests would be our families." This was truly important to me. I felt that Reverie deserved more than we had given her so far, and I had a driving need to correct that.

"I understand your desire to give my daughter this, and I applaud it, but with the latest attack on the town in Oklahoma, it's just not safe." Sly leaned down and kissed the pout that had formed on Adelaide's lips when he vetoed our plans. "That doesn't mean we can't arrange a day to go visit. I want to meet all the parents of Reverie's Faction members. Except for Storm's."

"You've already met them." Adelaide teased.

"Unfortunately, I have. That smarmy bastard is involved with the Dark Factions, and I think the Council has been helping him keep it covered up." His expression grew thunderous.

"I have no doubt that's true." I nodded my head in agreement.

"Do you trust Storm with your Nexus?" Before I could

answer, he fired off another question, "How can you be sure he's not spying for his father?"

I ran a hand through my hair, thinking of the best way to word my answer.

"I didn't believe that anyone could love my Nexus as much as I do. I would do anything to ensure her survival. Anything! Now that we've been marked, I would swear on penalty of death that each one of them feels the same. I can feel it here," I held my hand over my heart. "Storm loves her so much that it feels like worship. So, to answer your question, I do trust him, and I know he hates his father almost as much as you seem to. Maybe even more."

Sly nodded his head but didn't say anything, hopefully digesting what I said. He kissed Adelaide and then left to get clothes for Jet.

"He's going to be overprotective for a long time." Adelaide took the vegetables I'd chopped and put them in the hot pan to sauté. "Sly's told me some of the things he went through, but not everything. I'm not sure I want to know everything." She whispered the last part.

I didn't comment. I knew she was talking to herself more than me at that moment.

"Reverie has always been a special child." Adelaide didn't look at me. She just kept stirring the vegetables.

"She's very special to each of us." I agreed with her.

"No," Adelaide spoke sharply. "I mean special in ways that even she doesn't know." She stopped stirring and just stared at the pan.

"I don't understand?" This felt important.

Adelaide looked at me in a way that made the hair rise on the back of my neck.

"There are things that need to be discussed between her fathers and me before I can say anything else. Just know there is more at play than any of you know." Her gaze grew more intense. "You said before that you would do anything for her. Did you mean it?"

I didn't hesitate, "Yes, right down to my soul."

Adelaide gazed into my eyes as if trying to see into my very heart. She nodded slightly, "Grab the pie out of that box."

I handed her the pie, which looked and smelled amazing. I was confused when she pulled a pie pan out of the cabinet and placed the pie inside.

"I trust you'll never mention what you just saw?" Adelaide narrowed her eyes at me.

"Yes, ma'am." I had no idea what was happening, but my momma didn't raise no fool.

"Now get rid of the box," she said, turning to the oven and pulling the chicken out.

We finished cooking the food together in companionable silence.

Adelaide didn't elaborate on what she'd said about Reverie, and I didn't ask. I knew she'd explain when she was ready. At least I had my Faction to lean on. I trusted that together, we could handle anything that was thrown at us.

CHAPTER 27

REVERIE

I cleaned up and changed into some black leggings and an old football jersey of Nathan's. I tossed my hair up in a messy bun and hurried back to the living room, anxious to reassure my parents that I was fine. I hated to see them stressed over me when I knew they were still dealing with everything that had happened to Sly.

As soon as I entered the room, I could smell the delicious aroma coming from the kitchen. That was one thing I missed deeply. My parents had always believed it was important for us to gather around the table for supper and talk about our day. It wasn't always possible, especially as I grew older, but we all made the effort.

The condo offered ample space and a unique charm despite its older style and lack of an open floor plan like newer models. The master bedroom was situated on one side, with three additional bedrooms located in a hallway on the opposite side of the living and dining areas. A large swinging door separated the kitchen from the dining and living room.

I was ever so grateful that the master was located far away from my room. I was happy that my parents were still deeply in love after all of these years, but I definitely didn't want to hear it.

Grumpy had wanted to remodel a few years back, but Mom loved it just the way it was. He chuckled when she mentioned how she enjoyed having some time to herself while cooking. We all knew she wanted to serve the dessert she'd picked up from House of Pies in her own dish so that she could claim she'd made it from scratch. She did it every time we visited the city; it had become a running joke in our family.

Dad was sitting alone on the giant sectional near the fireplace. I plopped down beside him, and he pulled me close.

"Where is everyone?" I felt so at ease with him already. It was like he'd always been here.

"Jesse and John took the guys out to show them their new outdoor kitchen that Adelaide had apparently surprised them with for their last birthday." He sounded upbeat, but his expression didn't match. He had missed so much, and I knew it pained him.

I didn't comment and just smiled, leaning my head on his shoulder. He'd been through so much that it would take time to recover fully, if he ever did.

Dad cleared his throat.

"Are you doing well in your classes?"

I smiled inwardly at his adorable awkwardness.

"I'm doing great. Grumpy, Pop, and Mom taught me so much that this first year seems a little redundant. Mom, Grumpy, and Pop began teaching me about our culture at a very young age. Their unique way of explaining things made learning fun, and I am well ahead of my peers in most of our classes."

"I wish I could have been here." He sighed, then leaned his head on mine.

"I do, too, but you're here now." I sighed in fake misery, "I'm sure you'll have plenty of opportunities to torture me with all of your knowledge."

He chuckled, "That's not really my strong suit. I'd rather torture you in training. I've already talked to John and Jesse about some fighting techniques you need to learn."

We sat silently for a few minutes, enjoying the quiet moment together. He had a presence about him that made me feel safe and protected.

"I tried so many times to get to your mother, never losing hope that she was still alive," Dad mumbled into the silence.

I twisted to see him better. "I'm sure you did. I never doubted it." He turned so we were facing each other.

"I would have done anything to be here for both of you. I missed so much," he cupped my face in his large hands. "I still can't believe you're real." Tears welled in his eyes as he continued, "Rue always said he wanted a daughter to spoil. It pains me that he's not here to see you. I'll always regret that I couldn't find him."

"Dad, you did all you could. You stayed behind to search for him. You sacrificed so much to try to keep this family whole. No one could ask for more. I'm just glad you're here now." I hated how tortured he looked. If my mom hadn't already claimed the right to kill Selene, I'd do it. She had it coming even more than Kristine did.

"Me too, kid." He grabbed my hand and stood, obviously trying to lighten the mood. "Let's see if we can rush your mom along. I'm starving! I've had dreams about that Chicken Creole while I was gone."

❧

We gathered around the kitchen table, and Zeke placed the massive dish in the center, steam rising in the air.

"Damn, Momma, that smells good," Nathan was literally licking his lips. He loved my mother's cooking almost as much as I did.

I cuffed him in the back of the head, "She's not your Momma. She's mine."

The first time Nathan had referred to her as "Momma" was when we were nine, and he came over for a playdate. Apparently, I was a little possessive of her and hadn't liked it. I'd thrown an entire container of glitter at him, and he'd sparkled for weeks.

Now, I didn't mind, but it was fun to keep the argument going. Grumpy smiled at me in approval.

"Next time, hit him harder."

"I enjoy my Nexi using a firm hand." Nathan stuck out his tongue at Grumpy, then squeezed my leg under the table.

Dad's eyes bulged. "Was that a sexual innuendo?"

"Absolutely not!" Nathan looked and sounded affronted. He then leaned over and whispered, "It definitely was."

Mom was trying not to laugh.

"Everyone, eat while it's hot."

Zane piled his plate high with rice, added two chicken breasts, and then poured so much sauce onto his plate that it spilled over onto the table.

"Show some manners, brother." Zeke hissed.

"He's fine. It's nice to see my food being enjoyed." Mom said, glancing over at Dad and smiling gently.

He'd doubled the amount of food Zane had put on his plate and was eating it so fast I thought he might be sick.

The rest of us dug in before Zane and Dad ate it all. There wasn't much talking because we were all too busy stuffing our faces. After we finished and the table was cleared, Mom brought in the dessert. Staying true to tradition, it was a "homemade" pecan pie from The House of Pies.

"This looks amazing! We'll have to come over more often if this is the kind of dessert we get." Zane gazed at the massive pie in wonder.

"You could buy one yourself anytime," Pop mumbled under his breath, risking his life by commenting.

"Did you say something, Jesse?" Mom asked, eyes narrowed in suspicion.

"Not a word, my beautiful Nexus." He smiled innocently and then winked at me.

"That's what I thought." She smiled sweetly and waved her hand in the air. The pie was split into ten pieces and landed perfectly on our dessert plate.

It was wonderful to see my mother utilize her abilities. She had perfect control and made using them look effortless. I could only hope to be so accomplished one day.

Once she finished, Oren stated, "This isn't the first time that a Nexus has marked her Faction. Queen Lilibet marked hers in much the same way."

I suppose he thought it was best to rip the Band-Aid right off. My parents exchanged a glance that confused me. It seemed like they already had some knowledge of this.

"We're aware of that." Grumpy took a big bite of pie, not offering any further explanation. I guess I was correct in my assumption.

"I feel like there's something you're not telling us." Jet, who had remained quiet since we arrived, spoke up.

Pop smirked, "I'm assuming, after everything that's happened, you're finally admitting that you're not *just a friend?*"

"I'm not just a friend." Jet stated but didn't elaborate. We'd explained what happened in the barn, but I hadn't included what Kristine had done to Jet before we left. It was his business and nobody else's, and if he wanted to share the matter, he would.

"What brought on this change of heart?" Dad mumbled, his mouth full, shoveling the pie in at an alarming rate.

"Slow down, Sly. I'm sure Adelaide wouldn't mind baking another for you later." Pop grinned as he and Grumpy shared looks of amusement.

"Keep it up, Jesse, and you'll be sleeping on the couch," Mom raised her brow, far from amused.

Ignoring them, Jet said, "There were a lot of outside factors that didn't permit me to act on my feelings. I want to discuss some of those with you later."

I was proud of Jet, and I thought it was important for him to be honest about his work for the government. He now understood that our people would do everything possible to protect humans from the Dark Factions. Collaborating with us to achieve this would be easier than gathering information undercover.

Dad nodded his head, satisfied with his answer for now.

Hopefully, when they heard his explanation, my fathers wouldn't kick his ass.

"There are many things we're not telling you," Mom told Jet solemnly. "We have to walk a delicate balance between what we can and cannot say. One false move could alter the future of not just our family but of all our people. Reverie is special. There are things we need to discuss before we can share them with you. Just know that we'll help as much as we're able."

I was shocked.

"Were you just pretending to be surprised when I shared everything going on in my life? Did you expect Pantar and my mark?" I felt a bit hurt that they hadn't confided in me. While intellectually, I grasped the reasons behind their choice, our close bond made me feel excluded.

"No, baby! Even though we knew to expect certain things, seeing them materialize was alarming and still a little unbelievable," Mom explained rapidly. "We love you, and with the knowledge we possess, we hope to navigate a path that helps without jeopardizing our future."

Pop smiled at me reassuringly, "Your mother discovered the reference to Queen Lilibet in a scroll I had strategically relocated from Oren's father."

"Stolen," Zane coughed, then grinned.

Pop grinned in return and shrugged,

"Call it what you will. We needed answers, and I knew the windbag had been hoarding any information he could find about our history."

"You must have returned it later because I'm sure that's the same scroll that I found the information in," Oren remarked, unconcerned with the windbag comment.

"He returned it when we knew Remus would be at a gathering of Aurathions. I painstakingly copied it by hand to avoid an outcry at its absence." Grumpy finished his pie.

"Was it Professor Lee who told you all of these things about me?" I figured it must be since he had given them the note years before.

Grumpy nodded, "It was. He warned us to expect many unbelievable things where you're concerned. There's much that he didn't share with us. We learned a lot by following hints and clues in documents we've strategically relocated from others." He and Pop shared a grin.

"Is there anything else you can tell me now?" I pushed back my plate, unable to eat, and Zeke frowned, pushing it back in front of me.

"Eat Nexus, we're in this with you. No need to lose your appetite because of it." He put a bite on his fork and brought it to my mouth. I accepted the bite dutifully, and he nodded his head in approval.

"Good girl."

I squirmed at the way those words made me feel spoken in his deep, rumbling voice. They truly did something to me, and I wasn't entirely comfortable with it while sitting at the table with my parents.

Dad frowned at Zeke and cleared his throat.

"Continue to research Queen Lilibet. You're on the right track, and anything you find out about her will help you in the future."

"Why me? What's so special about me?" I didn't understand it.

My parents exchanged looks, and Mom gently asked, "Can you be patient and trust us? We need to confirm with Lee that what we say won't harm you or others in any way." She sighed, "And to answer your question, why not you? I can't think of one thing about you that's not special." Mom looked around the table, "I bet each one of these lucky men would agree. You are meant for great things, Reverie Cleopatra Hawthorne."

I wanted to demand answers, but respected them enough to honor their wishes.

"Okay." There really wasn't anything else to say. I knew they loved me, and I trusted them completely.

"We'll keep researching and let you in on what we can. In the meantime, keep those marks hidden and contact us the instant something new occurs, because there will be more. You can count on it." Pop said seriously.

"Sooo… if we have a daughter, I want her middle name to be Cleopatra." Zane smiled, threw his hands up, "What the hell? If it's a son, I still want to use it."

I narrowed my eyes at him, "Not no, but hell no!"

Mom gasped, "Reverie, I'm appalled. Cleopatra was your great-great-great-great-great-great…" She took a deep breath, "-great-great-great-great-great-great-great cousin thrice removed. I think it's sweet that Zane would want to do that."

I saw Zane smirk and decided to ask Chloe to help me get revenge on the asshead. It would serve him right if I did name our future son Cleopatra.

"My grandson will not be named Cleopatra," Pop stated, clearly alarmed at the idea.

"Do you all agree with him?" Mom looked at her other Faction and frowned.

The two tough guys shook their heads negatively, unwilling to stand with Pop.

"Pussies." Pop mumbled, narrowing his eyes at them.

The comment fazed neither man. I had to smother my laughter when Pop flipped them off with both hands when Mom turned her back.

"We've decided to send Nathan to the Dean to ask for Faction housing," Oren said, changing the subject. I'm sure Pop was relieved.

"I won't leave Chloe alone in our dorm." I was annoyed because it was apparent they'd been making plans with-out me.

"Chloe isn't the one in danger, and it might make her

safer. Until we come out with our bond, no one would think to get to you through her." Zeke ran a hand through his hair, "and anyway, she won't be alone if Oliver has anything to say about it. I think she'd spend more time at his place if she weren't worried about you."

"We'll make sure Chloe is safe," Zane said seriously, and that reassured me more than anything else. The boy was never serious.

I knew they loved her fiercely, and if they thought it was for the best, then I wouldn't argue.

"Okay, if that's what y'all believe to be the best option, I'll go along with it."

Oren nodded in satisfaction, "It is. I'll be able to put protective wards around the place with fewer people going in and out."

Dad frowned in disbelief, "You have that ability?"

"Yes, and I'm lucky that I do. It'll stop anyone from teleporting into the house and taking Reverie." He pushed his plate away.

I knew he had many abilities due to the injections his father had given him. Like Jet, he was entitled to share with my parents whenever he was ready... or not at all. The decision was entirely his.

"Can you tell us more about the attack in Oklahoma?" Jet asked.

Grumpy ran a hand down his face. "We were informed that the event occurred late at night. Despite the town's guards and protective measures, the attack could not be avoided."

"They weren't ready. Even though they'd been warned, nobody expected that level of malevolence and destruction. I'll meet with the Council and discuss steps we can take to help keep this from happening again." Dad got up and went to Mom, pulling her from her seat to his and then settling her in his lap. "Both Damien and I heard and witnessed things that will help us in the future if they listen."

"That's a good idea. Just be ready for the man Randall has become. He actually wanted me to replace you and Rue with two new Faction." Mom still hadn't gotten over that betrayal.

Dad growled and pulled her closer, "We'll be having words about that. I've seen what forcing a bond can cause, and they have no right to ask that of their people."

"Everyone was killed except for the children, and they were taken. Now everyone is in panic mode and even discussing going into hiding." Pop's incisors had lengthened, and his voice had an animalistic quality. Nothing pissed him off more than cruelty to children or animals.

I'd rarely seen it happen, but he sometimes transformed into one of his fiercest forms when his emotions were intense. And right now, they were definitely intense. Mom got up from Dad's lap and moved to Pop's.

"It's going to be alright, my love. We'll make the Council listen and prevent anything like this from happening again." She stroked his chest gently.

I studied my mother's actions. She was an expert in managing the emotions of her Faction and they her. We could all learn to help each other more, just by watching and learning from them.

"I'd like to help. I have contacts that could keep watch and perhaps give more of a warning." Jet spoke up.

"Who are these contacts?" Grumpy asked.

"The human military." Jet's expression remained calm, but I noticed his body tense.

"What the fuck?" Dad growled.

I took a page from Mom's book and got up from my chair to settle in Jet's lap. This was going to go one of two ways: either they would understand, and we could continue our discussion, or there would be shit talk, yelling, and cursing. Mom would then make them *pretend* to understand, and we'd continue our discussion.

CHAPTER 28
JET

To say I was glad I had pulled my head out of my ass regarding this girl was an understatement, I thought as she sat down in my lap to show her support for me. As she wiggled to get comfortable, I placed my hands on either side of her waist to still her movements. I didn't mind if she felt the proof of my desire for her, but I'd appreciate not having to hide it from her parents.

I knew they weren't going to like the thought of me being undercover. I'm sure it would feel duplicitous to them, but I considered it an honorable service to my country. I didn't grow up knowing about my heritage, so my loyalty had been to humankind. In part, it still was. My parents and family were human. Or so I thought.

Now that I'd learned more about Aurathia and the war that had been fought, I felt different. It was true that my feelings for Reverie were a considerable part of that, but not all of it. I'd seen the devastation and learned of the bravery Aurathions had shown fighting against the Dark Factions. I wanted to be a part of that.

The bonus was that I would have a role in protecting the planet I called home. I held Reverie tight, burying my nose in her hair to inhale her scent.

"After I was approached about my Aurathion blood and asked to join the academy, I was recruited into an organization that is buried so deep I'm not even sure who they are. I have a contact I report to, and so far, I haven't talked to anyone else."

"How do you know the military sanctions them?" John asked.

It was a reasonable question.

"I was called into my Sergeant Major's office, where a guy dressed in civilian clothes was waiting to talk to me. Not long after, I was given an honorable discharge from the Marines."

I'd never been one to talk much. Listening usually benefited me more. That's why I'd been perfect for undercover work. I understood that now wasn't the time to hold back. I wanted to be absorbed in Reverie's life as if I'd always been there. Getting her parents' approval was a huge step in that direction.

"He's right. Jet knew nothing of our world, and when he was picked due to his blood, the humans jumped at the chance to use him to find out more about us. They have been aware we exist for a long time." Oren had come around the table to stand behind me.

"You're the last person I'd trust with an explanation," Sly growled at Oren.

"Dad, he's my Faction. You're going to have to accept him sooner or later." Reverie frowned at him in disapproval. I felt bad for Oren. I knew Sly had been through some things.

I'd seen firsthand what war could do, but Oren wasn't his father and deserved the benefit of the doubt.

Sly grunted but didn't confirm or deny what she'd said. I knew it would take time for him to accept Oren. As much as he seemed to love his daughter, I was confident he'd make the effort. Between Oren's support and Reverie's comforting weight in my lap, I felt the stress I'd been carrying melting away. Being part of a Faction felt similar to the camaraderie and support I found in the military. Of course, none of my buddies sat on my lap to comfort me. They would have toted an ass whipping if they had tried.

I cracked a smile at the memories of the crazy shit we'd done. Now that I think about it, Josh may have tried to sit on my lap one night after we paid a visit to Bourbon Street. That nutty fucker was always trying to push my buttons.

"Just understand that I am loyal to Reverie and my soon-to-be Faction brothers. I have a large family who are unaware of this situation, but I'd like you to meet them. I also owe them some answers, and perhaps all of you would be willing to help with that."

Maybe meeting my family would help them understand why I'd had trouble transferring my loyalty for so long. Sly stared into my eyes and then nodded his head in the affirmative.

"I was taken by surprise when you mentioned the human military. I can understand your loyalty to your people. It shows character that you want to come clean to us now."

"You felt no loyalty to Aurathia until *recently?*" Jesse smirked.

I knew he was joking with me, but I took his question seriously.

"Why should I be loyal to something I knew little about? I have friends and family who I feared could be harmed or killed by Aurathions. Why wouldn't I try to prevent that if I had the chance?" I kissed Reverie on the head. "I'll admit the pull to your daughter had a part in my decision to speak up, but there were many deciding factors."

"I'm sure there were." Adelaide stood and began clearing the table. I gently removed Reverie from my lap and jumped up to help, along with the rest of the guys. Adelaide grabbed me and pulled me to the side after I set the dishes I'd gathered into the sink.

"I think you'll be a wonderful addition to Reverie's Faction. A man of your experience can help guide and teach the rest. The stronger my baby's Faction is, the better I'll feel. After hearing of the attack in Oklahoma and the damage that was done, I fear that things are going to escalate quickly." Her gaze became distant, "You must learn from our mistakes and remain together no matter what. You're stronger that way."

Adelaide patted my arm and then headed to the sink. Her words had instilled fear in my heart. It seemed like she'd had a premonition, but I wasn't sure if that was an ability she possessed. Either way, I would stick to Reverie's side like glue.

The thought of this Selene woman getting her hands on my Nexus was more than I could bear.

I felt a cold splat on my face, and everything went black. After my conversation with Adelaide, it startled me for a moment before I realized what had hit me. Pulling the wet rag from my face, I saw Nathan grinning.

"Heads up, Jolly, you wash, and I'll dry."

I threw the rag as hard as I could at his head, but he disappeared before it landed and reappeared behind me.

"You've got to be quicker than that." He laughed and teleported back to the sink. I loved Reverie for herself, but I couldn't wait until I had an ability to torture him with.

Maybe I would gain the ability to mute the bastard. One could only hope.

"I have a dishwasher." Adelaide hid a smile behind her hand.

"We'll take care of it. Go sit down and relax. You deserve it after that fantastic meal you just made." Zeke came in carrying more plates and glasses.

"Fine. Y'all talked me into it. I'm going to grab Reverie so we can gossip about all of you handsome men." Adelaide grinned and left the kitchen.

"So, what do you think our next move should be?" I looked at Oren.

"I think we go through with our plan of getting Reverie into the Faction housing, and we don't let her out of our sight. She's a badass, but not against the number of powerful Aurathions she'd be up against if they succeeded in taking her." He looked enraged at the very thought of it. Zane strolled in.

"What did I miss?"

"Besides the dishes?" Nathan raised a brow, handing me a plate to dry.

"My brother has a talent for avoiding housework. Just wait until we visit my parents, and you'll see him work his mojo." Zeke narrowed his eyes at his twin while he wiped down the stove.

"We were discussing Reverie and if there was anything else we needed to do to keep her safe." Oren used his ability to levitate the trash bag from the can and replace it with a new one.

I watched in wonderment, still just as amazed as on my first day at Emberhold.

"We stick to her cute ass like glue," Zane said, opening the refrigerator to examine the contents.

"What are you looking for?" I finished drying the last dish and put it away.

"Something to eat. What else would I be looking for?" Zane took out some ham and cheese and began making a sandwich.

"Are you fucking serious?" Oren asked in disbelief.

"As a heart attack. I'm a growing boy." He winked, "Does anyone else want one?"

"I'll take one." Nathan shrugged.

These fools were ridiculous. I'm glad I'd seen them in action, or I'd try to talk Reverie into trading the two of them in for better candidates.

"I know that look. I'd kill you in your sleep before I'd let you talk Reverie into replacing me." Nathan was watching me with narrowed eyes.

He was strangely perceptive.

"As if you could." He smirked. "I'm sure you saw the jersey she was wearing and the giant STRAUSS across her back."

"*I* did. It made me think how much better she'd look in my hockey jersey with *Moon* covering her back." Zane said before taking a giant bite of his sandwich.

"The hell you say, ginger boy?" Nathan growled.

I turned to Oren, tuning out the two morons. "I'm going to call a good friend of mine and see if he wants to meet with us."

"Is he with the same covert agency you're with?" Oren asked, watching in disbelief as Nathan piled an insane amount of ham on his sandwich.

"No, but he was a Marine Raider in my old unit, and I know he'd be willing to help." I smiled, just thinking of Deshawn's face when I explained all of this to him.

"Okay, let me know how it goes. If he's willing to meet, arrange it as soon as possible." Oren looked thoughtful.

I nodded as I left the room. Oren was brilliant, and I was glad he was on our side.

CHAPTER 29
REVERIE

Mom caught me before I could enter the kitchen and dragged me out to the patio. We sat on lounge chairs by the pool, and she grabbed both of my hands in hers.

"Tell me how things are going." She grinned, "Those men of yours are unbelievably sexy." Mom waggled her brows.

"Mom!" I tried to sound shocked.

"What? I'm bonded, not dead." She grinned.

I giggled, "Well, each one is as different as night and day, even the twins. Oren is so knowledgeable and commanding and, if I'm being honest, a bit of an asshole. But he's my asshole, so that makes it all good." I smirked.

"I know what you mean. You'll eventually learn that every man has a bit of asshole in them, but that's what keeps you from getting bored." She laughed. "How are you and Jet doing now that he's decided to admit he has feelings for you?"

"I want to take things slow until I'm sure he's all in. I feel bad that I haven't marked him like I have the rest of them, but I guess it's going to take time for my Nexus to trust him completely." I turned and stretched out in my chair.

"Trust takes time. Rue was the hardest one for me. He was so clinical and scientific. I came to the realization I would have to make the first move." She smiled slowly, "He was shocked at first, but it didn't take long for me to figure out that inside he was a *very* different man than he was on the outside.

"No matter how old I get, it'll never be old enough to want the details when you make statements like that." I grimaced.

Mom died out laughing, "I can understand that."

"I was terrified when that man showed up out of nowhere and grabbed me." I looked down at my lap, "For a moment, I forgot all of my training and just froze."

"Look at me, Reverie." Mom said in her no-nonsense voice.

I looked up hesitantly.

"There's nothing wrong with that. You've never been in that situation. The most important thing is that you didn't stay that way.

Oren told your Pop that you almost separated the asshole's nuts from his body." She smiled, "I can't tell you how proud that makes me."

"I wish I'd been the one to kill him." I scowled.

"I'm sure you do, but your Faction needs to prove that they're worthy of you. Even though you may not think it's necessary, their instincts will drive them to do it." Mom turned and stretched out in her chair, putting her hands behind her head.

"I get that." I sighed, "How bad do you think things are going to get?"

"Bad, my darling. Really bad." Now, it was her turn to sigh. "I think things are coming to a head, and we'd better be ready. We lost the first war, but we can't lose this one. I'm afraid they want to eradicate us and take this world like they did Aurathia. We can't allow that to happen... I WON'T allow that to happen, and neither will your fathers."

I stared at the stars, just processing what she'd said. I knew Mom was right, and it terrified me, not for myself, but at the possibility of losing all I held dear.

"I won't allow it either. Whatever this power is inside of me, I'll use every bit of it to prevent that from happening." I turned my head to meet her eyes, "I love you, Momma."

"I love you, too, my baby."

⟿ ⚜ ⟾

W e decided to spend the night here and meet Zeke and Zane's parents together tomorrow. I was both nervous and excited at the same time.

I really wanted them to like me. Not only was I in love with their sons, but their daughter was my best friend.

I'd called Chloe earlier, and she was going to join us along with Oliver. It seemed that the relationship was headed toward performing the ritual sooner rather than later.

I was happy for my girl. Oliver seemed like a great guy, and his personality complemented Chloe's. I'd bet she had a few more Faction waiting in the wings. It would take about twenty to keep up with her.

I smiled at the thought just as my door slowly opened, and Nathan slipped in.

"Hey, Nexi, mine. I hope you didn't think you were

sleeping alone after I watched you sashay around all evening in my jersey."

I frowned at him, "I don't sashay, and I hope you don't think we're going to be having sex while under my parents' roof."

"We had sex under your parents' roof that night after graduation." He waggled his brows and grabbed me around the waist.

"They were all here! And how was I supposed to resist you after that strip tease you performed?" I leaned in and bit his neck gently.

Nathan moaned and leaned down to whisper in my ear,

"Was that why? Or was it because you got jealous when you heard Shelly and Tonya talking about wanting to try to lure me behind the bleachers?"

"I knew they didn't stand a chance, but I'll admit to feeling the need to remind you of who you belonged to." Now it was my turn to moan when he licked my neck, then sucked it gently.

I heard a throat clear.

"What's going on in here, young lady?" Zane smirked.

I jumped at the intrusion, but Nathan never moved his attention from my neck. I tried to answer him, but instead, my head fell back, and I couldn't contain a moan.

"Looks like I got here just in time." I could hear the heat in Zane's voice.

Nathan raised his head.

"You're not invited to participate, but we don't mind if you watch."

"Don't mind if I do." Zane took a seat at the end of my bed.

"Are those minion sheets?" He laughed.

"Of course, and thanks for asking if *I* mind," I said sarcastically.

"Oh, I know you don't mind." Nathan shoved his hand down my pants, easing two fingers between my legs. When he pulled them back out, they were glistening with my juices. "You're soaked at the thought of him watching." He sucked his fingers clean.

"You want me to watch him fuck you?" Zane winked at me. "I would love to do it myself, but Zeke and I made a pact to wait until after our ceremony."

I felt my pussy clench at his words, but I didn't want to admit it. I knew they could feel my desire, but I didn't want to make it easy for them.

"No, I'm tired, and I just want to go to bed."

"Sorry, Nexi, that's not going to work for me." Nathan grabbed me around the waist and took my mouth in a filthy kiss made up of tongues and teeth.

When he crouched down to peel off my pants, I didn't say a word. I couldn't. I was overcome with desire.

"I'm going to fuck you in my jersey, but I want you on the bed on all fours so I can admire my name on your back while I do it."

Nathan rose and effortlessly flipped me over on the bed.

I did as he wanted and got into position. My ass so close to Zane, at the end of the bed, I could feel his breath on my skin. I'll admit to being a little annoyed that he and his brother decided to make me wait for a ceremony.

He deserved to watch.

"Looks like my Nexi wants to show you what you're missing."

Nathan laughed as he ran his hand over my ass and back down between my thighs.

I arched my back and let out a low moan.

"Why don't you help keep her quiet? She's enjoying this now, but if her parents hear us, she'll never forgive me." Nathan started taking off his clothes.

"I think I can help with that." Zane got up, walked to the head of the bed, and sat back against the headboard.

He took the rubber band out of my hair and gently combed his fingers through it, then abruptly grabbed a handful and leaned low to take my lips in a devastating kiss.

I moaned into his mouth at the desire I felt coming from him; he was burning up with want.

Suddenly, I feel a warm mouth between my legs and let out another long moan at the feel of Nathan gently sucking on my clit.

My hips start bucking as I try to get as close to his mouth as I could, chasing the pleasure he was providing. Zane lifted his head and stood, unbuckling his pants.

"I don't think my kisses are going to do the trick. Looks like I'll have to sacrifice and use my dick." He climbed back on the bed, and I got my first look at his penis.

It was beautiful, if a penis can be such a thing. Alabaster in color with a slight curve, the head smooth and perfect. He wasn't as long as Nathan but more girthy.

"Do you want this in your mouth, precious girl?" Zane crooned as he gripped himself, rubbing the smooth head on my lips.

I nodded my head eagerly and opened my mouth. I'd barely taken him in, when Nathan roughly inserted two fingers into my pussy, and I exploded.

Zane eased forward just enough to stifle the groan I could feel rumbling in my throat, but ruined it by letting out a long moan of his own.

"She's amazing at that, and I'd envy you if I weren't the one about to feel her perfect cunt wrapped around me,"

Nathan said as he rose and gripped my hips with his strong hands. There'll be bruises there tomorrow. Luckily, I was Aurathion, so they'd fade quickly.

He gently eased in, going much slower than I'd like.

"God, you're small. I love the feel of you gripping me so tight."

I clench my pussy around him, and he stopped moving, slapping me lightly on the ass.

"None of that, or I'll finish before Zane."

I know this asshole wasn't making a contest out of this too.

"That's a game I won't mind losing," Zane said but groaned out the last part as I sucked hard and took him deep into my throat.

"Fuuuuck, precious. That feels so fucking good." He grabbed my hair again and pulled it out of the way so he could watch himself slide in and out of my mouth.

The two of them found their rhythm, and I was just along for the ride. I felt Zane tense, and I reached up and squeezed his balls gently, and that was the last straw for him.

"You better swallow every last drop. I want my come inside your body too. Fuuuuck!!" He growled, holding my hair so tightly that I knew my scalp was going to be sore.

True to his request, I swallowed every drop as he curved his body over mine, keeping his dick in my mouth until he softened completely.

Nathan hit at just the right angle inside of me, and I stiffened in pleasure, cumming harder than I did the first time, with him following right behind me.

"Fuck my Nexi, I love you so much." He bit out.

All three of us collapsed, and the two of them cleaned me up and then took a spot on either side of me.

"I love you, precious girl," Zane whispered as he gently kissed my lips.

"I love you both more than you'll ever know," I whispered back.

Just before I drifted off to sleep, I could have sworn I heard Nathan mumble that he was king of the bedroom. That asshole turned everything into a competition.

CHAPTER 30
REVERIE

I found myself in a room with three other Aurathions. I didn't recognize any of them, but we were all restrained by strange, thin, bracelet-like handcuffs. The table at which we sat was crafted from the same stone found throughout the academy. The walls were adorned with a metallic material that sparkled peculiarly, almost as if crushed crystals had been mixed into the surface.

Torches were lit and mounted around the room, made from the same stone as the table.

Why would torches light a room that looked so high-tech? It was beyond strange.

Where in the hell was I?

There were two men and a woman. The woman had brown hair and brown eyes and was very beautiful in an exotic way. There was a guy seated on either side of her; one had mocha skin and soulful brown eyes, and the other was his exact opposite, with pale blond hair, alabaster skin, and light blue eyes.

Together, they were stunning.

It felt like we all knew each other. The men kept giving the woman and me looks of reassurance, even though both seemed extremely stressed.

The door opened, and a man with long, dark hair falling just below his shoulders walked in. He had striking green eyes and a cleft in his chin. He carried himself with confidence and a hint of arrogance.

"I hope your wait has been comfortable." He spoke in a deep, authoritative voice. For some reason, I was shocked at the sight of him and filled with an intense rage.

"Hello, my darling Reverie, did you miss me?" He smiled at me lovingly.

"You!" I can't believe you lied to me all this time." I struggled to get out of my cuffs.

"Calm down, little Bellator. There is no need to be angry with me. I'm here to help." He strolled to my side of the table and leaned down to kiss my cheek.

I jerked away, but he just smiled in affection and turned to address the others in the room.

"I assume you know why you're here?" He didn't sound nearly as kind as he did when he spoke to me.

"We know exactly why you took us. Let our Nexus and Reverie go, and we'll cooperate fully." The dark-complected man said in desperation.

"I'm sorry, that's just not possible." He smiled in fake sympathy, "If she does what I ask, then she won't be harmed. I give you my word."

"Please, don't ask this of me. Reverie has been a good friend, and this will be a betrayal." The woman twisted her hands together, and tears filled her eyes.

"That is why you should be happy to do this. I can protect her and keep her safe from everyone who would do her harm. Reverie was always meant to be mine." He ran his hand through my hair lovingly.

"Please, Tanya, don't listen to him. My men will find me!" I pleaded with her.

The man lost his smile and went to stand behind the pale man, putting a hand on either side of his head.

"If you don't do this, I'll end him. You know how effortless that would be for me."

The woman, Tanya, gave me a look filled with such sorrow that tears came to my eyes.

I couldn't stand to see it, so I took a deep breath and nodded my head.

"Do it. You can't lose Razor." I spoke in the strongest voice I could manage under the circumstances.

"Reverie, I'm so sorry." She closed her eyes as a tear fell down her cheek.

"Everything will be fine. You'll see. Reverie will be happy with me, and together, we'll fix everything wrong with our world."

He came back around to me and reached out a finger, dissolving my cuffs.

I took the opportunity to call fire to my hands, but at his touch, the sparks went out. I brought up my knee and threw a punch at his throat simultaneously, but neither landed.

He threw back his head and laughed.

"I love your spirit, little Bellator." He grabbed me around the waist, "Now, Tanya, I don't want to wait any longer."

"Please forgive me." She raised her hand and closed her eyes. A soft, green light shot out of her palm and enveloped us both in its glow.

I felt my heart break, and I knew things would never be the same. In my head, I was screaming for each of my Faction, but there was no answer.

~☖~

I woke up abruptly, drenched in sweat, Nathan and Zane asleep on either side of me. That was the most realistic dream I'd ever had. My heart still raced with terror at what the woman named Tanya was about to do. Even though I had no idea what that was, exactly.

I carefully slid to the end of the bed, my bladder about to explode, and made my way into the bathroom. I relieved myself and then started the shower.

I tilted my head back and let the water flow over me, starting to feel a little better. The dream was fading, and things didn't seem as dire as they had when I first woke up. I finished my shower and tiptoed into my room to get dressed.

The guys had gravitated toward each other after I left. Nathan was sleeping on his back, and Zane had thrown a leg over his, and they were both snoring. I smirked and grabbed my phone, taking pictures from several different angles. That ought to be priceless for blackmailing those two into doing anything I wanted. I owed Zane anyway, and I'm sure Nathan deserved payback, too, for something or other.

I looked at the pictures I'd just taken. I thought I'd have them printed in black and white. That would really capture the mood.

Pulling on a pair of ripped jeans and a hot pink T-shirt, I left my hair down to dry naturally, grabbed my kicks, and shut the door quietly behind me.

Zeke was frying bacon when I entered the kitchen. I sat at the kitchen island, and he stopped what he was doing to fix me a cup of coffee.

"Thank you." I yawned behind my hand.

"You're welcome, my treasure. Did you sleep well last night?" He smirked.

My face grew hot, "Yes. Please tell me you couldn't hear

us." I would be mortified if my parents knew what we'd been up to.

"I could *feel* your desire. The only satisfaction I got was knowing Storm was just as miserable as I was." Zeke went back to flipping bacon.

Before I could comment, the kitchen door swung open, and Oren walked in. He had dark circles under his eyes, and it didn't look like he'd slept a wink.

He went straight for the coffee, filled a cup, and drank it in one go. Zeke and I looked on in amazement.

"Damn, Storm, you probably scalded your throat," Zeke said.

"I got zero sleep last night, and I needed the caffeine in my system asap. Thanks for that, by the way, baby." He turned and gave me the stink eye.

"You should have joined us," I smirked, having zero shame about being satisfied by my Faction, as long as my parents were unaware.

"Don't think I didn't want to, but I need to win your parents over, and I didn't think that would help." He strolled over to me and kissed me on the head.

"They'll come around. Just remember that I'm your Nexus so your first priority is pleasing me." I joked and pressed a kiss to the underside of his jaw.

"Sounded like you were getting pleased well enough last night without my input." He grinned.

When Zeke started chuckling, I jerked my head around to stare at him accusingly.

"You said you couldn't hear anything."

"No. I said that I could feel your desire. Never did I say I couldn't hear it, too." He turned his back to me, trying and failing to hide his laughter.

Storm sat beside me, "Are you still going to meet the

twins' parents today? You don't have to be back at Ember-hold until the morning."

"I don't think our plans have changed, but it seems yours might have. You're not going with us?" I'd been thinking about our visit while I was in the shower, and I couldn't see any reason to delay meeting the Moons.

Zeke turned slowly, and his smile was so brilliant it was blinding.

"I'm glad we're still on for a visit. I'm dying to show you off."

Oren was quiet for a few minutes, and I knew he was working out the logistics.

"I don't see any reason not to go. You should be perfectly safe." He looked sad for a moment. "I'm not going to be able to go, because it's probably better that I show my face around the academy today."

"Why?" I knew we had to keep our relationship secret, but surely, we could trust the guys' parents.

"Yeah, man, why can't you go? My parents would never betray us for any reason." Zeke frowned at Oren, looking more than a little pissed.

Oren sighed, "It's not your parents I don't trust. My father has eyes and ears in all the Aurathion settlements. It would get back to him one way or another."

Zeke looked sheepish, "Sorry, I should have thought of that."

"We can just stay here. It won't feel right leaving you behind." I was aggravated that I couldn't claim my guys outright.

Oren pulled me onto his lap, "No, I want you to meet the Moons. They are amazing people, and you're going to love them."

He pulled me in for a kiss. "Plus, I wasn't lying when I

said I needed to show my face at the academy. After learning about the attacks in Oklahoma and Selene trying to have you taken, it's more important than ever that my father believes I'm on his side. The information I get from him could be invaluable."

Zeke set a steaming platter of scrambled eggs, bacon, and biscuits in front of us.

"It's settled then. We'll head over as soon as everyone gets dressed. Do you think your parents are still interested in going?"

"Still interested in going where?" Pop walked into the kitchen.

"To meet Zeke and Zane's parents." I hopped off of Oren's lap and sat back in my chair.

Pop poured a cup of coffee and then took a long sip before answering.

"Of course we are. Your mom was even more disappointed than you when we shot down the idea of a bonding ceremony. She'd never forgive us if we canceled this, too."

Grumpy entered the kitchen and, like Pop, headed straight for the coffee pot.

"I'm going to wake Adelaide up." Pop smiled and left the room.

"Wake Adelaide up for what?" Grumpy grumbled, still not completely alert until he'd had his first cup of coffee.

"To let her know we need to get ready to meet the Moons." I felt like I'd had this conversation several times already.

"Get y'all's asses up! We're going to Ohio."

Done.

Dad walked in, "Why is Jesse waking Adelaide?"

I laughed. I guess I'd be repeating myself a few more times anyway.

CHAPTER 31
REVERIE

Mom was over the moon that we were going to meet with the Moons. I was going to have to rethink the use of some of my expressions. Nathan and Zane were reluctant to get out of bed. Zeke and Oren were more than happy to help them along.

"What the fuck?" Nathan squealed.

"Storm, I'm going to fuck you up!" Zane jumped out of bed after Oren doused them with cold water.

Just wait until they look in the mirror and see the new facial hair they sported, thanks to Zeke and a permanent magic marker.

Jet didn't participate, looking on with amusement. He wasn't completely innocent, though. He'd been happy to give Zeke advice on his part of the prank.

"I told you to get up," I smirked.

Nathan walked over, slapping me on the ass on his way to the bathroom. "You wore us out, Nexi."

Zane was dripping wet when he pulled me in for a long kiss, getting my clothes soaked in the process.

"You might have worn him out, but I'm up for another round. Join me in the shower?"

Suddenly he jumped in the air and grabbed his ass as the sound of a whip hitting its target echoed throughout the room.

"Son of a bitch!" Zane yelled before turning to Oren.

A stream of fire shot out of his mouth, headed directly for Oren's face.

Oren threw up a shield made of shadows and deflected the flames.

"Zane, stop!"

I yelled and put my arms around his waist, laying my head on his back. He was burning up.

Out of nowhere, a blast of ice enveloped Zane's fire, and the flow of the flames stopped abruptly.

When I raised my head, Oren was staring at Zeke in amazement.

Zeke looked as stunned as Oren, and when he turned his head in my direction, I noticed his pupils had transformed into those of a reptile. His beautiful sapphire eyes now featured a black, slitted pupil occupying the center.

Zane turned, gathering me close, and I saw his eyes mimicked Zeke's exactly.

"What the hell is going on?" Zeke asked in disbelief.

"Looks like your ability is showing itself in a spectacular fashion," Oren said wryly while smoke rose from the burnt sleeves of his shirt.

I ran to him, "Are you hurt?"

I frantically checked his skin, but it looked as smooth and gorgeous as it always did.

"No, baby. I'm fine. I couldn't contain the entire force of the flames, and my clothes suffered some damage."

"Damn, did you two gingers get dragon powers?" Nathan

frowned, obviously pissed at what he thought to be the Moon's good fortune.

"No. I think they have the ability of the Draxon. No one has developed that ability since..."

"Let me guess. Queen Lilibet's reign?" I interrupted Oren.

"Yes, Queen Lilibet's Faction, to be exact." Oren pulled me into his arms. "Baby, this has to stay under wraps. I can't imagine what my father would do with this information." He shuddered at the thought.

"Things just keep getting more dangerous for our Nexus. Deshawn is going to meet us in Ohio. It's time we upped our game." Jet rumbled, abruptly leaving the room.

"Everyone, get dressed. You need to leave so you can spend time with the Moon family, and I need to get back to the academy." Oren kissed me on the head and then left, following Jet. I'm sure he was going to find out precisely what he had planned.

~⚘~

The Moons lived in a small Aurathion settlement approximately fifty miles east of Cleveland, on the shores of Lake Erie.

I arrived in their backyard with Nathan and my dad. Neither of them was willing to let me out of their sight until they assessed the situation. I would have loved to see the town, but we were trying to stay away from public spaces in case Selene had eyes and ears in all the settlements.

The rest of the guys and my parents appeared seconds after we did. I was impressed that no one had spilled the beans about the new facial hair Nathan and Zane now had.

However, both had looked at all of us with suspicion when we burst into laughter at odd moments.

I heard a squeal, then was wrapped in my bestie's arms.

"I'm so glad you're here. My parents have been dying to meet my best friend and roommate."

"I'm sure meeting the Nexus to their twin sons wasn't even on their radar." Zeke rolled his eyes at his sister.

Chloe stuck her tongue out at them, then did a double-take and died laughing.

"What the hell is on your face?" She asked Zane in between chuckles.

Zane looked bewildered for a moment, then his expression cleared in understanding.

"I thought it was just Nathan."

"I thought it was just you, ginger boy," Nathan growled.

"I don't know how you two even made it into a Faction."

Chloe gasped out, still laughing at them both.

"That's enough, la'u alofagia. Quit provoking your friends."

Oliver walked out of the house, his grin huge.

I raised both brows at Chloe, and she shrugged her shoulders and winked.

"Gesundheit," Nathan said to Oliver with a grin, already over his anger and, if I knew him at all, probably plotting revenge.

"Very funny." Oliver laughed, pulling Chloe away from me and into his arms.

"What did you call my sister?" Zeke asked, raising his brow.

"Probably brat in Samoan," Zane smirked, as he put an arm around my shoulders.

Chloe glared in his direction.

Oliver smirked, "She can be." Chloe redirected her glare to him.

He squeezed her tight, "But most of the time, she's perfect. I referred to her as 'my darling' because she's precious to me."

Chloe melted at his words, and I could see the stars in her eyes. This guy was good.

"Hey, quit jabbering and bring my new family into the house!" A beautiful redhead scolded the twins and Chloe.

That had to be Meredith.

Two big, burly guys joined her. They were both blond and reminded me of the Vikings I'd seen on several popular television shows.

Zane whispered proudly, "That's the triple M's."

He hustled me to the porch, and I was engulfed in a tight hug from their mother, while their dads greeted my parents.

"I'm so glad to meet you. You've made my boys happy, and there is no way to repay that." She kept an arm around me and turned to the others. "Welcome to our home. Adelaide, I can't tell you what an honor it is to meet you and your Faction."

She actually bowed to my mother. It was surreal to see how Aurathions felt about my parents. They were truly heroes, even though we lost the war.

"Everyone, come in. Michael has prepared an amazing lunch." Meredith announced.

"Zane, take your friend and wash those ridiculous mustaches off your faces." She rolled her eyes, "Boys will be boys."

Zeke grabbed my hand, "You're in for a treat. Poppa is almost as good a cook as I am."

Zane and Nathan headed to the bathroom. I wished them luck with washing the marker off; it wouldn't be easy.

"I heard that boy." The man in question dropped back to cuff Zeke on the back of the head. "I'm the one who taught you, and I left a few things out. You're not ready for all of my secrets." He sniffed in disdain but ruined his haughty look by winking at me.

The house was beautiful. It was a stately, two-story, brick home. The backyard was massive with a pool and outdoor kitchen to rival the one at our condo. It was a large neighborhood with each house sitting on about a half-acre or so.

We entered through French doors that led into a cook's dream kitchen: white cabinets, granite countertops, and a large kitchen island with a butcher block top.

The kitchen was undoubtedly beautiful, but the smells emanating from it made it even more so.

"I wasn't hungry after that wonderful breakfast Zeke made this morning, but the delicious smells coming from your kitchen have built up my appetite." Mom rubbed her stomach.

Michael smiled then nudged Zeke with his elbow.

"Told you, kid. You still have a lot to learn."

Zeke rolled his eyes, "Whatever, old man. I could outcook you with one hand tied behind my back."

Mark started laughing, "We'll have a cooking contest at a later date. Then you two can settle this argument once and for all."

"I'll be a judge." Pop grinned.

Grumpy smiled, "I also volunteer as tribute."

Everyone laughed as we entered a beautiful dining room with a massive table. The table was huge, but with the amount of food on it, I was scared it was going to collapse. There was a huge salad, corn on the cob, grilled pork chops, and a large loaf of freshly baked bread.

"Wow, this looks amazing!" Pop rubbed his hands together, ready to dig in.

"No need to wait, everyone, dig in," Meredith said.

"You don't have to tell me twice." Nathan walked back into the room and started filling his plate, with Zane right behind him.

Somehow, the two had managed to get all the marker off.

Oren and Zeke better be on high alert. I wouldn't want those two teaming up against me.

Unless they were working together in the bedroom.

We all ate our fill of the delicious food, then made our way into the den, everyone spreading out on the oversized sectional and large recliners scattered throughout. It was amazing how quickly we all felt at home here. Now I understood why Chloe had put me at ease so fast. Some people just had that talent. I was fortunate enough to stumble into an entire family of them.

"The boys told me that you shot down their idea of a bonding ceremony." Meredith frowned at Dad.

"He was right to do so, Meredith. After what took place in Oklahoma, it's too dangerous." Mark commented.

"We all agreed it was a bad idea," Grumpy said, not wanting Dad to take all the heat.

She sighed, "I know you're right, but I'll admit to being disappointed."

"I'm upset about it too, but maybe after everything is resolved, we can plan one." Mom smiled slightly.

Dad nodded solemnly, "I didn't think it was wise to expose Reverie like that, especially after her attempted kidnapping."

"Say what now?"

"The hell you say?!"

Mark and Michael spoke up simultaneously.

"Kidnapping?! The children didn't mention anything about a kidnapping attempt." Meredith frowned at the "children" in question.

"We wanted to tell you in person." Zeke wrapped an arm around me, drawing me closer.

"Jet and Nathan made sure he wouldn't be kidnapping anyone in the future." Zane ran a finger across his throat.

"Do you know who it was and why?" Mark asked.

"It was one of Selene's Faction." Dad grimaced.

"Selene? The Selene that we battled against in the Dark War?" Michael looked more worried than before.

"The very one." Dad nodded.

"Why? Why did they want her?" Mark questioned.

"To get to us." Mom shook her head.

"It was because of me. I was assigned to her Faction before I escaped and reunited with my beloved Adelaide." Dad pulled Mom onto his lap, apparently needing her even closer.

"We all heard of your return. It was all anyone talked about for several weeks." Meredith said, solemnly.

"How bad is it in Aurathia?" Mark asked.

"Bad. The Brummond is running unchecked with the power of Trent Storm behind him. True Factions have been broken up.

Terrible people who wouldn't have been Nexus in the proper order of things have been made Nexus by the serum." He shuddered.

"I'm sorry. I didn't think about how my question would dredge up horrible memories." Mark apologized.

"No apology necessary. It's difficult for me, but I'm one of the lucky ones. I made it out." Dad said grimly.

"I don't know what Aurathia was before, but now people are pitted against each other and placed in Factions. What's even worse is the younger Aurathions born into that world know nothing different." Nathan looked at Dad, "You'll have my thanks for eternity, helping me get out of there. I can't imagine having to go through what you did and being forced to break my bond with Reverie. I think I'd die." Nathan got up from his chair and leaned back against the couch, pulling my legs over his shoulders.

"We need to have a meeting between the leaders of all the Aurathion settlements. The Council should've already called us together." Michael got up and started pacing.

Jet stood and leaned against the fireplace. "I'm meeting with a friend of mine tonight to assist me in convincing the human government to help us."

"I'm sure there's an explanation as to why you have connections with the government," Meredith spoke up.

"There is, but we'll explain all of that later." Chloe stood. "For now, let's talk about what kind of bonding ceremony my best friend wants. Even though we're going to have to put it off for now, it never hurts to start planning early."

Our moms got excited and started babbling away about the ceremony. I gave Chloe a grateful look, and she winked at me. I didn't want to talk about Jet's military involvement or anything else to do with the attempted kidnapping. I just wanted to let my food baby digest and enjoy the wonderful people around me.

Tomorrow would come soon enough.

CHAPTER 32
JET

My meeting with Deshawn wasn't until midnight, so we would be exhausted for classes tomorrow. I really liked the guy's parents and couldn't wait to introduce Reverie and her family to mine. Of course, I'd have to come clean about my Aurathion heritage and what I was involved in. One or both of my parents had to be of Aurathion blood also, finding out which one would be entertaining.

The guys showed us around their home, and Chloe took Reverie to her room.

"I want to talk to you about your sister," Oliver said as soon as we closed the door to Zeke's room.

We'd briefly looked into Zane's room, but it was so messy that no one wanted to stay too long. How he and Zeke were twins was beyond me. Personality-wise, they were complete opposites.

"What about our sister?" Zane frowned.

"I'm 100% positive she's my Nexus, and I want to do the ritual."

"What kind of name is Oliver anyway?" Nathan cut into the conversation, his question having no relevance whatsoever.

"Yeah, it doesn't seem very Samoan." Zane piped in.

Oliver rolled his eyes.

"My mother is a big Charles Dickens fan."

Nathan's eyes widened, and he fluttered his lashes.

"Please, sir, can we have some more?"

He and Zane died laughing.

"Like I've never heard that one before." Oliver rolled his eyes again.

"Enough, you two. You know you can't do the ritual until Chloe completes her initiation." Zeke said seriously.

"I'm aware of that, but I wanted to get your permission," Oliver said.

"You know that's not necessary, and if it were, you should go to our fathers." Zane plopped down at the end of the bed.

"I plan to. And it is necessary because I'm old-fashioned like that." Oliver smiled.

"Let me give you a word of advice about our sister. She's not the type that would appreciate you talking to us about this before you speak to her." Zeke pushed Zane off his bed and smoothed out the wrinkles.

Zane rolled his eyes and sat in the chair in the corner.

"I agree with the clean freak. Ask Chloe first."

"Thanks for the advice. I'll talk to her tomorrow after class."

Oliver leaned back against the door and crossed his arms.

"You're going to meet with Deshawn tonight?" Zeke asked.

"Yes, around midnight," I confirmed.

"Why don't you take our girl for a walk?" Zeke smiled.

"I thought we decided it wasn't safe to have anyone see us?"

Zeke nodded, "That's true, but there's a gate at the very back of our yard that leads to a trail in the woods."

"Yep, it's extremely private and it leads to a beautiful view of the lake." Zane yawned and leaned his head back, closing his eyes.

"Why are you helping me?" I was confused.

"We need you to get close enough for my Nexi to mark you. We all agreed that we need a fully bonded Faction, and you're the last holdout, my friend." Nathan explained.

"I'm not arguing. Now that I realized how wrong I was keeping her at arm's length, I want her tied to me in as many ways as she'll allow." And some she won't, I thought to myself.

~☬~

I knocked on Chloe's door, and Reverie pulled it open.

"Would you like to go for a walk with me?"

"Sure, I'd love to get some air." She whispered, "I thought we were on lockdown. Are you breaking me out?"

I smiled and leaned down to whisper in her ear

"No, we're going for a walk in the woods behind the house."

Reverie shivered, looking up at me with heat in her eyes, "Let's go."

When we went downstairs, Adelaide and Meredith were still talking about the plans for the ceremony.

"Where are you kids going?" Meredith asked.

"I'm taking Reverie for a walk to see the lake," I answered.

Adelaide frowned, "Is it safe? We don't want to advertise that we're here."

"It's safe. No one is ever back there, and the path goes deep into the woods." Meredith reassured her.

"Okay, just don't be gone too long or I'll worry." Adelaide tried to make her words sound teasing, but we both knew she was serious.

"We won't, Mom," Reverie leaned down and kissed her cheek.

We left through the back door and luckily didn't run into the other parents. I was reasonably sure that Reverie's dad would stop us, and I really wanted this time alone with her.

Leaving through the gate, the path was clearly marked. It led through a small field and directly into the woods.

I took Reverie's hand.

"Are you really okay?"

"Yes, why wouldn't I be?"

"Well, it's not every day someone attempts to kidnap you." I smiled.

"Oh, that." She grinned, "How could I not be okay when my five big, strong men rescued me in seconds?"

"It was only fair, since my little, tiny Nexus rescued me a few days ago." I brought her hand to my mouth and kissed her knuckles.

"I may be tiny, but I pack a punch."

"Nobody knows that more than Kristine." She laughed, and the sound made me smile.

We entered the woods, and the temperature dropped several degrees.

"I wish I could have killed her like y'all did the guy that attacked me." She ducked her head and kicked a rock off the path.

I stopped and turned to take her into my arms, the lake within eyesight.

"The fact that you helped me when I've been such an asshole to you shows your character. I know you couldn't kill her without putting yourself in danger, and I wouldn't want that." I lifted her so she was eye level to me. "You're safety will always come first."

"I wouldn't want *that*. You're important to me, too, Jet."

"You're *everything* to me, Reverie. Absolutely everything. The military has been my life and other than my parents, it's the only thing I've ever cared about." I stared deep into her amber eyes, "For you I gave it all up and with not a single regret. I'd steal and kill to keep you. I love you." I kissed her like this was our last day on Earth.

Suddenly, I felt a burning sensation that enveloped my entire chest. I set Reverie on her feet before falling to my knees.

She gasped, then pulled off her sweatshirt and stared at her chest.

"Jet look."

I raised my eyes to her even though I was still in pain. When I saw her mark, I forgot my agony, and a grin broke out on my face. The last place in her mark was filled. It was a crimson shield with a tree of life dead center.

I tore my shirt off, and my entire chest was covered with the exact shield in Reverie's mark. I threw my head back and laughed with sheer joy.

Getting to my feet, I grabbed Reverie and spun her around in circles.

"Put me down, crazy man. The guys are going nuts. You'd better answer them, or they'll come looking for us."

I stopped and listened, stunned, when I heard them in my head.

"Did the last piece of the puzzle just fall into place?" Oren sounded distracted.

"Jolly finally got tagged! Just remember, I was first." That was Nathan of course.

That dick.

"Glad to have you as a brother," Zeke said solemnly.

"Fuck yeah! Way to go, big guy." Zane laughed.

I kneeled in front of Reverie and lay my head on her chest.

"I'll never forget this day for as long as I live."

"You're fucking right you won't," Kristine said as I was jerked back from Reverie by a clawed hand around my throat.

"Get away from him!" Reverie screamed.

"That depends on you bitch. Did you really think I'd let you try and humiliate me in the arena?" Kristine snarled.

"Let him go, and I'll call the whole thing off." My Nexus begged.

"Fuck that. I'm going to kick your ass here and now so my beloved stepbrother can't help you cheat." Kristine laughed, "Did you two think you were fooling anyone. I could see the look of worship on his face every time he looked at you."

I was pulled to my feet and dragged backwards. I turned my head slightly and saw two strange-looking creatures holding each of my shoulders.

Both of them had to be seven feet tall. They were grey, with only patches of hair on their head. The only thing I'd ever seen, similar to them, was a week-old corpse. Dare I say they resembled what I imagined a zombie would look like? What the fuck were these things?

I attempted to pull away, but I couldn't move. Whatever

these creatures were, they were powerful. I jerked my head up when I heard Reverie let out a grunt. There was another creature holding her while Kristine punched her in the face repeatedly. Blood was running out of her nose and mouth.

I struggled and managed to headbutt one of the creatures, but he was so tall that it didn't do enough damage for it to release me.

Shit, I was such a fucking idiot. *"Come now! We need help!"* I called the guys.

There was no answer.

Kristine continued to punch and kick Reverie, and I was only able to look on in fury and helplessness.

"Fuck, Come NOW!"

Still no answer.

Suddenly, Reverie began to glow intensely, and the creature let out a howl and it released her, its hands were nearly melted off.

Reverie delivered a roundhouse kick that jerked Kristine's head back, causing her to fall to the ground. Reverie sat on top of her, throwing punch after punch at the bitch's face without letting up. The creatures that held me suddenly released their grip and headed toward my Nexus.

Not fucking likely.

I pulled the knife I always carried out of my boot and jumped on the back of the creature closest to me and started hacking on its neck. He screeched in pain and tried to pull me off his back, but that wasn't happening.

The other creature lumbered back my way, grabbing me by the neck, and pulled me off. Lucky for me, my knife took the head of the first one on my way down.

The creepy fuck picked me up again but this time I stabbed him anywhere I could reach. Unfortunately, it seemed to have no effect on him. I tried to aim for the throat, but he had me turned and in a headlock before I could hit my target.

I could see Reverie now, and she wasn't on Kristine any longer. Instead, Reverie looked like she was in a trance, and Kristine had a knife, holding it close to Reverie's face.

I heard a battle cry, and suddenly the creature dropped me.

Oliver was breathing hard and holding a knife even bigger than mine, and the creature's head was on the ground.

I turned and saw Chloe hit Kristine in the head with a limb and pull Reverie into her arms.

"What the hell, bestie? How dare you kick that bitch's ass when I'm not here to watch." Chloe was crying and yelling simultaneously.

Reverie pulled out of Chloe's arms and kicked Kristine in the side. Chloe followed Reverie's lead and kicked Kristine on the other side. She grunted but didn't wake up.

Chloe grabbed her wrist and started screaming. Oliver rushed to her in panic, then grabbed his shoulder and groaned in pain.

I was stunned when Chloe raised her sleeve, and a tree of life inside a perfect circle was on her wrist. Oliver unbuttoned his shirt and pulled one arm out, stunned at the same tattoo as Chloe's on his shoulder.

"What the fuck? Are you my Nexus?" Chloe asked Reverie, staring at her wrist in shock.

"No. It's not that kind of mark." I knew what this was. Oren had mentioned the possibility, but none of us actually believed it could happen.

We didn't notice Kristine slipping closer to Reverie until suddenly she wrapped one hand around Reverie's ankle and flipped us off with the other just before a portal appeared beneath both of them.

Reverie and Kristine were gone before I could take a single step in their direction.

I felt agony like I had never experienced before.

My Nexus was no longer in this world.

TO BE CONTINUED...

PANTAR

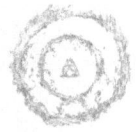

I felt it when she was taken, and I let out a roar of rage.
Who dared to take my Nexus? Whoever they were, they
would pay with their lives for this.
"Pantar, what is wrong?"
Mira asked, standing and dislodging Rubbish, who had been
napping on her back.
"My Nexus has been taken. I must find her."
"Where is she?" She asked in fury.

"Aurathia."

ACKNOWLEDGMENTS

Thanks to everyone that made this book possible. Hayley and Adaira, none of this would be possible without you two. I can't tell you how much I appreciate you.

My BETA Ladies are invaluable and I am forever grateful that you take time out of your busy lives to keep me from making a fool out of myself. Chantel, Jamie, Angie A., Angie B., Sydnie, and Charlotte. Thanks for all of your help.

Thanks to all of my ARC readers. The fact you were interested enough to ask to participate amazes me.

Thank's to my son Garrett. You didn't do a single thing, but I promised your name would be in the acknowledgments. I love you, BIG.

Thanks Mom for being the top buyer of my paperback. Thanks to everyone for being patient with her when she pulls one out in the grocery store, post office, dentist office … I love you for being the kind of mother that is proud of me, no matter my age.

Thanks to my sweet husband for all your support. I'll love you forever.

And as always, I love you Frank James. No one ever had a better father than you, and you will be forever missed.

ABOUT THE AUTHOR

Frankie James is a brand-new indie author. She's been an avid reader all her life and decided to try her hand at creating her own stories. She raised her babies in a small town in Texas. After they left the nest, her husband decided to take a job traveling. They bought a fifth wheel RV and haven't looked back. Seeing this beautiful country gave her all the inspiration she needed to put pen to paper.

When not reading or writing her favorite things are loving on her grand babies, cooking, and hanging out with her husband. Come hang out her at her.

Also by Frankie James

Emberhold Academy Series:

Exordium

Inter

Exitus (Pre-Order)

SCAN ME